THE REVEREND BURDIZZO'S HYMN BOOK COMPILED AND EDITED BY MATTHEW CASH AND EM DEHANEY

Burdizzo books 2017

Copyright Matthew Cash Burdizzo Books 2017

Edited by Matthew Cash, Burdizzo Books
All rights reserved. No part of this book may be reproduced in any form or by any means, except by inclusion of brief quotations in a review, without permission in writing from the publisher. Each author retains copyright of their own individual story.
This book is a work of fiction. The characters and situations in this book are imaginary. No resemblance is intended between these characters and any persons, living, dead, or undead.
This book is sold subject to the condition that it shall not, by way of trade or otherwise, be lent, resold, hired out or otherwise circulated without the publisher's prior consent in any form or binding or cover other than that in which it is published and without similar condition including this condition being imposed on the subsequent purchaser
Published in Great Britain in 2017 by Matthew Cash, Burdizzo Books
Walsall, UK
Cover artwork by www.matthill.co

Order Of Service

Foreword - Em Dehaney   5

Foreword - Matthew Cash   7

The Dancing Man - Christopher Law   11

We Plough The Fields And Scatter - Kitty Kane   19

J. C. Wants Me For A Sunbeam - Matthew Cash   31

Hail Mary - Paul B Morris   37

Cow Made God - Mark Nye 59

Come Away To The Sunday School - Dale Robertson   63

Some Strings Attached - C.L. Raven   77

The Old Rugged Cross - Michael Noe   81

Morning Has Broken - Matthew Cash   89

Onward Christian Soldiers - G. H. Finn   99

The Brutality of Faith - Andrew Bell   117

For Those In Peril On The Sea - Em Dehaney   139

Bind Us Together - Dani Brown   149

Lord of the Harvest - Mark Lumby   161

Olaf Lily-Rose - G. H. Finn 181

Bring In The Children - Betty Breen   193

Take My Life And Let It Be - Lucy Myatt 203

Aum - J.G Clay   213

This Little Light Of Mine - Edward Breen 223

The People That In Darkness Sat - Pippa Bailey   233

The Lord's Prayer - Kevin J. Kennedy   253

Author Biographies 259

Foreword - Em Dehaney

Faith is a funny thing. You need faith to have religion, but you don't need religion to have faith. In these troubled times, we all need something to hold onto. Our friends. Our family. Our faith that human beings aren't all monsters.

And in dark times, the light can come from the strangest places.

In a previous incarnation, I worked within the Major Investigation department of my local Police force, dealing with the up close and personal details of murders, rapes, kidnaps. These were the most serious and violent crimes, and I lived and breathed them every day. It was through this work that I met a man who experienced vile sexual abuse as a child, but who had chosen to take his experiences and use them to help others. He had come to talk to our investigation team about how to help survivors of abuse, and how to understand why many victims only have the strength to come forward and report their crimes many years after the event. This man set up a charity called NAPAC (The National Association for People Abused in Childhood), to support other adults like him coming to terms with the abuse they had suffered as children. All proceeds from the sale of this book will go to NAPAC, to help bring some light to survivors of abuse.

I have more recently found my light within the writing community, I have found my people. Writers of the macabre, the vicious, the gory and the gross. To outsiders, the idea of a horror writer is a morbid, hunched figure, afraid of the sunlight, bashing away at a tortured typewriter at 4am with a bottle of bourbon. Well, we all have our moments…But I have found a world full of funny, warm, creative, generous people who all just happen to have sick and depraved imaginations.

I have faith in these tales. Each one inspired by religious songs and themes. Each one entirely new and blasphemous its own unique ways. But this is not an anti-religion collection, this is a pro-creativity collection. Bodyshockers, night terrors, post-apocalyptic psychedelic sci-fi, well-known characters re-imagined and folk tales re-told.

Tales by the firelight. Songs in the dark. Hymns sung with a heavy heart.

All are welcome in The Reverend Burdizzo's congregation, so come one come all. Be you Muslim or Methodist, Anarchist or Atheist, Buddhist or Brahman, pull up a pew and prepare to be terrified, tantalised, disgusted and delighted.

Em Dehaney AKA The Black Nun
☐

Foreword - Matthew Cash

For those of you who like the odd little autobiographical encounters I sometimes add in my solo collections I thought I would include this one in my foreword, as it is partially religious.

"Footpath Deity"

As a teenager I had a lot of questions, aside from the ones about physical intimacy between myself and ladies, and the fantastical ménage à trois between me, Michelle Pfeiffer and Cindy Crawford of which I had neither the experience or stamina to pull off even if this event miraculously happened, I had questions of a religious matter.

I was brought up in a church of England background, I'd like to say my parents were religious, they said they believed in God, but surely if you believed that some epic deity was looking down on you you would do more than visit churches for funerals and carols? Oh and not forgetting the weekly singalong to Songs Of Praise on the television. I don't know whether their view was "well if He's everywhere why do I need to go to a church?" but I had often heard my father praying before he went to sleep and up until my teenage years I did too, just in case.

My mother died when I was nearly twenty, I think I had been suffering with depression for a year or so beforehand but that kind of thing wasn't known to us and our family. I was still a loner virgin who only had a few workmates to communicate with during my laborious hours working at an agricultural growing farm. My best friend, the one person I spent almost all of my waking hours with, was my big brother. He rescued me from desolate obesity which ballooned after I left school at sixteen and talked his boss into giving me a job. And through months of constant emotional blackmail and bullying, although I know it was for my own good, made me stick at it and shed a fair few stone.

The family who we worked for were baptists and proper die-hard believers and even though I was respectful, I had a lot of questions to ask them. They would always have their smartass answers and I was always left unsatisfied.

My mum died after a week of being in a semi conscious vegetative state caused by a bout of pneumonia, a stroke and heart attack.

It was a horrible week.

When it happened I was the first to find her, to try and wake her up. Once we were at the hospital I did not want to leave the waiting room, I didn't want to see what state she was in. But I did, I was made to.

That week my sisters and father, and I think my brother too, did more than their fair share of praying. I did too. I think I was the only one who was pessimistic enough to pray for death, whilst my sisters mentioned how they would give up work and spend the rest of her time nursing mum, I didn't want the constant reminder of what had happened. If there was no improvement then it wouldn't have been any life for her.

Anyway Mum died and my Dad and sisters had the comfort that their faith gave them, that one day they would be reunited. I didn't have that at all. I just had questions but no satisfactory answers.

My depression became worse, when I wasn't at work I would spend most of my time with my headphones on listening to music and facing the sofa cushions.

Months after one summer day I had an epic migraine and in the fugue that followed it, and the fact that for the first time in my life I didn't have my mum as a comforter, I had a massive anxiety attack. I fled my darkened room and needed to be outside.

Where I lived, the little village that features in a semi-fictional form in my book Pinprick (plug, plug, plug), was quite rural, and I found myself wandering along country footpaths alone, no doubt crying and muttering like a madman.

I climbed up to what I've just realised was the highest point in my village and sat on a bench by Goswells Wood ranting and raving and taking out all my frustrations on the trees and fields surrounding me. I shouted and bawled and shrieked at the blue sky. I wanted to be someone different. Popularity, body confidence. I wanted a sign. I distinctly remember sitting there alone in the middle of nowhere, at the top of one of the steepest footpaths I've climbed, on a Bench surrounded by the aromas of wild catnip, looking out over the fields of corn, the river stour a twinkling triangle between the buxom cheek rolls of the declining and inclining fields, asking God for a sign.

A few seconds went by and a figure came round the bend after mounting the crest of the footpath hill, a man dressed in normal clothes, a mass of white hair and a big bushy white beard like Santa Claus. Like most people's interpretation of God in human form. I was gobsmacked as this man, this sign, this deity walked past me, nodding a hello as he passed by. My depression lifted like a veil and I burst out into uncontrollable, belly-shaking, fucking head-pounding after my migraine, laughter.

I hadn't found Jesus or God but I had definitely rediscovered my sense of humour

I have always been interested in religion. Churches were visited occasionally at Christmas, Easter, for weddings, funerals and christenings. I was always fascinated but simultaneously fearful of the great archaic buildings built hundreds of years previous as places of worship. When the congregation of churchgoers would speak in united prayer I used to visualise the words gaining mass and firing from the pointed steeple like some epic lazer, into the Heavens. I still like old churches, cathedrals, they still hold that fascination, but with not so much terror these days.

I would never call myself religious, it's a wonderful idea and a big part of me envies those who can pledge to having absolute faith in their chosen belief. Like I say, I have, however, always been interested and loved the imagery and frightening aspects of certain areas of Christianity. Though most of my own research has been gleaned from films such as The Omen, and reading the 'interesting' parts of the Bible, I have always been drawn to it, especially if manipulated into the horror genre.

As I grew older I took interest in and found out about other religions, myths and legends and loved learning about them. Greek and Norse mythology played a big part in my upbringing, plenty of vengeful gods and monsters.

With this collection I not only wanted to conjure up the fear of forgotten gods, the punishment of disbelievers, I just wanted to see if my fellow authors got inspiration from the same things as me.

At Primary school in the village of Brantham, just near the Suffolk/Essex border, we would be made to sing Hymns each morning in assembly, and say the Lord's Prayer. Often the songs would spark wonderful images, and sometimes terrifying. From the joyous Spring morning wanderings that Morning Has Broken inspired, to the desolate wastelands that Think Of World Without Any Flowers conjured.

'Think of a world without any people,
think of a street with no-one living there,
think of a town without any houses,
no-one to love and nobody to care.
We thank you, Lord, for families and friendships,
we thank you, Lord, and praise your holy name.'

This hymn book is based on Hymns, inspired by Hymns and religions. Not necessarily blasphemous, but blasphemy may occur. It is not my intention to offend people but like everything this may be interpreted this way. As ever I wanted to bring you guys an awesome anthology that I'm proud of with an, as yet unused by me, different theme. I am proud of the entries within and the wonderful work the authors have done and the brilliant job my right hand man, Em Dehaney has done with editing. Em joined Burdizzo Books earlier this year and it was the best decision I have ever made. She is ruthless and not afraid to stick a big black cross on stuff that she thinks doesn't make the standards. She is helpful, insightful and quite often inspirational. The Reverend Burdizzo teabags her routinely with his overexcited ideas and is always happy when her alter-ego The Black Nun breathes upon them and buffs them with her pristine wimple.

I hope that with her help, we'll bring further great charity anthologies to you from Burdizzo Books.

So this book is also for her, to welcome her into the fold.

So without anymore blithering, here is the HymnBook, pull up a pew. And so endeth today's sermon.

Matty-Bob, April 2017

The Dancing Man - Christopher Law

The performance is about to begin. I wish that I could stop it, the way I do every time, but there is nothing I can do.

The house lights dim and, even though I am the only one here, I can hear the audience fall silent, their murmuring chit-chat ending. A few seconds later the curtain is raised and The Dancing Man appears, centre stage and spotlit. I want to scream and sob but my jaw is wired shut and my lips sewn together. I'd close my eyes or look away if I could; I'm not strong enough to overcome the brace keeping my head still and it is a long, long time since they cut away my eyelids.

"Ladies and gentlemen!"

He is dressed in a top hat and tails, a cross between a ringmaster and an undertaker. He grins as he talks, always the consummate performer.

"Ladies and gentlemen, it is an honour and a delight to welcome you this evening. You grace us with your presence and it is with some trepidation, and a pinch or two of confidence, that we venture to come before you. Tonight, we are sure, you will be amazed, all but swept away, by our agility and acrobatics, all our other contortions," he pauses for a few seconds, humbly accepting the silent applause. "So, without further ado, let me present our first act – the incomparable Missy."

The spotlight goes out and I sit in the dark for what feels like an eternity, my stomach and heart twisting with anticipation. I've seen the show before, so many times that my life before this theatre seems like a false memory, but I'll never become used to it. Knowing what I am about to witness, every horrid detail burned into my soul, only makes it worse.

The spotlight comes back on and, in the middle of the empty stage, my eldest daughter begins her routine. She is dressed like the ballerina she never wanted to be, on the tips of her toes, the bones breaking because he won't give her ballerina slippers. Her head lolls to one side and her arms are at shoulder-height, sticking out to the sides, lifeless below the elbows. Her hands dangle and jerk like a marionette as she begins to pirouette to the discordant strains of the atonal orchestra, feet awkwardly kicking in time to the percussionists – there are at least a dozen of them down in the pit, thumping and pounding on kettledrums and glockenspiels. Her eyes are wide in her emaciated face and I can hear her trying to scream, her whimpers only a little louder than my own.

It is part of my punishment that I know it is really her down there, and that she is as awake and as aware of it all as I am. Even stronger than my wish for this to end is my wish to let her know that I am sorry, that I'd change everything if I only could.

I first dreamt of The Dancing Man when I was a child, six or seven years old at the most. He was only one of the monsters that plagued my nights until adulthood killed my imagination, almost taking my heart with it. The selfish part of me, the part that led me here, wishes that my heart had died with my imagination – I wouldn't be able to feel this torment if it had. I wouldn't understand what I've done to my children and I wouldn't think it worthwhile to learn.

Psychologists and other therapists will tell you that The Dancing Man is just another manifestation of my night terrors, no different to the looming black figures with red eyes that visit every winter or the ghosts that like to take over my body and wake me so I can feel the heavy paralysis of possession. There are others, ones that like to make me bite my tongue or thrash my limbs so I wake with bruises and broken bones, but we would be here for days if I described them all. If you've ever suffered with a sleep disorder you've probably encountered most of them yourself – it is where the old myths about succubi and other nocturnal visitations come from, as well as the postmodern convictions of the silly alien abductees.

Unlike all the others, terrifying as they are, The Dancing Man has always been as real as my waking life. The red-eyed loomers can stop me breathing and the ghosts make me feel that my arms and legs have been severed, there is one who could makes me feel like an invader in my own body for days after she visits, but only The Dancing Man can talk. Only he has breath I can feel, warm and damp against my cheeks, sinking into my ears. Only he tells me what he wants me to do, offers me the chance to keep his attentions benign and distant.

You'd think that, given the vividness of his visits, I'd never have been able to forget him. Looking back, with every benefit of hindsight, I can't explain how I did. My psychologists will tell you about repressed memories, the plasticity of children's minds and other kinds of twaddle. There might be some truth to what they say. I have found a whole host of memories that shock me with their intensity in the few weeks since he came back into my life, demanding his payment, his protection money. He is a crude gangster; the classless child of psychopaths, a loan-shark charging a thousand percent APR.

It is blood that he wants, spilled with as much lingering pain as possible. Something I never shared with my head shrinks, I've seen so many over the years, is how many animals I killed to satisfy his demands. The stray dogs and cats, lured in with mock affection and food, the badger with a broken leg, my younger sister's hamster. They all died slow, savage deaths I had forgotten before I turned twenty-one.

If the adults around me had known what I was doing when I disappeared into the woods for hours on end I'd have been medicated and monitored, everyone knows these days that serial killers take their baby steps by goading the RSPCA, but I got away with it all.

I never did it for the fun of cruelty I did it to keep myself alive. If I'd remembered to keep doing it, to keep tearing fur and cutting throats, I wouldn't be here now, watching the twins emerge from the wings to join Missy on stage.

Shoulda-woulda-coulda. That's my life story.

Missy's real name is Melissa. It's a terribly American nickname for a family as English as we are, but it's the only one that suits her. I'm innocent on that count. It was my wife that started calling her Little Miss because she wouldn't stay still in the last trimester.

"She's got a laser-lock on my bladder, won't stop using it for a pillow."

It was my thirty-seventh birthday the day my wife said that. It was an amazing day, I was spoiled rotten and sprawled on the couch with her and the bump in the crook of my arm, I was happier than I've ever been, both before and after. I'd not thought about The Dancing Man in over twenty years and all the other night terrors had been silent for a decade. I was making good money and it didn't matter that I knew the machines I was selling were shit – I was in sales, not quality control or R and D. The dice kept rolling in my favour and that was all that mattered.

I'm fifty-four now and Melissa is still Missy because, from the second she popped out, she's been precocious, stroppy and awkward. She started walking before her first birthday, talking not long after. We spoiled her, myself more than my wife, but she was never bad, not really – there isn't a malicious bone in her body. There were tantrums and dramas when the twins arrived, Missy was eleven, but they weren't so bad, certainly not as atrocious as I thought they were at the time.

I'd like to claim that I've always been reasonable and balanced, that I'm one of the genuine latter day saints. I spent the last five years before I died, before I found myself in this theatre, the only warm body amongst the ghosts and echoes, telling myself that I was.

If I'd been able to think back then the way that I think now – shoulda-woulda-coulda.

Missy was twelve the first time she dreamt of The Dancing Man. The twins were teething and starting to crawl. My wife did the best she could to handle the crisis but, to my shame, I was too busy with work to listen, let alone care. I was a department head by then, our plush lifestyle dependant on my staff hitting the targets I told my CEO we could achieve. I didn't have time for awkward teenage girls and the tricks they like to play, the horror stories they tell their younger siblings.

"Daddy," her eyes have always been big, almost Disney. She was half-asleep. If I could close my eyes now I know I'd see her the way she was that evening, the way she was when I failed and The Dancing Man came back. "The weird man wants to take me waltzing. He says you haven't paid."

The penny should have dropped then, hindsight tells me that. It was three in the morning and my alarm was set for six. I had to drive to Gatwick to catch a flight to Munich, people to see and machines to sell. If the penny did drop I chose not to see it.

"It's just a nightmare. You're a big girl now, go back to bed."

"I'm scared. I don't want to go back to bed. Can I sleep with you?"

"Get in by your mother. I have a flight to catch."

The dreams kept coming after that and I now know what was happening. I didn't see it back then and, harassed by work, life and middle-age, I took the easy route and blamed Missy for it all. She was a teenager, not a saint, and there are some areas where I was right and she was an awful brat, but not enough for me to be excused. The last big fight we had, before he came to take us all, I threatened to throw her out on the street if she didn't stop putting ideas in the twins' imaginations. They were dreaming about him as well by then, another sign I didn't want to see.

The scales come down on her side more than mine, all I can do is apologise, strain my jaw against the cage it's in and hope that, one day, I'll be forgiven.

Hell can't last forever, can it?

It isn't hard to keep him happy, just a few minutes a week and an animal or two. You can make it elaborate if you want, make a fetish out of your sacrifice, but he doesn't really care. Back when I was a kid, in the days I wish I hadn't forgot, all I ever did was bash a brick against a dog's skull or hold a cat under water. I got bit and scratched a lot but never enough to hurt, and we don't have rabies in Britain unless you go fucking around with bats. It was a fairly safe pass time, I wish I'd kept it up.

Dogs are easier to kill than cats. Those numbnut critters will let you do whatever you want in exchange for a sausage but cats are easier to disembowel. I imagine that the little dogs, those yappy little terriers and arrogant toy-poodles, are as easy to slice open, their innards as diminutive and slick, but I never found a small dog to kill. So long as they die quick and you dance for a while with the entrails around your neck, a minute or two will do, you'll keep him happy. You'll need to do your best to be graceful and coordinated but, so long as something has bled and suffered, he's pretty easy to please. If he comes for you and yours next my only advice is to keep the colons intact they really stink if you don't.

Missy was trying to please him when I caught her standing over the twins with a steak knife in her hand. She was crying so hard the tears were dripping from her lips and the tip of her nose. Her eyes were larger than normal and her cheeks almost concave. At sixteen was long past the days when her father can see her in her smalls but that's no excuse for my failure to see how emaciated she was – she liked baggy clothes because they hid the jut of her hips and the void below her ribs. She's wearing them now, up on the stage.

"He wants blood," she said. "Not yours. Someone else's. Someone human. He wants me to dance. He said the animals aren't enough anymore, not for what you owe."

That's the moment when I remembered, when my childhood came flooding back. I tried to stop her but my body turned to lead and the air into toffee. I thought she was going to kill one of her siblings. The twins, Freddie and Hannah, are only five, young enough that we can let them cuddle as they sleep.

She didn't, the knife went into her own throat and, surfing her jugular wave, I met The Dancing Man again.

I should have tried to save Missy as she slumped to the floor, blood gushing from her ragged throat. I should have ignored my enemy. I should have been a hero a good man at the very least.

Instead, I took the knife from Missy's hand and looked her in the eye as she died. I told her I loved her, that I was sorry I had to do what came next. It was hard to grip the knife, the handle was slick with blood, but I managed to push it through Freddie's throat, gobbets of his larynx falling out when I tore it free. Hannah woke as her twin died but she was so small, only five, that she could do nothing to stop me cutting her throat.

At the time, with The Dancing Man jigging and cavorting in the corner, it seemed like the only thing that could be done to save myself from the trauma of his return. The feeling stayed just as strong when I went back to my own bed and drove Missy's chosen blade through my wife's left eye and into her brain. It didn't stop as I called the police and paramedics, my mind skipping like scratched vinyl in an attempt to make them all alive again.

I put the knife into my own chest when the approaching sirens made it clear what I had done. It didn't hurt, nothing like the way hindsight does. I was dead and bloodied when they found me check the tabloids headlines for my new name.

I wish that I'd found oblivion when I tried to follow my family, I was sure that I would. I am alone in the stalls while The Dancing Man makes them prance and twirl, peeling their flesh in spirals from their fingers and toes, Maypole ribbons of skin, muscle and bone stripping upwards to their skulls.

I will be in this theatre forever and the agony will never stop. I want them to know I am sorry, but I cannot speak, my jaw is wired shut and my lips sewn together. All I can do is whimper as the house-lights dim and the invisible audience falls silent, wishing that my lidless eyes could look away.

We Plough The Fields And Scatter - Kitty Kane

Rolling out of bed, Jim's bones creaked. His bones creaked and his body ached. Farming all his life had taken its toll, and he knew it was beginning to fail him. Hell, it already had failed him. It scared him thinking how many more years he might be able to eke out a living from his farm.

Jim had no family, not any more. He and his wife were alone. She had given birth six times and only two of the children had survived their births. The remote farm was treacherous to get to, and Meredith had a dispensation for going into premature labour. Jim was a simple man, but set in his ways. His way was to lack sympathy. He lacked it for everyone, even those he loved, if love was what you could call it.

Also a violent man, he often wondered, though not actually cared, if he had caused some of the stillbirths. Meredith stoked his ire, and often found herself on the wrong end of his fists. Those fists were gnarled now, and clawed with arthritis, caused by so many years hard labour. The two children that had survived their births had grown into sturdy young men, but that had not prevented them too being the subjects of his temper from very young ages. Cowed and obedient, the small family had run the farm well, on occasion taking cheap labour from passing drifters and the like.

Not one to romanticise, Jim did miss his two now deceased sons, but not because of any emotional attachments. No, Jim missed the labour they offered. Alfred, the eldest son, had perished on the farm itself. Out working on the hay baler alone, Alf had gone around the rear of the tractor, hoping to sort out a jam, and had somehow fallen into the working parts of the machinery. When Jim finally missed his eldest son, and made his way out to the field, with the intention of laying into him for tardiness, he was in for a visceral shock.

As he approached the stricken baler, he squinted in an attempt to make out what was wrong with the machine. It was a strange colour, and had peculiar protrusions that shouldn't be there. Increasing his pace slightly, when he realised what it was his stomach lurched. Arms and legs at impossible angles, Alf was stuck head first in the baler. His limbs sat at impossible angles, impossible because his eldest son had been torn in two. Entrails were still steaming where they lay glistening in the September sunlight.

Even as hard nosed as he was, Jim lost the meagre lunch that remained in his belly, and it spattered upon the land. Bile burned as it poured from the pit of his stomach, up his oesophagus and sprayed forth between his weather worn lips. He noted with annoyance that the baler was going to need fixing, and huffing his displeasure he turned tail to fetch his wife and younger son to clean up the mess that was left of his firstborn. And that was how he had lost his son.

The loss of his second son needed little explaining, certainly not to Jim anyway, because Jim killed him. Killed him the same as he had likely killed his unborn offspring, and done it with just as little care. There had been talk in the small village pub for near on a year. Jim didn't go to the pub often, preferring to consume copious amounts of homebrew that couldn't be categorized, it was simply rocket fuel. He frequented the inn on his visits to the village to collect his farmers weekly, and on occasion, an almanac.

The talk Jim heard was about something he had feared for a while, but had as usual buried his head in the sand. But this time the talk was right. His youngest son, Eric, had always been a sickly and weak, almost effeminate child. Never truly happy getting his hands dirty and his muscles buffed on the farm. The lad lacked the stature of his beefy brother, and lacked the sturdiness of his father. No, he was his mother's child, and in need of heavy handed guidance. But no matter how he tried, how many bruises and shattered bones he wrought upon his child, the boy never manned up.

Jim had risen early on the day in question. Instead of heading straight down to the sheep fields, he had veered off towards the cattle barn. It was soon tupping season and he wanted to be sure the dye he used for the ram, to tell whether it had serviced all the ewes, was still useable. As he headed into the barn, a strange sound greeted him. Not the usual lowing of the cattle, but another animalistic sound. Grunts came from one of the stalls, and concerned one of his cattle was in difficulty, Jim fastened his pace to the stall. What he saw sickened the hard nosed farmer.

Lost deeply in what could only be described as the throes of passion were his son Eric and a young blonde man Jim vaguely recognised from the village. Feeling both his anger and his gorge rise, Jim stormed into the stall and ripped the pair apart. The village lad scrambled for his clothes, and Eric froze in terror seeing his father stood there with apocalyptic rage across his features. As the boy scrambled clear, Jim picked up the nearest item which was a pitchfork, and thrust it into his back. Blood spurted everywhere, spattering straw and people alike. Eric shaking now with fear faced his enraged father, looking in horror at his dying lover on the manure clad ground. He knew this would hurt, and braced himself for the fist which flew towards him. He had felt those fists many a time, but this time they beat rapidly and hard, his jaw and nose exploded. A snap as his ribs broke, as he collapsed to the ground he felt his back snap. Loss of sensation prevented him from feeling his father stomp on his ankles and feet, but he heard the grinding of his bones. The last thing Eric did feel, was when his father twisted his head so far and fast, his neck broke. Cursing, Jim set about once more burying his offspring in his field, his disgusting lover too.

The village of Souldrop bustled with whispers about what had happened to young Sam, the young man had vanished. Rumour had it he had been seeing young Eric from the farm, and a lot of the village suspected foul play, but then, a lot of very strange things happened in Souldrop. Nobody dared voice their suspicions too much, lest any of the unusual factions in the odd village catch wind of it, but many an odd happening occurred in Souldrop.

That is not to say that the boys were not missed. In the nearby city of Southampton, in a club which the pair had frequented, suspicions were raised. The men of the club began to talk frequently of where the young pair had vanished to. One brave lad decided he was going to search for them, so he made his way to the remote and ragged farm. Knocking on the door of the farmhouse the clubber was met by a downtrodden looking Meredith.

'I'm looking for Eric, I'm his friend Alex , from the city? We haven't seen him for a long time, has he left town?"

The old farmers wife's eyes misted up. "In the field. Both of em...All of em...In the field" she whispered, but then her eyes widened as she saw her husband approaching.

"Who are you? Whaddya want?" he growled at Alex. He thought to himself this was without doubt another of the gay men from the city.

"I'm looking for Eric, and Sam actually. We haven't seen them for weeks, Sam at least was very regular at the club, and we last heard he was heading up here to see Eric?"

"Well I'm fucked if I know where the little slacker is, buggered off almost three week gone, ain't welcome back here at all"

"But where has he gone?"

"Look you little prick, I don't know, I don't care, and I want you and any others of your ilk off my land, freaks of nature the lotta ya"

"Well I'll go, but I'll be back, you best have some explanation ready."

"I'm gonna explain my shotgun to your scrawny ass in a minute faggot!"

So with that Alex took to his heels, but he wasn't satisfied, and neither were the boys at the club. They missed their friends, and with their strong suspicions together they planned their revenge.

As the season rolled on, Jim found the time for sowing to be upon him once more. Seed was becoming more and more expensive each year, and the farm was bringing in very little. Knowing he needed to sow a fodder field, he decided to use the vile tasting but cheap turnips that did so well for sheep and cattle alike, plus he had been offered some cheap seed by a fellow in the pub down in Souldrop. The seed looked rather unusual, almost purple in colour, but he simply frowned and yoked up his worn out old cart horse and set to sowing the field.

His oxen had ploughed it into satisfying and almost straight furrows a couple of days before. He had been careful not to allow the blades of his rusted old plough to delve too deep, lest he dig up any of his children, long gone or more recently dispatched. He and the old horse toiled for the best part of a day, and then he headed back to the farm house, aching bones and tired brain making him cranky. He thought to himself Meredith had better have a decent meal on that table tonight, otherwise his fists would be letting her know of his displeasure.

Having eaten a relatively satisfactory meal, but still having given his wife a beating simply because he felt like it, Jim settled in front of the TV for the evening. Not long into Emmerdale, the cattle and fowl began to make a racket. Yelling at Meredith to go and see what the problem was, Jim didn't get an immediate response and went looking for his errant wife. Finding her bleeding in a heap on the floor, he huffed and sighed to himself, and pulled his manure covered boots on and set off in the direction of the noise.

Now Jim certainly had seen a few things in his time, but the sight that greeted him as he approached the fodder field he had just sewn beat them all. Lit by some small bonfires were several scantily clad, obviously homosexual men. As they saw him some turned and he could see clearly for the first time what they were doing. They were masturbating, all furiously tugging their hard cocks in unison. As they saw him approaching they began to chant.

"Tell us where they are, tell us what you did, tell us where they are, tell us what you did!"

As the chant reached fever pitch, the pace of the mass masturbation increased, and some started to groan their pleasure as a multitude of climaxes were reached at once. Everywhere that Jim looked men were orgasaming and spurting their seed all over his fodder field. There was so much semen flying around Jim doubted that there would be much of this field unaffected by the dirty little bastards. This field had seen it's share of secrets, but for once in his miserable life, amid the jeers of these young men, Jim found his rage so white hot, he was unable to think. And doing something he had never done before, he walked away.

Two months later.

The seasons rolled around once more, and the arable farming and husbandry worlds became due to meet again. The ewes were all serviced and due very shortly. The scrawny dairy heard that Jim had once been proud of would offer one more calving this year, but the slaughter house would be their next stop. The crops had begun to pop their heads through the dry, lime heavy soil. The harvest would not be a heavy one if early indications were correct, however one field was thick with its crop. The turnip field in which the shocking and unholy show of onanism had been performed was lush and green. Taking his timid but loyal old sheep dog, Jim moved the flock of pregnant ewes up to the field to eat the iron rich turnip tops before he thought about turning his hand to digging up the roots on which he would also feed his dairy herd.

The ewes seemed to be happy chewing on the tough green turnip tops, so Jim ensured the hedges were secured and went off back across the tracks down to the farm to change the broken belt on his decrepit old tractor. Several hours passed, and as is often the way with practical problem solving on a farm, the quick fix he had hoped for turned into a few hours of cursing, injuring himself and generally stirring up his increasingly quick temper.

Since the night he had found all the vile young men in his field performing the mass abomination of debauchery, his wife had been having an even harder time than usual. He had on a couple of occasions wondered if he had gone too far on Meredith, leaving her in pools of blood, her body more bruise than white skin. He was furious with the time taken to fix his old Massey Ferguson, and wanted someone to take it out on. He had already kicked the dog until it yelped and dragged itself to the corner of the tractor shed, and had he cared one jot about its welfare, he may just have noticed the old dog cocking its head to one side, and seen the fear in its eyes, but he didn't care, not ever.

The ewes out in the fodder field had been happily eating the turnip tops when he left them, and had he cared about them too, he might have been concerned by the frantic noises they began to make as they attempted to continue their feast. But he didn't care about them either. He cared about nothing but himself.

The ewes had loved the new, bitter tasting crop they had been set to pasture to consume, and they begun to do so with gusto, but not for long. The purple green topped roots of the plants began to rise up from the dry ground. Bulbous heads squeezed out of the earth, followed by stick thin arms, rounded bodies and stumpy little legs. Sheep usually showed no genuine fear, just being flighty, stupid creatures they would blindly follow one another, but these small humanoid plant creatures emerging from the earth caused the sheep to scatter. They scattered and they ran, screaming their fear, but of course nobody heard, and nobody cared.

The creatures being born of the earth looked very much like human foetuses, but their heads bore the purple, green and off white colour of turnips. The bodies carried a similar hue, but also a vaguely human pinkness existed within the spindly and deformed limbs. Each not much bigger in height than a domestic cat, they had the voracious appetite of the newly born. The desire to gorge was strong. To consume their first meal, the life giving energy that would sustain their birthing trauma, and power their steps into the world.

The creatures did not however crave the milk of a mother, they craved the warm, pulsing innards of hot blooded creatures. As more and more of the homunculi burst forth from the soil, they fell upon the scattered ewes, using the razor sharp appendages they had at the end of their spindly arms to split open the growing bellies of the pregnant ewes. As the almost fully formed bodies of the unborn lambs fell from their wombs, the plant babies gleefully rent huge tears in the lambs, rapidly consuming the visceral organs of both dam and unborn offspring. The teeth contained within the turnip heads were many, and they were razor sharp. Blood, bile, shit, urine dripped from the creatures. As they consumed they all began to wear matching, inane grins. They wanted more, much more.

Once the tiny plant/man hybrids finished eviscerating every one of the sheep, some of them catching the odd shrew or hedgehog and quickly dispatching those too, they collectively turned their thoughts to more. More steaming entrails, more iron rich blood, more kidneys more livers, just more.

Finding themselves outside the cattle shed, the horrifying creatures knew what they desired was inside. The hens in the henhouse made the mistake of clucking curiously at the new sounds, and some of them gathered around that too. The fastenings upon the doors of the cattle shed and henhouse alike were no match for the ravenous beings. The faction that besieged the henhouse chattered their delight as they gorged upon the hens, finding the undigested corn in their gizzards was a bonus, but the half developed eggs they found inside of the unfortunate birds sent the small devilish men into rapture. Sucking the manure from around the semi-formed shells, they sank their sharp teeth into the eggs with gusto.

The cattle in the shed fared much the same as the sheep in the field. Bellies were torn open, steaming piles of entrails were fell all around. The creatures were now bathed in blood and shit, and with each mouthful they consumed, the more they desired. They craved something else too, something they had not found yet. None of the creatures they had decimated had contained the substance they desired being as they were all of the female persuasion. What they really wanted was the calorie laden, life giving nectar that only the male could produce.

So strong was the desire for semen that they forged on with their search, even after each and every cow and hen was dead. They must find males, the craving was immense. Sniffing the air they sensed living presences close by. Not many though, maybe this was the male they so desired.

First they found the scrawny cock, once a proud servicer of all the hens on the yard. The creatures delightedly fell upon the bird, clawing and suckling at him in an attempt to find the precious elixir. Next they found the ram, his swinging testicles with which he had valiantly impregnated the entire field of ewes were ripped from him before any killing blow was struck. Last of the unfortunate farm animals to fall was the bull. The sheer size of the balls hanging under the huge creature caused utter delight among the homunculi, the first to reach them swiped with its mantis like hands, blood spattered as warm drools of white fluid dripped out, the creatures shoved and trampled one another in their intense desire to taste the salty substance. The bull bellowed and managed to trample a few of its tiny tormentors, but they were too many, and the old boy, rent testicles being rapidly eaten, fell away and breathed his last.

In the farmhouse, Jim and Meredith were both laid down for the night. Jim in his bed, his wife once more in a heap upon the floor where she had fallen when his beating had finally finished. He had considered dragging her up to bed when he found himself slightly horny, but hadn't bothered as he had soon lost his hard-on when he flashed back to that night in the field. All those men, all jerking off, he still couldn't quite believe he had witnessed it. That damn field, his children, all of them, were there. Damn field.

A noise stopped his thoughts, sounding much like the bull. And it sounded in pain, not that he cared if it was, but even with his herd on their last birthing year the bull still would be of some use. Bull semen was valuable if it came from good stock. Might be one of his last commodities. He supposed he had best get up and see what the issue was, but just then the old wooden bedroom door burst open. Jumping up with the intention of slapping his wife down for daring to be so bold as to slam open a door, Jim was bewildered to see no outline of his wife stood in the doorway. Fumbling his fingers upon the bedside light, Jim gasped as the room, now bathed in light, showed what was coming through his door.

Small creatures, covered with blood and excrement poured through his doorway and fell upon him. He let out a high pitched squeal as he felt the most awful pain in his scrotum. The creatures swarmed over him, his testicles fell from their sack, plopping onto his legs and he screamed even louder as several of the creatures bit into his de-bagged bollocks. They swarmed over his entire body but Jim was transfixed by what they were doing to his testes. He didn't notice as they split open his belly, burying their strange heads into his vital organs. As two of them inserted their mantis blade hands into his ears and began to scoop out his brain, he didn't care.

They were eating his balls like apples and he felt every bite of the sharp little teeth. He stared at his tormentors, he could swear that he had seen them before but surely he couldn't have could he? He wasn't even awake was he? But the pain told him he was, and he realised why he thought he had seen them before, they looked just like the unborn children he had kicked from his wife's womb. And in his last, selfish thought as he died, Jim the farmer once more blamed anyone but himself. In one final throe of agony the mandrake imps tore his entire body apart, and gorged upon his living tissue.

The creatures sensed one more living being existed here. Its life force was weak, but a few of the tiny terrors investigated. They found an already bloodied human, cowering upon the stone floor of the kitchen. At first disappointed to sense it being female, some primal instinct swayed the creatures. Curious, they looked at the woman, and through bruised eyelids she looked back at them. The creatures found some confusing force preventing them from falling upon and killing the woman. Seeking not to murder, but some other urge, some of the creatures snuffled around and found the woman's breasts. Taking the nipples gently into their sharp toothed mouths, the creatures began to suckle on the woman. At first to no avail, but soon a creamy, sweet warm substance flowed into their ever hungry maws.

Meredith looked down, at first horrified, then a warmth spread around her. The tiny creatures suckling her breasts were beautiful. Her beautiful babies. All of them stolen from her, now returned. She stroked the blood and viscera soaked beings, and they chuffed their pleasure at the contact. Yes, her children, her babies, this time she would protect them, this time they would live.

Many of the creatures stayed, surviving on Meredith's milk and killing hedge row animals. Some however moved on, into the woods surrounding the town of Souldrop. There they set up home, among the other beings that lived in the magical woods, but that is another story…

J. C. Wants Me For A Sunbeam - Matthew Cash

When Jesus appeared in the skies religious fanatics had been wailing about his imminent return for decades, maybe even hundreds of years. The Earth had been juggling numerous balls of possible global destruction for some time. The bookies favourite was nuclear war, closely followed by some new-fangled super flu. Some favoured the mysteries of space and predicted that a mega asteroid that had been hurtling through the cosmos for millions of years would accidentally veer off course and obliterate us. Whoopsie-daisy.

There were, of course, all the usual global conflicts; insane leaders that made Adolf Hitler seem pleasant, threatening to hurl even bigger missiles at one another. As a result, those in favour of the prophecies in the Good Book all bowed their heads and bent their knees more frequently.

Even without the continuous killing of millions of innocents, which was, pretty much, common place on this planet, the biggest and most detrimental effects were being unleashed upon Mother Nature. This poor weathered old battle-axe had taken so many beatings since Mankind stained her flesh with its permanent pockmarks and concrete corruption. Those in the knowledge of environmental matters had been warning for years about us destroying the planet but we only started doing something about it when the damn thing was on its deathbed.

The prophesying Bible bashers paid heed to the destructions of both Mankind and the environment. They were correct in assuming that the increased temperatures, more horrific storms and earthquakes, were a sign from above. These were the End Times.

Aside from the obvious delirium that came with the appearance of The Christ in the skies, there rose more than a fair share of doubt. Conspiracy theorists insisted that this colossal icon which circled the atmosphere like another moon was nothing but a massive con. For years they had been laughed at when mentioning things like Project Bluebeam, a supposed plan to beam images onto the world's largest blue screen, the sky, to convince man that we were under attack by extraterrestrials, or in order to pull the wool over mankind's eyes ready for the Antichrist's New World Order.

Millions threw themselves about in religious ecstasy at the serene, bearded, olive-skinned face in the sky. Of course even more wars began amongst different religions who each mistook the image in the sky to be their particular God.

The skeptics began to question everything. Aircraft were sent up to investigate, to communicate with Him.

Evil doers wrung their hands in fear, begged for forgiveness, pleaded to the heavens.

For three weeks the image in the sky just smiled down, like someone peering into a goldfish bowl, entranced by the immeasurable patterns the fish made in the water. Any aircraft that got in close proximity to Jesus vanished without a trace, drones and other unmanned machinery would not work anywhere in the vicinity of Jesus's trajectory.

Nothing happened for a few weeks. Mankind did clean up its act a little, and more people turned to religion. This, of course, majorly irked those who had been devout before the Messiah physically poked his head into our business, but they did nothing to discourage or shun the newly converted. They knew they were being closely watched, knew that the all-knowing entity above would know who His true believers were and who had absolute faith before he made his second appearance.

A lot of these religious folk were flabbergasted when, what can only be described as, The Rapture happened and they were all left behind. It seemed that the only people who had mysteriously vanished were the bad ones. Prisons around the world were silenced in the same second, guards staring in disbelief as those they guarded disappeared before their eyes. Murderers, rapists, people of violent natures, all vanished, not just those incarcerated. Family members gasped in shock at what suddenly vanishing loved ones must have done to feel the Lord's wrath.

Religious leaders came up with the theory that God was going to rebuild the Earth, and had toiled over the lands to pluck out the offending weeds so that the good could prosper. Celebrations surged around the world as finally the nations were joining as one, they realised that their religion didn't necessarily matter, in a way they had all been right in simply believing in a higher realm.

Then Jesus spoke.

His voice filled everyone's ears and minds both audibly and telepathically. It didn't matter what language He spoke in or what language each individual understood, every ear heard and every knee bowed.

"My Children," His voice was pure love, it washed over the Earth's inhabitants like a cleansing balm, soothing any ailments and any possible doubts. "The world is close to its end."

Everyone already knew this but confirmation from 'the One in charge' still scared some.

"But it is not beyond salvation."

Thousands of voices from all over the planet, those that weren't still singing delirious hallelujahs, cried out their love, their promise to give themselves totally to the One God.

"The Sun is dying."

No one questioned this, they were convinced that they were the Saved, their God would wrap them and hold them in the safety of his His ever-loving embrace.

"You are God's chosen ones."

The world went wild upon hearing that, people fell to the floor in the throes of religious ecstasy.

"Those who have already been taken have prolonged the sun's demise by half a century."

This baffled Mankind. It was common knowledge that all evil doers had been taken, to make way for the glory of God's chosen. Well, that was what they thought.

"The Sun created us all, created God, your Creator. And the sacrifice to continue its blessed light must be bigger."

This was a lot to take in, people began to worry, to doubt the Lord's word. If God was the Creator of the Earth then this new revelation would change everything they ever believed in.

Footage from all over the globe replayed Jesus's message.

"My Children. The world is close to its end. But it is not beyond salvation. The Sun is dying. You are God's chosen ones. Those who have already been taken have prolonged the sun's demise by half a century. The Sun created us all, created God, your Creator. And the sacrifice to continue its blessed light must be bigger."

Religious leaders were confused by this message and with the confusion saw the resurgence of doubt. Was this the true Christ? Had they been duped by the Great Deceiver, Satan? Most went back to their bibles, searching for some hidden answer. They found nothing.

Two days passed and Jesus spoke again. Since his first uttered word people had witnessed the miracle of never-ending daylight the world over. Where the sun couldn't reach, its light was reflected from The Christ's face.

"It has been decided, by God, that fifty percent of His Chosen will be taken, given to The Sun. This will give life to the sun for one thousand years, after all You are God's most powerful creations. Everything that came from God is His to use. This second rapture will happen in two hours time."

Silence cloaked the world. Everything stopped. Then panic ensued. The bad people of the world had already been taken, only the devoted remained and there fast became less of those. Anyone of them could be taken and there was nothing they could do about it. New theories ignited even though they wouldn't have much time to flourish. Was this all part of His Master plan? An elaborate hoax, whether it be man-made or something worse? "Everything that came from God is His to use."

If The Sun made God, and The Sun was dying, and God had the power to use His own creations to stoke its fires was He doing it to save Himself? Did this mean that he was not the most powerful thing in the universe? That he could, in fact, be harmed?

It only took the remainder of Mankind thirty-five minutes before one of the rare un-corrupt world leaders to type in a few coordinates, press a few buttons and launch one of the planet's most powerful nuclear weapons into the colossal face of Jesus.

People were shocked at Mankind's retaliation against their Creator. Those still undecided, mostly the religious leaders, insisted that a nuclear onslaught wasn't the best of ideas against a being as powerful as God. You just didn't go firing nuclear missiles into Jesus's face.

Unsurprisingly the missile, as yet untested as it was predicted to make the Tsar Bomb, the biggest nuclear bomb ever detonated, look like a firecracker, was simply absorbed into Jesus's face.

It did nothing.

Mankind launched everything they had in the last half an hour before the second rapture. Missiles collided in the sky, missing their target or exploding too soon, raining radiation down upon every country, killing millions.

When the two hours were up Mankind had created its own night time, the atmosphere clouded in a thick blanket of radioactive ash. The charred, sickened survivors clawed their way to the highest points, atop the debris of collapsed buildings and screamed into the sky at Mankind's collective idiocy.

The voice of Jesus hurt their already poisoned minds as He said His final words and addressed Mankind as one. "Now that you have destroyed more than half of your population, God shall take the rest. You have all been Chosen."

Mankind's scream was cut off abruptly as all human life was eradicated.

Within the soil and the Earth's polluted air, the aftermath of Mankind's weapons seeped into the very fibres of the planet, changing everything back to how it was. The World still spun, The Sun still shone, and even with its inhabitable atmosphere the genesis of new life began deep underground. And God looked down and saw that it was Good.

Hail Mary - Paul B Morris

Charlotte left her boyfriend's house at 11:00pm to make the short walk home, as she had done many times before. Despite her parents preferring that she take a cab, Charlotte didn't mind the walk. At least she could smoke before arriving home. It was a pleasant Thursday night and the weather was kind to her. Moving briskly through the deserted cul-de-sac, Charlotte made her way to the opening of the woodland walk. Whilst not a deliberate pathway, it was a useful short cut to the main road that led to her house. As Charlotte stepped from tarmac to grass, she stopped to light a cigarette. Despite the absence of light, she knew exactly where she was heading. Her parents would have a fit if they knew she came back via this uncharted route. Charlotte often argued with her parents about such things, pointing out they lived in 1994 and not 1894.

Half way along the roughly trodden track Charlotte stopped to extinguish her cigarette which had stuck to her lip and couldn't simply be flicked away as usual. She didn't hear the movement behind her. A small hand grabbed her across her mouth and she felt the ice of a blade being stuck into her stomach. The assailant was stronger than Charlotte and held her tightly, preventing her from screaming. She was stabbed a second time in the chest, sending an explosion of pain throughout her body. One further blow struck her hard forcing her legs to give way and she collapsed in a heap, close to death. Charlotte struggled for breath. The attack had been sudden and deadly accurate. She looked blearily upward at the hazy figure standing over her. Pain of recognition caused her face to contort and tears roll freely down her cheeks.

"Oh my God. It's you." mumbled Charlotte weakly.

"I'm far worse than your God, bitch. I told you awhile ago that I would kill you. Didn't want to disappoint." spat the figure in black.

The assailant looked downward at the stricken body of Charlotte stabbing her again and again, taking her life in a brutal frenzy. Once satisfied that Charlotte was indeed dead, the person from the shadows ceased the butchery. Pausing momentarily to survey the area, the dark figure then disappeared into the shadows once more, leaving Charlotte's body where it fell, in a pool of her blood.

It was Friday afternoon and Alex Swinton made his way into his A-Level English Literature lecture a few minutes later than the rest of the class, who were all there but one. He silently cursed his unreliable car and sat down at his desk. There was an uncomfortable silence within the group of students and a few of the girls whose names he couldn't recall, looked visibly upset. He'd heard some rumours of something happening to another student, but wasn't exactly sure what. Professor Wyatt finally entered the classroom looking solemn and distressed.

"Dear students. I'm so terribly sorry to have to make this announcement." he grimaced with anguish and was clearly fighting back tears. The class was silent.

"I'm afraid I have the most unbearable news to share with you. Charlotte King, a member of this class, was discovered in the early hours this morning, brutally murdered."

Gasps of horrified shock filled the room with some of the girls at the back of the class bursting into uncontrollable tears. The whispered rumours had been true. Alex looked around somewhat bewildered as Professor Wyatt broke down in tears also. He'd known of her, sort of anyway, but couldn't display the same level of outpoured emotions as the others did. He kept his head bowed, out of respect for the loss of life if nothing else. Professor Wyatt regained his composure and addressed the class group once more.

"As far as we know, the Police do not have any leads but are currently investigating as one would expect. I'm sorry, but I really do not have any more news to share with you at this point." He took a deep breath once more, clearly devastated by the nature of the presentation he'd had to make.

"My dear students, I feel it would be inappropriate to begin today's class in light of the tragic circumstance and respectfully ask you to head home. The College counsellor is..... well, you know what I mean. Please, go now. I'm so very sorry!"

With that, Professor Wyatt left the classroom, too distraught to continue. Alex was one of the first students to exit behind the lecturer. He wasn't one for group communication and so opted to discreetly disappear, leaving most of the students to comfort each other in their own way. Alex felt the sadness within the room but had hardly known the girl.

Alex exited the College into the pouring rain. It hammered down with a fury like the heavens were trying to avenge the taking of a young life. He made his way to his car, a battered Austin Allegro that once belonged to his Grandfather, getting soaked in the process. He got inside and tried to start it up, but the starter motor just whirred. Alex banged hard on the steering wheel. He cursed at it's inability to start, recalling the insults that were thrown at him by Jack Groves, the rich prick. Yeah, he'd been none too polite about Alex's car as he drove around in his brand new VW Golf which had been bought by his Daddy. Alex didn't give a fuck though. His car had been lovingly passed to him by his Grandad whom he loved dearly and he respected the gift. It was just a shame that the fucking thing wouldn't always start first time. Patiently, Alex fired the engine for a third time and it reluctantly spluttered into life. He began to navigate his way out of the student car park when he caught sight of Mary Carter stood by the entrance, drenched to the skin. Alex wound down the window and called out to her with the offer of a lift.

Mary eagerly entered Alex's car, dripping rain water over the aged upholstery and dashboard. She ran her fingers through her wet black hair, droplets of water ran gently over her pale face, pausing only when they reached her pouting red lips. Alex was silenced by her beauty.

"Thanks, you're an angel. This rain is surely the work of the devil or something." laughed Mary.

"Yeah, it's pretty damn bad. I'm Alex by the way."

"I'm aware of that. I don't just jump inside any guys car you know." She replied sweetly.

Alex blushed a little, delighted that she had not only acknowledged his existence but also that she knew his name. Mary went on to divulge that she'd seen him around college and thought he was nice looking. She'd also seen him on Sundays at Saint Peter's Catholic Church, but she'd not had the chance to introduce herself. They chatted for a bit and then Mary politely asked Alex if they could listen to some music, pointing to the impressive looking stereo cassette player that was of more value than the car. Proudly, he announced that he had 'The Downward Spiral', the latest album from Nine Inch Nails. Mary responded positively and they drove onwards to the sound of Trent Reznor's embittered lyrics. Twenty minutes later Alex arrived at Mary's and pulled up outside.

"Thanks for the lift. Do you wanna catch up soon Alex?" asked Mary seductively.

"That would be great, yeah. I'd love to!" Alex drooled in response. Mary laughed.

"Okay, well, I've got things on tonight and tomorrow, so I guess I'll see you at Church on Sunday and we can go from there if you want?"

"Amazing. I look forward to it!" Alex replied overly eager. Mary laughed sweetly again and kissed him on the brow. Then she exited the car into the darkness, making her way inside the house. Alex felt the tightness of his crotch and the lump in his throat. He wanted this girl.

19 year old Darren Potter had enjoyed his Friday night out. He was determined to make his way home without falling over and injuring himself. Darren was fucked. Too much alcohol and one spliff that he didn't need had seen him being far from compos mentis. He was the last to be dropped off by the taxi, his friends living closer. Darren got too abusive whilst on his own, the driver pulled over and told him to get out before he battered him. Darren managed to do this and made the rest of the way home on foot.

Feeling unwell, Darren made his way from the footpath and down the steps that lead to the river where he promptly threw up. Somewhat better, he acknowledged the nagging feeling from his bladder and made best attempts to rectify this. Unable to fathom out the combination of his buttoned jeans, Darren simply pulled them down and answered the call of nature. It was all too easy for the figure in black who emerged from the shadows, to smash him over the head with a branch, crumpling Darren to the floor.

"You absolutely disgusting fucker Potter. I told you that you wouldn't get away with it. How dare you flash your fucking cock at me. " Raged the figure in black to the prostate Darren, who was now concerned at the slow trickle of blood emitting from his head.

"What the fuck man. I don't even know who you are. What's going on?" bleated Darren who tried unsuccessfully to get to his feet.

The assailant laughed and lifted the balaclava to reveal a face that Darren recognised.

"No fucking way. Not you. I was only joking for fucks sake." Pleaded the stricken Darren who shuffling on the ground like a lame animal.

"Too fucking bad you cunt. I told you that it would end badly for you. But you wouldn't listen." Spat the dark figure, before lunging forward at the grounded waster. Screams filled the air, but nobody heard them.

The body of Darren Potter was discovered the following day, stabbed multiple times. His penis had been sliced from his body and taken.

Sunday morning worship at St Peter's Catholic Church saw a large congregation. The weather was good, there was a feeling of hope in the air.

Father Jacobs was on good form as he led the congregation in prayer for the two murdered teenagers, comforting all with the promise that their souls were now at peace with God. He asked them to consider the Mothers of the 'children' who had their lives taken from them as the faithful then entered into 'Hail Mary full of grace, the Lord is with thee, blessed art thou among women, and blessed is the fruit of thy womb'. At that point, Alex couldn't resist but look over to the right hand pews at Mary, head slightly bowed. Alex's Mother noticed this and casually slapped his leg to express her contempt.

At the end of the service, Mary hung around in the vestibule waiting for Alex. His Mother looked at them with disapproval, but moved along eager to join her circle of friends in the church hall. The couple exited the church and paid respect to Father Jacobs who was thanking the passing congregation with a firm handshake.

"Bless you Alex and Mary, for coming today." He said with great reverence.

Alex shook his hand while Mary looked onward into the distance. Father Jacobs replied to Alex whilst looking directly at Mary who refused to make eye contact. Alex thought it strange, but let it pass by without issue. Unperturbed by this, Father Jacobs spoke.

"Mary, you should bring Alex along with you to the next Friday night gathering. I'm sure he would find it, stimulating." he cooed.

Mary swirled back on her haunches and flashed him a sarcastic smile. "Why of course Father. I intend to." She said with a sense of menace that Father Jacobs and Alex didn't know how to register.

"Well, yes. Of course child. A prayer to you both. Stay safe and The Lord be with you!"

There had been many rumours about Father Jacobs, but none substantiated. He was a good looking man in his fifties, tanned and athletic. He had a suave, sophisticated style like a Hollywood actor. It was alleged that he had quite a way with the ladies, particularly women who were vulnerable or lonely and that he didn't practice a life of celibacy as per holy orders. Reputedly, the Diocese and congregation turned a blind eye to his womanising ways, because he was an excellent Priest who was devout in his work. Plus, there were many other priests inflicting far worse sin on children for him to become anywhere near a relevant cause for concern. Still, the way he looked at Mary troubled Alex.

Mary encouraged Alex to go with her for a drink at the Black Flag, a pub in town for bikers. Alex initially protested given that they had just left church, but Mary pointed out that they were dressed in black so would fit in. She won the argument.

After a long and enjoyable evening getting semi pissed and listening to heavy rock music, Mary suggested they leave and invited Alex back to her house. In the taxi they made their way onward, kissing passionately. Alex, somewhat love-struck and inebriated, started singing 'without you in my life, I'd slowly wilt and die!' until Mary punched him playfully in the arm, expressing her hatred for Mötley Crue songs.

Twenty minutes later, they arrived at Mary's house, a suburban end terrace. Alex was surprised that she lived on her own, given that she was only nineteen. He couldn't comprehend it and was jealous of her freedom.

They entered and made their way through to the kitchen, Mary produced some alcohol and decided to fill in the gaps rendered necessary from Alex's blank expression. Making their way into the living room, Mary placed the latest Nine Inch Nails CD that she bought yesterday into the Hi-Fi. Alex was suitably impressed. She began to tell her story to the background of 'Mr Self Destruct'.

Abigail, Mary's mother, had committed suicide fourteen years ago. Mary was only five at the time. She never knew her father and although her mother obviously did, it was never revealed anymore other than he was an abusive, selfish bastard. He never wanted her and made his best efforts to encourage Abigail to terminate the pregnancy. Abigail suffered emotional and physical abuse during Mary's infancy but stayed strong. Yet, she never revealed the name or identity of the child's father or more importantly, the magnitude of the abuse she'd endured. Eventually the bullying and abuse took its toll on poor Abigail and she ended her life by cutting her wrists in the bath one night. Her sister Rachel and Mike, her brother-in-law, took Mary in and raised her as their own. All was well until Mary reached puberty and her temper tantrums became too excessive for Mike. He split from Rachel not too long after Mary turned thirteen. Mary herself, suffered many years of abuse from her peers, which would continue into adolescence. Despite the fights and fallouts, Rachel looked after Mary until her 18th birthday. On that day, Rachel presented her with a box containing Abigail's most personal belongings, including a letter for Mary which would reveal all the secrets of her life. She was also left £200,000.00 with instructions to use it wisely. Mary did just that, buying herself a home of her own and going to college. She also promised Rachel that she would one day, somehow, avenge her Mother.

Alex sat silent as Mary finished her tale, not knowing what to say to her that would be of any comfort. He offered Mary a smile and contemplated giving her a reassuring hug, but wasn't sure if it was appropriate. He wasn't good at these situations. Mary wasn't aware of Alex at the time, she stared silently into the distance, her gaze fixed on nothing. She was motionless apart from the regular movement of her chest as she breathed. Her face lacked any expression but her eyes told of the pain she experienced. Mary was somewhere else and this unnerved Alex somewhat and he jumped up from his chair disturbed. He called out her name. It was not until the fifth time of doing so when he shouted out loud, that Mary returned from her trance and joined him in the now.

"What's wrong Alex? Why are you shouting?" Asked Mary bemused.

"I don't know? You tell me. You went into a trance after you told me your story. It was quite scary." Explained Alex who was a little freaked out.

"Did I? Shit. I'm sorry. I don't know how or why that happened."

"Has it ever happened before Mary?" asked Alex sympathetically

"What? You mean 'zoning' out? No, I don't think so. I'm not sure." replied Mary casually.

"You up for another drink Alex? I've got plenty in!"

Alex nodded and watched bewildered as Mary bounced off into the kitchen to fetch more alcohol. He was confused and couldn't quite work Mary out. He wondered what had just happened to her. Had she done it to on purpose to freak him out or were the blackouts something that occurred regularly? He felt uptight, his brain aching from over thinking. Mary was all smiles and full of exuberance when she returned carrying a tray of alcohol and snacks. Alex decided to forget the blackout and lighten up.

"Come on, let's drink, rock out and have fun."

"Yeah, that sounds cool." replied Alex as he took a beer.

Mary grabbed hold of Alex and gave him a kiss. She looked at Alex happily and he could see her beautiful eyes had softened once more. Alex felt an incredible sadness for Mary, but also thought that she wasn't as vulnerable as she sometimes looked. He didn't know why but Alex sensed that there was something not right about Mary. Although she was incredibly beautiful and fun, he wasn't sure he wanted to fully enter her world.

The night had grown old and dark. Mary allowed Alex to stop over for the night as he was too pissed to travel home. She found some spare bedding from a cupboard in the hallway and threw it in the direction of Alex who sprawled halfway across the sofa and floor. Mary's face signaled that she was ready for sleep, so she waved at Alex and made her way gingerly upstairs to the bedroom. Alex heard the door close and the sound of Mary clumsily getting undressed before a clicking of a light switch suggested Mary had managed it to her bed. Alex fashioned the blankets and pillows into something that he could reasonably sleep under then located the downstairs bathroom. As Alex washed, he was drawn to a wooden plaque on the wall. The hand painted words appeared to be an old Catholic Prayer which he hadn't seen before, but were somehow familiar,

'Soul of Christ, sanctify me; Body of Christ, save me; Blood of Christ, inebriate me; Water from the side of Christ, wash me; Passion of Christ, strengthen me; O good Jesus, hear me; within Thy wounds, hide me; let me never be separated from Thee; from the evil one, deliver me; at the hour of my death, call me and bid me come to Thee, that with Thy saints, I may praise Thee forever and ever. Amen.'

Alex felt an uncomfortable sensation flow through his body as he read the words, from 'the evil one deliver me'. Sensing a presence, he turned around sharply to see Mary standing naked in the doorway. Her gaze was lost in a place unknown and she was clearly elsewhere once more.

"What the hell Mary? What are you doing?" demanded the disturbed Alex.

Mary didn't focus on Alex, continuing to look straight ahead at the wall. She raised her arm and without looking, pointed at the plaque, knowing that Alex was looking at it.

"It's a prayer that some Priests use in exorcisms. It was a gift. Given to keep me safe from evil." she spoke without feeling, her voice monotone.

"Okay, okay, I understand, I think?"

"You're safe Alex!"

"I am? Well, that's good Mary, thanks."

"You can fuck me Alex if you want?" offered Mary, voice and eyes still devoid of emotion.

"Thanks for the offer Mary, but, I'm kinda wasted. I'd be no good to you. Need some sleep. I hope that's okay with you?" Alex replied sensitively and cautiously.

After a pause, Mary replied blankly, "of course Alex. That is fine."

Mary turned and slowly made her way back upstairs. Alex stared at her beautiful formed body as she ascended the stairs. Her milky white skin appeared to shimmer in the soft light. Alex noted with interest the tattoo that almost covered the whole of Mary's back. From distance, he couldn't clearly make out what the image was, but it looked as if it were a winged angel or a demon?

Morning arrived and Alex was relieved to see it. He hadn't slept well during the night, waking at the slightest noise. He was somewhat perturbed by Mary's behaviour in the bathroom and had found it difficult to settle. Hearing sounds of activity from the kitchen, Alex dressed and made his way through. He didn't want to hang around any longer than necessary, plus he had to go to college in the afternoon. Mary sang as she made toast and coffee, looking fresh, beautiful and angelic.

"Morning Alex. I hope you slept okay? How's your head?" she sweetly enquired whilst handing him a mug of coffee.

"I think I'll live. How about you?"

"I'm great thanks. I remember heading off to bed, falling over as I got undressed. Got into bed and then, here we are, in the kitchen the following morning." She laughed casually.

Alex noted that the appearance outside of the bathroom wasn't referenced. Was this because she was too embarrassed to bring it up in conversation, or had she blanked out again entering into a trance state? Could there be any other reason? Alex decided to say nothing of it. If it was relevant, then perhaps Mary would bring it up at some point and they'd have a laugh about it. He thanked Mary for a great evening and made ready to head off home en route to college.

"So, are you still up for The Church of Darkness this Friday night?" enquired Mary. Alex paused on the spot unsure how to respond.

"Hey Alex, don't get standing me up now. It will be a spectacular night that will blow your mind. I promise." she cooed seductively and with quiet authority.

"Put like that, how could I refuse?"

"Fantastic. You won't forget it. I'll speak to you beforehand, but we'll go from here. Say about 8:00pm?"

"Sure, that sounds cool." replied Alex before he made his way to the door.

Mary watched him as he left, smiling in the process. Alex waved and then was gone. Mary turned to face the mirror in the kitchen, her smile changing to one of malevolence.

It had been two weeks after she'd been killed, before Police discovered the body of 20 year old Suzie Jasper on the grounds of the derelict Red Fox Tavern. The nature of the murder was similar to those of Charlotte King and Darren Potter, only more brutal. Suzie's body was found with her hair cut from her head and shoved into her throat. Stabbed multiple times in a frenzied attack, there were wounds to her stomach, chest, arms and face. It was clear that whoever killed Suzie wanted to prove a point and make pretty damn sure that she was dead. A horrific and brutal attack that shocked even the most hardened of Police officers and forensic investigators. It was merciless. Senior Police officers didn't want to suggest that there may be a serial killer at large so reported it to the public with sensitivity. While they admitted to not finding many clues at the crime scenes, they did believe the murders were linked and they would continue with their vigorous investigations until the murderer was brought to justice.

News of yet another local murder had already circulated college by the time Alex arrived. Although not a student, Suzie Jasper was known to a few people, so naturally the news of a brutal murder caused some distress. Alex didn't know of her but still felt saddened by yet more tragic news, especially after his evening with Mary had left him on edge. Alex had decided to go to the library before his first lecture. He wanted to check on the origin of the prayer that was on display in Mary's bathroom. He found an old Catholic prayer book and scanned through it until he found the prayer he recognised. It was the 'Anima Christi' which dated back to the 14th century and was still popular as a communion hymn. It was also used by some Priests when performing exorcisms. Alex wasn't sure what his research meant in relation to Mary, but reconciled that the prayer plaque was significant to her in so much as providing some protection against evil. But why was it relevant? Was it simply just Catholic ornamentation which is found in many households of faith? After all, there were many in Alex's home. Or was it something of significance to protect Mary, particularly from herself?

The afternoon lectures passed without issue or excitement for Alex, so he made his way home. He had not seen Mary around today which he thought was unusual. Concerned by her absence, he decided to drive to her house to check if she was okay. He arrived twenty minutes later, happy he could remember the way. Despite knocking the door and ringing the bell several times there was no answer. Quickly returning to his car, Alex tore a page from his college notepad and wrote a short message, asking Mary to call him. He drove off wondering if his emotions would have been less conflicted if he had not offered Mary a lift the other week. He was infatuated with her. But, he was also equally troubled by her.

Arriving home, Alex found a note in the kitchen from his mother, informing him that she and his father had gone out for a meal with friends. Had he come home on Sunday after church, he would have known this. A meal hadn't been prepared for him, but there was plenty in the freezer. They didn't know what time they would be back. Alex made his way through to the living room and switched on the TV with the intention of finding the MTV Rock channel. BBC local news was presented first and Alex's attention was instantly caught.

'Police have reported that they are interviewing Robert Hill, who is helping them with their enquiries into the three murders committed locally within the last two weeks. At this moment, it is not known if Hill is a suspect.'

Alex felt a slight sense of comfort from this. Especially as it allowed some freedom from the thoughts that sat gnawing away in the back of his mind. The sound of a telephone ringing brought Alex back to his senses. He answered and it was Mary.

"Hey. Sorry, I missed you. I've had a few things to sort out today. Are you okay?"

"I'm good Mary thanks. Didn't see you at college, so wondered if all was well."

"Yes, I'm fine thanks Alex. Just a lot to do. So, you're going to be okay for Friday then? You haven't changed your mind now have you?"

"I'm going to be fine for Friday. I'm intrigued."

"Good. That's good. Okay, I'll see you at mine at 8:00pm. Gotta go now, bye."

Alex didn't know how to react. Sure, it was good that all was okay with Mary, but something seemed strange. Once again, he considered what it would be like not knowing Mary and came to the conclusion it would be dull. Yes, he was very intrigued about Friday and was sure as hell going to go. After all, he could always make it to confession at some point after.

Father Jacobs sat alone in the main living room of the parochial house, almost asleep through boredom. He was stirred by the sound of a crash and that of breaking wood from outside in the garden. An animal or intruder perhaps? Making his way through the corridor that lead to the back door, Jacobs grabbed his coat and torch. He wasn't overly concerned and was confident enough to investigate the disturbance on his own and deal with what may be evident. He had faced conflict in the past and despite his Holy Orders, was more than capable of taking care of himself. Scanning the garden area to the left of him, he noticed that a fence panel had been damaged. To the right, he could see under the light of his torch, that the statuette of the Holy Virgin Mary had been desecrated. The head had been cut off and the hands broken. Walking closer he found that the head was lying intact and blood had been poured over the torso from the neck downwards, particularly over the hands. He sighed heavily and then looked around once more, before speaking out to the night sky.

"I take it that this act of degradation is a sign my child? It was to be expected in truth. But know this. It solves nothing. I am ready. I have always been ready. None shall judge me other than God."

Father Jacobs quickly surveyed the area once more, before returning inside. After locking the back door, ensuring that all windows and the front door were secure, he made his way into the study. Pouring himself a generous glass of fine malt whisky and taking the contents in one mouthful, he opened the middle drawer of the desk to produce a handgun with plenty of ammunition.

"I'm ready child. Ready for anything you want to throw my way."

Newsflash: 'Police have formally charged Robert Hill on three counts of murder after he voluntarily made a statement confessing to the killing of Suzie Jasper, Darren Potter and Charlotte King. We'll bring you more news on this story as soon as possible.'

Friday night arrived and Alex made his way over to Mary's place, prior to heading off to The Church of Darkness. The night was already quite black, cold and with an air of mystery. Alex wasn't too sure how his emotions were fixed at this point. On one hand he was somewhat comforted by the news the killer had been arrested, thus quashing the bizarre notion he had in his head. Secondly, he was excited and yet terrified about the evening out with Mary. He knew nothing about The Church of Darkness and was somewhat apprehensive. It didn't help matters that Mary was being too damn secretive. As requested by Mary, he had made an effort with his outfit, choosing black leather trousers, black silk shirt and his trusty beaten old biker jacket. In his mind, he looked like a rock God. Mary was suitably impressed when she answered the door to Alex and this pleased him. Alex thought she looked incredible, dressed in a figure hugging black lycra catsuit, knee length black leather boots and a mini red leather jacket. The devil herself in all her dark majesty.

Alex drove to The Church of Darkness. Mary reassured him that the night was going to be one he would never forget and that they could get a taxi back if all went well. He accepted this as reasonable and followed her directions, excited about what lay ahead. The venue was located thirty minutes outside of town, situated in a field in the middle of nowhere. Alex parked the car outside of an old building that was once a chapel. The sound of loud rock music seeped through the heavy stone walls, whilst red and amber light flickered through the concealed windows. Getting out of the car together, Mary slung a heavy looking backpack over her shoulders.

"What the hell's that for?" enquired Alex robustly.

"You'll have to wait and see dear Alex. Let's just say it includes toys for the evening." replied Mary mischievously.

"You're really fucking tripping me out tonight. This better be safe Mary, I'm warning you."

"Ooh, I do like it when you swear Alex, you naughty boy. Now, let's get inside and have fun. I've already told you, this is going to be a night you will never forget."

Mary led on to the large oak door of the 'Church' and knocked. A porthole opened revealing the centre part of a black guy's face. He saw Mary's smiling face and promptly opened the door, revealing quite a considerable frame behind it. Mary offered two ten pound notes into the 'voluntary' collection box before she and Alex were allowed through into the main hall of The Church of Darkness. Mary smiled as Alex could only mutter "Oh fucking hell."

The room was dimly lit with a seedy reddish glow and there were no windows evident, presumably they were behind the black-out curtains. Opposite the entrance, a seven foot cross took centre stage, dominating the view. Spotlights were trained directly on it, providing an almost divine effect. Leather chairs and sofas were positioned around the perimeter of the room,some were occupied by a few people in varied levels of undress,performing sexual acts on each other. There appeared to be at least eight people in the room, not counting the guy on the door. Loud electro ambient music pumped rhythmically from the speakers. Father Jacobs, left the chair that he was sharing with two young women and made his way over to greet Mary and Alex. His white shirt was unbuttoned revealing his hairy chest and the buttons were undone on his trousers. He smiled at the latest visitors, running his hands through his hair before reverently bowing before them.

"Welcome lost souls to The Church of Darkness. Take what you will from me and offer what you wish. Let free your desires, share your fantasies or simply sit back and enjoy the experience. Anything goes in my congregation of the damned." said Jacobs with a smooth and reassuring elegance.

"Thank you Father. We certainly will enjoy the experience." replied Mary coldly. Alex remained silent. Father Jacobs nodded before turning his attention to the stage.

"Ah excellent. A beautiful devotee is offering herself to us. Come, let us celebrate this gift!" said Jacobs, leading attention to the front of the room.

"This is fucked up Mary. What are we doing here?" rasped Alex angrily.

"Relax, I told you that I was going to blow your mind. This is only the beginning." replied Mary flashing Alex a mischievous smile. He nodded in return.

Father Jacobs took to the stage where Jessica Lloyd stood naked in front of the cross. He directed the two people standing either side of her, to help her into position and strap her hands to the cross beam. Her opened legs were secured by a spreader bar at the foot of the cross.

"Hear me oh acolytes of darkness and sin. Jessica has given herself willingly so that you may enjoy her beauty!" Jacobs concluded his speech by caressing the 'crucified' Jessica's breasts, before encouraging another acolyte to follow suit. Jessica clearly enjoyed the experience, even more so when Lucas Hopwood knelt in front of her and proceeded to lick her vagina. The congregation circulated around each other, drinking, smoking and sharing their bodies. The smell of cannabis, sweat and sex hung heavily in the air.

Mary pulled Alex away and took him to the middle of the room. She pulled a wooden chair from the side and invited Alex to sit on it, which he did somewhat unsure. Mary then proceeded to tie his hands to the side of the chair and ankles to the chair legs with rope from her backpack.

"What's this for Mary? What's going on?" Alex enquired nervously, his breath quickening.

"I have something special in mind for you Alex. I want you to enjoy it." she replied seductively, running her hands over his firm chest.

As Mary busied herself, Alex stared directly ahead at the still bound and clearly ecstatic Jessica, who was being fucked hard by some guy he didn't know. To the left he could see Father Jacob's being pleasured by two girls he recognised from college and church. Lucas Hopwood, Selina Giles and Melanie... surname he couldn't recall, all danced together while sharing a spliff. He really didn't know why he was here or what Mary had in mind for him. In truth, he was afraid and wanted nothing more than get home. Mary jumped on Alex's lap and kissed him.

"A few more minutes and then it's show time Alex. Just sit back and enjoy." she grinned at him darkly.

"What are you going to do?" pleaded Alex.

Mary didn't answer, but stared at him without expression. She got off his lap, picked up her backpack and made for the entrance. Alex tried to turn his head to her direction but couldn't see her. No one else had noticed her move. She smiled to herself, then stepped silently through the curtain. The big black guy who answered the door to them earlier, was sat wedged in a chair, in a cramped corner watching a small TV. He had his back to Mary and was unaware that she was behind him. All too easy. Mary carefully withdrew a hunting knife from the backpack, paused for a couple of seconds, then pulled it fast and hard across the guy's throat, blood spraying over the wall. Startled, he tried to make a sound, but Mary had her left hand pulling his head backward whilst slashing hard over the already gaping wound. She was too quick and the guy was dead. He didn't stand a chance. The bulk of this giant man rested uneasily against the wall, his head hanging limply to one side. Mary locked the door and prepared herself. Opening up the backpack, she took out a holster and belt, tying it quickly around her waist. The revolver was already in place. Breathing in deeply, she cleared her mind of everything else other than what was planned. Mary was ready to begin.

Taking the revolver in her left hand with the bloodied hunting knife in her right, Mary re-entered the room unnoticed by anyone. She knew she had to be quick. With the pace and stealth of a wild cat about to strike at it's prey, Mary was upon Lucas. She smiled as did he in kind unaware of what was to come. Before any word was uttered, Mary struck out, slashing the hunting knife across his throat with such force, it almost cleaved his head from his shoulders, spurting red liquid over her. As he slumped to the floor, Selina and Melanie screamed so loud they could have been heard in another continent. The show was well and truly underway. Mary aimed the gun at Selina's face, blowing most of it away with just one shot. Alex screamed out Mary's name with all of his might, but it was no use. Everyone started to scream and panic as chaos erupted. Father Jacobs ran towards Mary, but he wasn't quick enough and was felled with two shots to his chest. Three down.

One of the girls sat next to Father Jacobs, took one bullet in the head before she could get up. The other ran. Mary chased down Melanie, before stabbing her through the heart, stomach and throat. Melanie's lifeless body slumped limply to the floor. Alex still tied to the chair, threw up all over his chest and into his lap. He cried hard. The guy who had been busy with Jessica tried to hide and run for the door. He didn't make it as the bullet tore through the back of his knee, sending him to the ground. Jessica screamed loudly as the advancing Mary turned and smiled at her.

"It's not your turn yet Jessica. Please be patient." she snarled.

Mary found the other girl who had accompanied Father Jacobs, cowering behind the stereo unit. "Gun or knife, gun or knife?" muttered Mary in front of the hysterical girl.

"Any preference?" asked Mary. "No? Gun it is then!"

Mary fired the last bullet downward into the top of the girls head, causing it to explode, showering blood and bits of brain over her and the wall.

"MARY. Why the fucking hell are you doing this?" shouted the distraught Alex.

"Shut the fuck up. Can't you see I'm busy playing with our new friends?"

Simon, who'd been shot in the knee, was trying to crawl away to the door despite the immense agony. He began to panic, eyes filling with terror as Mary drew near. Within seconds she was stood over him laughing maniacally, before stamping on his damaged knee. Simon screamed almost passing out in the process. "You get knife I'm afraid." she said blankly before plunging it deep into Simon's heart, twisting it several times causing warm blood to spew over her hand.

Mary turned to face Jessica, then made her towards her. Alex shouted out, pleading with her to stop, but she dismissed it with a shake of her head. Mary was soon on the stage where Jessica was still tied to the cross.

"Guess what, you're the star of the show now Jessica. This is a bit surreal isn't it? A little bit disrespectful too maybe don't you think?" quizzed Mary

"Please, please, please Mary. I'll do anything, ANYTHING." Jessica screamed, tears running uncontrollably down her beautiful face.

"Recite the Hail Mary to me Jessica!"

"Hail Mary.......... full of grace.......... Our Lord is with thee." mumbled Jessica through her tears.

"Lies Jessica. It's all fucking lies. There's no Mary full of grace and there certainly isn't any Lord the saviour. Sorry, you don't get to live."

Mary took a breath, before thrusting the knife into Jessica's chest. The scream was deafening. Mary used all of her strength to pull down on the blade, carving through bone, skin and sinew. Jessica's screams became more subdued. Mary continued to butcher Jessica, cutting through her stomach down to the groin. Jessica fell silent after Mary plunged the knife into her heart. Mary who was now covered in Jessica's blood, pulled the knife free and made her way over to Alex. He was beside himself with fear and loathing. His face burnt from the tears that were shed and pain inside, as the blood soaked demon stood right in front of him.

"I told you this was going to be spectacular didn't I Alex?"

"Why Mary? Why the fuck have you done this? WHY?"

"They all deserved it Alex. Every fucking one of them."

"It was you who killed the other three wasn't it?"

"Yes Alex, it was. You see, they all fucking abused me in some way and bullied me for years. They had to fucking die. Charlotte took advantage of me when I blacked out for the first time. She thought it was cool to stub her cigarettes out on me. Then the fucking bitch encouraged Darren Potter, a mate of her boyfriend, to fuck me when I'd blacked out again. Suzie, the fucking bitch, was the worst. The bullying was constant from the age of five upwards. She even cut my hair off and made me fucking eat it. I promised I'd get revenge."

"Mary, I know you've had a shit life, but did it need to come to this?" Alex tried to remonstrate.

"You know fuck all Alex. Jessica was friends with Susie. She used to love it when I was being picked on and thought it was a fucking great show to watch. As for Father Jacob's, I've been waiting to kill him for a long time. That fucking hypocritical sack of shit was the one who got my mother pregnant and then drove her to commit suicide. It's just a shame he died so quickly. I really wanted to make him fucking suffer."

Mary fell silent, unaware of the shuffling in the background. She stared at Alex for a moment, undecided what to do with him.

"So where do I fit in? Why am I here?" Alex asked scared of knowing the answer.

"I really liked you. But then I realised who your Mother was. She was responsible for causing my Mother torment within the Church circles. Your mother believed it was wrong that my mother was carrying a 'bastard child'. It wasn't right for the church. I mean what a fucking contradiction. So, I wanted to make her suffer, through you."

Alex wept. It was all too much to take in. His only crime was to fall for Mary's beauty and zest for life. He had concerns and wished that he had listened to his self doubt. In fact, he wished he had never offered Mary that lift, that he never entered into her world of darkness.

"So, what happens now?" he asked weakly.

Mary stood silently in front of him, contemplating her next action. She was about to speak when the sound of gunfire erupted. A bullet flew straight through Mary's chest and then a second quickly followed, penetrating the back of her skull and through her forehead. Alex watched startled as Mary fell to floor, dead before impact. He looked around frantically and made the sight of the stricken Father Jacobs who had managed to crawl from where he had fallen. His wounds were clearly terminal as evidenced by the extreme loss of blood, but not as instant as Mary would had thought. He managed to muster enough of the air that remained in his damaged lungs and spoke out to Alex.

"I'm sorry my child, truly. I was ready, always have been. I'm sorry............." Then he died.

Alex sat alone. The music from the stereo had long since ceased and the only sound he could hear in the room of death was his own heart beating. He cried deeply and then passed out.

It was the early hours of Saturday morning when the Police discovered Alex, the sole survivor in The Church of Darkness. They had been on the trail of Mary Carter since Friday evening when Robert Hill broke down, confessing the truth and named her as the true killer. Mary had a previous record of convictions for minor assault and threatening behaviour. Apparently, Robert Hill, a local heroin addict, had tried to rob Mary one night, much to his regret. He pleaded with her not to kill him, stating he was desperate for money to feed his addiction. Mary had offered him several thousand pounds if he took the heat off her by confessing to the killings, so that it would buy her some time to complete her plan. Mary had even given him £150 cash upfront, so he saw no reason not to go along with it. He didn't have anything to lose. But, Friday afternoon, when faced with the charges of three counts of murder, Robert changed his mind. The Police managed to discover that Mary Carter was with Alex Lawton on the Friday night. Searching for the location of Alex's car, registration provided by his mother, was a good starting point.

They had been too late.

Cow Made God - Mark Nye

Something flickered at the edge of Phil's vision. He snapped his head around to stare at the machinery behind him, but beyond the wire grill there was only darkness. He slid off of his stool and walked around the mammoth metal machine to look behind it.

The cow at the trough hadn't moved. It stood in a languid state, its head resting on the metal bars. No longer aware of where it was, its tongue lolled from one corner of its mouth leaving a trail of saliva from tip to floor.

Phil reached out; his hand ran over its soft skin. He looked around the hanging head and saw its stomach split from throat to crotch. The crimson sack of organs and guts hung loose from the belly of the beast, awaiting removal to the dog food bins.

He took shallow breaths through the handkerchief across his nose and tried to mask the rotten stench of offal, copper and shit that permeated the abattoir. But his nose still filled with stale death. As Phil ran his hand down the cow's neck, an unexpected wave of sympathy washed over him. It may have been his job, but it didn't help him to sleep at night.

'Godspeed,' he whispered, placing his forehead upon the nape of the cow.

'You're looking for God in wrong place, flesh bag.'

Phil jumped. He glanced around the shack but no-one was there. Turning back to the cow, he watched as one stomach escaped the organ sack and slapped onto the gritted ground underneath.

'Trying to figure out how I work, boy?'

Phil took a step back and peered past the cow. The cow's stomach slid across the floor and rested against the side of his boot.

'I'm here flesh bag, look at me, at what you've done.'

The colour drained from Phil's face as he watched the cow's jaw move in an abomination of oral articulation.

'Why would you do this?'

'This can't be real, can't be true.' Phil mumbled as he stepped further back towards the machinery. His foot connected with the stomach, its contents splashed over the floor as the weight of the boot caused it to explode.

'It's true, it's real.'

'But how? Why?'

'You killed me! You tore me open and left me hanging here. I was still breathing when you walked away.'

Phil's eyes drifted to the gore covered knife on the table in front of him then back to the cow.

'But you're dead, and you're a cow!'

'What I am does not matter. This is your fault, your hand that held the blade and now it's time for you to reap what you have sown. It was only a matter of time until you found one of us. You have mercilessly slaughtered our kind for as long as we've been on this earth, and yet you never knew of our existence.'

'Existence of what? You're just a fucking cow.'

'I am so much more than just a cow. You think you are the only species that worships deities and idols?'

'What? You trying to tell me you're a God?'

'No. I am not A God, I am part of a larger collection, and we are God. We have watched over cow-kind since the dawn of time. There are three of us in total. I am the most lenient of the triumvirate, and I have a gift for you Phil,' the Cow-God's head rolled to the side and a lifeless eye fixed on Phil.

'What the fuck is going on?' Phil's back connected with the wire mesh and he grasped it with his fingers.

'It's the gift of death, Phil. All day long you blow our brains out and carve us with your cruel, curved knives. For you it's a job, but for us it's the end. We see it coming, we try to avoid it where we can but we must all go to the diamond pasture in the sky. But before I leave and rejoice in rebirth, I want you to know what we feel.'

'What do you mean?' Phil stepped towards the Cow.

'We want you to be the killer we know you are. We can't control our future but we can change yours. This isn't a gift of flesh or leather, steak or milk. This is a gift of bovine brutality, our internal conflicts, and the emotions you never knew we held.'

'B-but I don't want it.'

'Killing is an act of self-realisation, boy. It shows a man his true nature, and when you know this, the petty world you tie yourself to with things and money falls away, and your true self is revealed. You do not get a choice in this, meat bag. Your path has been chosen. Accept it.'

'No,' Phil screamed as he turned to run. His foot skidded in the pool of coagulating stomach contents and he fell backwards, cracking his head on the table.

'Now is your time boy, and our time for retribution.'

The Cow-God lowered its head over Phil's mouth. Its neck convulsed and throbbed. If the cow had been alive, it would have been hacking and coughing, but instead its throat heaved in a hypnotic rhythm. Neck skin stretched to breaking point as a deep red clot slithered its way out of the God's throat and rolled over the cow's tongue, slapping its way down its flaccid, pallid length. It reached the end and dangled as a pendulum, then dropped the small distance to Phil's mouth with a dull plop.

The God clot popped as it ground past the teeth and a bovine parasite slurped its way down his throat. Black trails of fetid cow blood leaked from the corners of Phil's mouth, giving his face a painted grin. More rancid bovine blood oozed out of his nose and mouth as the parasite violated his body.

Arms spasmed and legs kicked eliciting clouds of dust from the killing room floor as the parasite worked its way into his system. Its distorted cow face sprouted fine, translucent tentacles. Each tentacle latched onto the inside of the throat with tiny brown claws and dragged itself past the tonsils and into the warm depths.

Phil gagged and choked as it wormed through his body and set his nerves on fire. His eyes glazed over and rolled back into his skull.

The spasms stopped.

A blank expression crossed his face as he picked himself up from the floor, bit by bit, as if his legs weren't his own. He turned to face the cow corpse.

'Good boy,' the Cow-God slurred, 'Now go. Be our hand of vengeance.'

Phil picked up the God-killing, crusty gutting knife and headed towards the slaughterhouse.

'Good flesh bag,' the cow whispered, its head lolled back to its chest, a wry smile peaked the corner of its mouth. Screams echoed around the farm as he went on to the diamond pasture.

Come Away To The Sunday School - Dale Robertson

Dark clouds lingered in the clear blue sky, threatening to outweigh the brightness.

A storm was definitely brewing.

The doors of the village church opened wide as the vicar sent the child on his way. He looked up at the sky and smiled, then directed his head back to the young boy walking along the concrete path to the garden exit.

The boy never glanced back as he turned the corner and disappeared behind the stone wall.

"Go forth," the vicar muttered to no-one, as he spun back into the church, closing the doors behind him.

At twelve years old, John Turner never really felt like he fit in at school. Probably the same feeling most teenagers had. He had his own small group of friends whom he was comfortable with but watching others, he envied them. The way they could mix with anyone at all without awkwardness. To be shunted miles across the country to some tiny village in the middle of nowhere didn't help matters – leaving his friends behind and being hauled from his comfort zone. When his parents divorced, he had the choice who to live with but opted for his mum; she was nicer than his dad, even if it did mean he had to leave the things he loved behind. His father was mean to his mum. Never physical, not that he saw anyway, but was always shouting at her. She rarely smiled and John hated that. He thought maybe this move would put the happiness back on her face. Unfortunately for him, it meant he was back to the very bottom of the social pecking order.

The village wasn't big at all; a couple of streets crisscrossed and lined with houses with a church stood at the far end, up high, almost like it was keeping an eye on everything. A small shop for the essentials, a park consisting of a slide, two swings and a climbing frame, and a school made up the rest of the meagre hamlet.

It didn't take John long to explore it all when they first moved. A quick trip round on his BMX and that was it. He was disappointed there wasn't much else to see. There was a forest with bike tracks and a lake somewhere in there. He hadn't ventured that far yet, as his mum didn't want him to go off on his own, in case something happened.

As he lay in his bed, staring at the ceiling, he heard his mum calling him.

"John? Johnny?" she shouted. "You'll be late for school. Come and get your breakfast."

He rubbed his eyes and glanced towards his Avengers clock, swinging his legs onto the floor and resting his head in his hands.

"Coming," he replied.

Ambling down the stairs yawning, John went into the kitchen when he reached the bottom step. He glanced at the table to see his breakfast set out with a glass of apple juice. His mum had her back to him, standing at the sink washing the dishes. He dragged the chair out from the table, causing a loud squeal to echo throughout the kitchen.

"Oh, good afternoon Mr Turner," his mum said, without turning round. "Glad you decided to grace us with your presence."

"Very good, Mum. You know, that joke wasn't funny the first time you said it."

His mum turned from the sink and smiled. "I just don't want you being late for school, that's all."

"Mum, it's a two minute walk. There's no risk of me being late. In fact, this place is so small I doubt anyone could be late for anything."

"Okay, okay." She held up her hands in mock surrender. "Oh, before I forget, we are going to church on Sunday. They have a Sunday School that all the kids go to."

John dropped his spoon into his bowl with a clatter and stared at her open mouthed. "Sunday School? I'm a bit big for that. Why can't I just stay here while you go to church?"

"Because, for one, we are new to this town and we have been invited along so it's only courteous that we go. And two, I don't want to leave my twelve-year-old son on his own at home."

"I'm old enough to survive without you for a couple of hours, you know," John tried to argue.

"Not yet you aren't. We are going. End of."

John knew better than to argue any more. He sat with a grimace and carried on with his breakfast.

Sunday School. Fucking hell.

John couldn't help but notice the lack of kids on the street. It was as if the place had been abandoned. He thought there would be others like him, leaving it to the last minute to make it to school. He checked his watch and saw that there were still another few minutes before the bell rang. He glanced around again. Nope, still just him.

Approaching the school, he was amazed at how un-school-like it was. It was more like someone's house rather than a place of education. His previous school had been an enormous structure plastered with windows; each one allowing the children to vacantly stare into oblivion whilst their teacher rattled on about a subject that would, no doubt, be useless in their future.

John stood at the school gates, which led into a small playground circling the school house, staring at the other kids. He frowned as he realised there didn't appear to be anyone older than he was. It was something that hadn't dawned on him until now. He looked left, right and behind him to confirm what he already knew – there was no other school. Just this one.

Strange, he thought as he stepped into the grounds.

The timing couldn't have been better as the ring of the bell blared out upon him passing by the gates and into the grounds. The children all lined up by the entrance in neat rows. John ambled slowly over making the journey last as long as possible before he had to enter class.

John found a spare table by a large window. Slipping his jacket on the back of the chair, he sat down and got out his pencil and books. He turned his head to the left and looked out of the window as the rest of the class settled down. There was a nice view of trees and hills in the distance, marred only by the encroaching dark clouds that seemed to linger with intent. Directly outside the window was a small plot of grass; rusted goalposts at either end and faded white paint outlining the football pitch. Further off to the side sat an obstacle area.

"Hey," a voice called.

John continued to stare out through the glass, ignoring it.

"Hey!" a bit more persistent this time and accompanied with a nudge on the arm.

John turned with a look of anger on his face. "What?" he growled.

"You're the new kid, right?" A spotty faced boy with straight, greasy hair asked.

"Yeah, so?" John replied curtly.

"You'll like it here. Takes a bit to get used to but you will. I was the same at first, until it saw it." He began to giggle as if someone had told him the funniest joke in the world. That was until John noticed the rest of the class had gone silent and were glaring at the spotty lad. The boy also noticed this as he stopped abruptly and looked down at the floor. John was amazed, it was as if time had frozen – no-one said a thing as they eyeballed the abashed child. John wasn't sure how to end this awkward situation and continued to look at the rest of the class. Their eyes never left the person beside him. Fortunately, he didn't have to do anything.

"Good morning class," the teacher announced brightly, strolling through the doorway and heading to his desk.

Time unfroze and everyone resumed their activities as if nothing had happened. "Good morning, Mr. Seers," they said in unison.

John kept quiet and looked over at the red- faced boy next to him. He never lifted his head to meet John's gaze. John turned back to the teacher as the lesson began.

'It', what the hell did he mean by 'it'?

Lunchtime came around quicker than John thought; either that or he had actually fallen asleep in class. Surely not, the teacher would have noticed and chastised him. It was strange, he couldn't remember a thing from that morning's lesson.

Shit, it must have been boring.

John wandered through the large room that was classed as the cafeteria. The room was crammed with tables and benches with a section against one wall where the meals were served. John was itching to get outside for some freedom but it looked like everyone sat here whilst eating. He scouted the room for a free space but saw none. Maybe by the time he was served, a space would crop up. He felt the eyes of everyone on him, weighing up the new boy. This was exactly why he wanted to be outside, away from the claustrophobic dining room.

"Cold or hot?" a voice startled his wandering mind.

"Huh?" he said.

"Cold food or hot foot, dear?" the dinner lady repeated.

John ran his eyes over the options; sandwiches, baguettes, chips, beans and some other food he didn't recognise. He opted for good old faithful. "Ham sandwich please."

He took the sandwich and put it on his tray, grabbed a carton of apple juice and headed to the till. Fumbling for the correct change, he paid the stony-faced woman behind the counter and turned to see if a space had become free. He was in luck. There was a space beside three girls who were deep in conversation. John advanced towards them, aware of each table he passed, the conversation hushed until he was by. Upon approaching, the girls stopped talking and looked him up and down with blank expressions. He felt as if he was on trial.

"Do you mind if I sit?" he asked.

They continued to stare for what felt like an eternity before the cute one with long, mousy brown hair tied in a ponytail smiled. "Sure, new guy. We were just about finished anyway."

"Don't leave on my account."

"It's not because of you, just bad timing. We are heading outside to play."

He watched as they each stood up and took their empty plates and glasses to the designated area. The cute one turned to look at him. He smiled awkwardly, mesmerised by her beauty. She blinked, and when her eyelids lifted, her eyeballs were completely black.

John's eyes opened wide in surprise and he looked away quickly. Glancing back, he saw that she was still looking at him but her eyes were normal, a deep green colour. She smiled again and gave him a wave before disappearing out of the room.

The rest of the day passed without incident, just an average, boring day in school, listening to the teacher talk about something he wasn't interested in. The school bell rang just in time to stop his eyes from fully closing. Any longer and John swore his head would have hit the table. He packed up his books and pencils and headed to the exit.

Stepping out into the chilly afternoon air, he let out a big sigh and lifted his head back. The dark clouds had invaded the blue sky, and were winning the battle easily.

Better run home, looks like a storm is coming

Gail Thomson had just settled her nine-year-old son, Ross, back down in bed since the wind battering his window woke him up. He stared at his mother, emotionless and vacant in his sleepy daze. Gail put her arm around his shoulders and directed him back to his room and into bed.

He had given her a fright when she first happened upon him. She was downstairs and had walked past the staircase, looking up to see a figure standing at the top, gazing blankly downwards.

"Oh, Ross," she said, holding her hand to her heart. "You almost gave me a heart attack. Come on, let's get you back to bed."

Walking downstairs now, she thought back to her son's face, devoid of expression and thought it peculiar. She put it down to him still being half asleep. Maybe he was sleepwalking. He went back to bed happily enough, and was soon snoring away.

"What was all that about?" Ross' dad, Neil, asked.

"I found Ross standing at the top of the stairs. The wind and rain beating against his window must have woken him up," Gail replied. "He's back asleep now."

Neil turned back to the television to concentrate on the football highlights. Gail picked up her phone instinctively and checked her social media accounts for any gossip, local or otherwise. She sometimes felt this was her only connection to the outside world. Nothing interesting was happening. She dropped her phone onto the cushion next to her on the sofa and let out a big sigh. Neil ignored her. She let out a second sigh, putting more emphasis on it.

Neil turned to her. "What?" he barked.

"Don't you just wish sometimes–"

"What? Wish what?" he snapped.

"Never mind. I'm going up for an early night. I'll probably end up reading for a bit. I've found a new author and want to check out some of his stuff." She knew there was no point in trying to have a "what if" conversation with him, especially when the football was on. He seemed to be content with the way his life had turned.

"Okay," he replied. "I'll be up soon."

She knew this was a lie. He would often stay up until the early hours, watching sports or a film. There was the odd occasion when he wouldn't go to bed at all and she would find him asleep in the chair when she came back down to check on him.

Never mind, she thought. An early night never hurt anyone.

She grabbed her Kindle off the bookshelf and made her way up the stairs.

Neil was glad when Gail went up to bed; he was getting sick of her moaning about being bored every night. She should find herself a hobby, he often told her, but nothing transpired. He gave up – if she wasn't going to help herself then he wasn't going to help her. At least he was getting some peace tonight. Years ago, before Ross came along, an early night meant he was "in luck". Not nowadays – an early night meant exactly that, an early night. Picking up his lukewarm beer, he downed the dregs from the bottom as the football highlights finished.

Sitting back in his chair, he sighed and browsed the channels for something else that he could watch, hoping a good film was on. Hearing a creak from the stairs, he turned round, expecting to see Gail standing there, but when he looked, the staircase was clear.

"Gail?" he called. No answer. He turned back to the television to resume his search.

He found an old action film called Hard Target that he hadn't seen for a long time. Van Damme in his hey-day, nothing better. He flicked it on and noticed it had just started. He paused it and jumped up off the chair to get himself another beer. Taking another look for Gail in the hall and failing to find her, the kitchen light was on. Must be getting a drink of water. The kitchen door stood open a crack and he pushed it open fully, struck immediately by Gail's absence. She must have forgotten to switch the light off, or maybe I did. Crossing the patterned, lino floor, he opened the fridge door and pulled out an ice cold bottle of beer, relishing the coolness. He popped the top off and took a big gulp, then headed back to watch Van Damme kick some ass.

Sitting back down and getting himself comfortable, he failed to see the figure that seemed to materialise out of nowhere, standing behind him. As he was about to resume the film, a slight movement caught his attention in his peripheral vision. As he turned his head round further, he finally saw the figure and jumped slightly, spilling his beer. "Jesus, Ross! You scared the crap out of me. Let's get you back to bed."

Before he had a chance to get out of the chair, Ross placed his hand on his father's head, spread his fingers out and gripped with an unnatural strength. Neil was so confused by the situation, he was dumbstruck. It took him a few seconds to regain his power of speech but by then he felt like his head was about to implode. He lifted his arm up to release the vice-like grip but Ross' other hand slapped it away as if it was an annoying fly. His hand then joined the other on top of his dad's head and twisted it sharply to the right. A sickening snap, like a branch being snapped in two, echoed through the house.

Gail awoke with a start, not realising she had fallen asleep until a noise roused her from slumber. She wasn't sure whether it was real or if it was in her dream. Momentarily confused by the object resting on her face, she moved the Kindle to her side, the bright light from the screen lighting up the bedroom. She laughed to herself at the amount of times she had fallen asleep reading, only to wake and find her Kindle at a random page she had no recollection of or a bunch of text that had been accidently highlighted by her lethargic hands.

The light from the screen drew attention to the fact that Neil hadn't made it to bed yet and she glanced towards the clock that sat on the bedside unit – 00:30. Still early for Neil, she thought. I'll check he hasn't fallen asleep anyway.

Kicking her legs out of the bed she stepped into her slippers and made her way out of the room to the landing. Standing at the banister at the top of the stairs, she saw the glare from the T.V. illuminating Neil's shape on the chair. "Neil?" she called, keeping her voice low enough not to wake Ross. She automatically glanced to his bedroom door at the thought of his name and saw that the door still sat open, just as she had left it. She turned back to the stairs and took a step down, when a creak from Ross' room stopped her. "Ross?" she whispered, a little too loudly.

"Yes, Mother," the voice came from directly behind her, rather than the direction of her son's bedroom, startling her so much that she lost her balance on the step. She would have been safe, grabbing hold of the banister to steady herself, had it not been for her only child's hands giving her a firm push, helping her on her way.

Gail's last vision before falling to her death was her son's sly smile and a pair of black, shiny eyes.

Waking on Saturday morning, John found the day to be dull but dry, so he decided to defy his mum's orders and take his bike to the woods for some exploring. He was excited to go somewhere new but felt a slight guilt at the lie he would have to tell his mother.

Sitting at the table eating breakfast, he told her he was going to a friend's house for the morning. He made up the name Sean and honestly didn't know if that was the name of someone in his class or not. His mum smiled and told him how pleased she was that he was making friends. "Told you it would happen," she said. .

John felt bad about deceiving her but he needed to get out of the house and the town held nothing interesting for him to do. The only place left was the forest.

John took his bike from the old wooden shed that sat in the bottom corner of the garden, zipped his jacket up to his chin and clipped his helmet on. Wheeling it round to the front of his house, he hopped on and cycled along the street that led up to the church. He knew where the path was that led to the forbidden place; it wound off to the right, just before the church. There was a path that led downhill and into the unknown. Pushing the pedals faster to gain enough momentum that he could free-wheel some of the way, he looked at the houses he passed and it struck him that a good few of them still had their blinds drawn. It wasn't exactly early – 10 am, so he expected more activity in the sleepy village which he now had to call home. He glanced behind him and saw there was no sign of life on the street at all.

Maybe everyone sleeps in on the weekend, there doesn't appear to be anything else to do.

As his mind was preoccupied with wondering where everyone was, he turned his head forwards and realised he was just about at the turning to the path. The off-road path was pretty obvious, now his eyes were facing the right way, as it broke up a long wall that ran parallel to the road. John stopped his bike and stared at the church, he was amazed it was still standing. The weather-beaten stone and wood of the structure and an adjoining building was well worn and looked as it if it might not make the next hard storm. John looked to the sky and thought that wouldn't be far away. Moving his eyes to the attached building, he guessed that's where the Sunday School was held while the adults were singing about Jesus in the church itself. Fucking hell, Sunday School, he sighed to himself. He turned to face the path and pushed himself off the pavement, launching himself down the hill onto the rough track.

He loved riding his bike – the speed he could get up to and tricks he could pull, and now, freewheeling down the dirt path with the wind blowing through his hair, with a big grin spread across his face. Coming to a corner, he touched the brakes slightly, lifted his feet off the pedals and coasted round, only cycling again when his momentum waned. He approached the entrance to the forest; two tall oak trees sat either side of the path, like sentinels guarding a private location, while the other smaller trees stood side by side as their backup. A flutter of fear passed through John's body at the sight of the intimidating trees but the feeling soon passed as he sped by them under the canopy of branches and leaves.

Carrying on past a few more bends, he suddenly realised he was now deep in the forest, underestimating just how far he'd travelled. He slowed to a stop and took in the surroundings. Not that there was much – trees, trees and more trees, nothing of noticeable interest. Fear began to creep back into his body as he looked around. In the distance further up ahead of him, it looked like the lane split in two. He decided to carry on. If it turned out his eyes had betrayed him then he would turn back. His eyesight proved correct as the path veered off to the right, while the other road carried on deeper into the trees, disappearing out of sight. He saw the end of this new pathway and it came out of the trees into daylight. He decided to follow it, promising himself that he would turn back soon as it seemed he was the only person left on Earth right at that very moment but the curious side of his teenage brain couldn't let him turn back just yet.

He came to a large clearing filled with short grass, the path cutting through it, up and over a hill at the other side of the expanse. He wheeled his bike to the bottom of the hill and got off, looking to the top of the knoll. He abruptly became aware of the silence that surrounded him; no wind blew through the leaves and there were no birds or animal noises. He turned a full circle to look about – either side of him was lined with tall grass that eventually led back into the woods. As his eyes followed the grassy trail, his vision caught something above the trees. John leaned forward and squinted, trying hard to focus on what he thought he could see. It was the church, he soon realised. The building stood watch over the town and the woodland that lay behind it. An unexpected shiver ran down his spine and he shook automatically.

"Watch it!" a voice from nowhere called.

John jumped at the sudden break in the calm and turned in all directions trying to locate the source. The only other place, it dawned on him, was over the hill. He left his bike at the bottom and crept up the incline. As he reached the top, he ducked low and peered over the other side looking for who the voice belonged to. He didn't have to look far. The other side led down to a small lake enveloped by a stony flat that led into the water. On the near side to John, there were five boys. One of the boys stood further away from the group of four with his back to the water. He had a stone in each hand and his stance was defensive. The other four advanced, one of them rubbing his shoulder, his face etched with pain.

John recognised the boy near the water as the spotty kid who sat next to him in school the day before and frowned to himself as he tried to work out what was happening. Before he came up with an answer, the group of four were on the lad, grabbing at him.

"Hey! Stop it!" he barely recognised his own voice as it involuntarily left his mouth.

The group of youths turned, dropping their victim onto the stones, and fixed their gaze firmly on John. He met their stare but was too frightened to shout anything else. His heart thumped faster and faster. Both parties were stuck in a strange void, neither moving nor breaking eye contact. One of the boys turned to his fellow tormentor and whispered something in his ear, who in turn, smiled without replying. The clear leader of the group nodded in John's direction but his line of sight was no longer at John, it was over his shoulder. He turned instinctively, seeing nothing out of the ordinary. He returned to his eye contact battle to find that the boys were in the same position as when his eyes left them, but with one difference – the group staring back at him now stared with glossy black eyeballs. John gasped and took a step back, not taking his eyes off them. Until, that is, the moment they charged forward.

John spun round, nearly tripping and tumbling down the hill. He just managed to keep his balance as he made it to the bottom and lifted his bike. He jumped on it and peddled as hard and as fast as he could, racing through the grass and into the forest, not even looking back to see where the boys were.

The group of four stood at the top of the hill and watched him escape before lifting their inky eyes to the church.

John thought his heart was about to explode and his legs fall off as he reached home. He stopped in his driveway before turning to check on his pursuers. They were nowhere to be seen. He sat on the front step as he tried to restore his breathing to a normal before entering the house. His mum would no doubt have questions if he ran in puffing and panting. That made second place in his mind. Making first was; what the fuck was going on with the black eyes?

He didn't understand any of what he had seen, or at least, thought he had seen. Maybe he was going mad. One thing was for sure, he couldn't tell him mum, she would think he was insane. Children with black eyes indeed, she'd laugh. He made his way into the house, grunting a quick hello before heading straight up to his room, not even waiting for a reply. He closed his bedroom door and lay on the bed.

Black eyes, black eyes, black eyes.

John didn't sleep much; his nightmares filled with evil kids with abnormal eyes chasing him. Sometimes it switched to something else - the episode at the lake replayed with the outcome differing from reality each time – he would get caught and dragged down to the lake where they would hold him under the water, or beaten at the top of the hill, or taken to the church and surrounded, the threat of impending death imminent. Every time they were about to catch him or finish him, he would wake up, saving himself from the resulting scenario.

He felt anxious as he sat opposite his mother at the breakfast table, his eyes glancing up to hers then back down to the cornflakes that he hadn't bothered to touch.

"Mum," he started, "I don't feel well today, can I skip Sunday School?"

She gave him a look over and said, "I'm sure you'll be fine, it's only for an hour or so. We can see how you are after that."

"But, Mum..."

"But nothing, John. This village is our new home and we have to do our best to fit in." She sighed. "One hour, that's all. Okay?"

John kept quiet and pushed his spoon through his breakfast, never raising the food to his lips.

Walking alongside his mum on the way to church, he noted the lack of people about again. There's never anyone about this stupid town, he thought.

"Where is everyone, Mum?" he asked.

"Probably already inside. If it hadn't been for you dragging your heels getting ready, we would be too. Come on!"

The vicar stood at the entrance to the church as they approached. "Good morning, do come in." He glanced at John with a smile and said, "the Sunday School is next door, the entrance is to the side." He raised a hand to point the way.

John's mum turned to him. "On you go then, I'll see you when it's finished." Turning back to the vicar she said, "Sorry about that, Vicar..." Her voice trailing off as she was led inside. The vicar turned to John with a strange look on his face– it wasn't a smile as such, more a sneer. Before his brain properly registered it, he had already vanished in the church with his mum.

John walked by the wall of the attached building and found the door, which was closed. He reluctantly knocked on the wooden entryway; secretly hoping no-one would answer. His hopes were dashed as the door swung inwards. Stepping inside, he recognised kids from the school scattered around the room. Some stood talking, others sat drinking juice, but they all stopped to turn their focus on the new kid.

John heard the door close behind him, and turned automatically to look at it then turned back to face his audience. Every single one of the boy's and girl's eyes had turned the same nightmare coal colour. He started to panic, his breaths becoming short, rapid bursts. He circled round and grasped at the door handle, finding the door locked. He froze, tears forming in his eyes then slowly dripping down his cheeks. He thought this was some kind of weird joke the whole village was playing on him, until he heard a low murmuring chant that rose in volume. Every black eye was fixed on him, and John began to wail for his mum, begging her to hear his sobs. He was on his knees banging on the door with his tightly closed fists. All the while, the chant was ringing in his ears.

Hands latched onto his shoulders, dragging him back to the middle of the room. The children surrounded him. John closed his eyes and put his hands over his ears, trying to shut out the ever-growing mantra.

>Then away, haste away!
>Come away to the Sunday School!
>Then away, do not delay!
>Come away to the Sunday School!
>◻

Some Strings Attached - C.L. Raven

"Dance for me."

Their movements were stiff and awkward, their steps out of time. Like they couldn't feel the music throbbing through their veins and quivering in their limbs. Had someone replaced my dancers with mannequins when I wasn't looking?

"You're dancing for your messiah, not an office Christmas party. Copy me."

I danced for them, my movements fluid, my limbs firm but flexible. The men playing James and John followed me. The fishermen watched. I leapt up, doing the splits in the air. Watching them attempt it was…painful. I stood behind James, holding his arms as we skipped. Maybe I should strap myself to each dancer so I could be the master of their success.

"Obey the music."

I sighed. It was like watching a zombie prom dance, without plummeting body parts and the terrible stench. At least zombies had an excuse for their lack of coordination. Being dead tended to be detrimental to hobbies and exercise.

"The Easter performance is in a fortnight and you're not ready. We can't perform like this! The audience will leave. They're expecting something new, something different. People are sick of chocolate eggs, cuddly bunnies and Mary Poppins on repeat. We have to remind them Easter was about betrayal, death, rebirth."

"Wasn't Easter about worshipping a fertility goddess then the Christians hijacked it to force people to accept their religion, hence the bunnies and chocolate eggs?" Jesus asked.

"My musical isn't about chocolate eggs and cuddly bunnies. This isn't a two hour advert for Cadbury."

I'd spent my life performing on stages, drowning in the audience's adoration. Then one day it was all over. Teaching others to dance cured the depression I'd wallowed in. Until I met this lot. They'd been keen at the beginning but when they realised how hard they'd have to work, they gave up their enthusiasm for Lent.

Remember, Jesus didn't kill anybody. Although apparently he kicked over bankers' tables and chased them with whips, so maybe he wasn't against maiming.

"Let's do the crucifixion scene."

This Easter performance would be my masterpiece. People knew the story of Jesus's crucifixion and resurrection. But they'd never known the story told my way – Jesus as an inspiring rebel murdered because he was dangerous to the old regime. I wanted them to leave knowing they would never forget what they witnessed on my stage.

Jesus tripped over the crucifix and face planted at his executioners' feet. That wasn't a man who would inspire a religion. All he would inspire was an internet meme. And not a flattering one. At this rate, the audience would remember the musical for the wrong reasons. Jesus's death wasn't supposed to be a slapstick comedy performance. I helped him up then they continued the scene. There was no grace, no style, no enjoyment. I doubted even the real Jesus looked this miserable waiting to die.

"I've seen dental patients who looked like they were having more fun. I can give your roles to people who actually relish hard work. If that happens, I guarantee, you will never dance again. Is that what you want?"

Some of them shook their heads. Others avoided eye contact with me. I was giving them a rare opportunity and they weren't grateful. Maybe I should have been more selective in my audition, but I was desperate to get started and not many auditioned. Easter musicals weren't 'cool'. Religion could start wars, but it couldn't draw people to the theatre.

I clapped twice and they started the scene with more passion; fake smiles painting their faces. It would do, for now. Though if those smiles weren't genuine on opening night, I'd make them wear masks. Or staple their smiles in place. I was tempted to give them Chelsea smiles, but squeamishness hampered my plan.

While everyone was on break, I retired to my office. 'Director murders entire cast' wasn't the headline I wanted associated with Messiah, the Musical. Sighing, I walked over to the little theatre stage in the corner and picked up the marionettes' control bars. They danced beautifully under my command, the strings guiding their every move. If only I could control my living dancers the same way and regain my title of Lord of the Dance.

I smiled at the figures sprawled on the stage, waiting for me to bring them to life. Easter was the time for resurrection and I was about to raise my career from the dead. Unfortunately, changing my cast to marionettes meant fewer dancers but what was success without sacrifices?

I peered down at the stage and raised Judas's control bar. He was heavier than he looked but I eventually hauled him to his feet. He twirled as I poured silver coins onto him. I frowned. His movements weren't as smooth as my other marionettes, but maybe I had to adjust to the new material. These weighed more but their natural joints allowed for realistic movements and they didn't have the dead doll eyes that turned most puppets into horror film material. This show starred Jesus, not Annabelle.

Sadly, I had to change the choreography for the men whipping Jesus. Before, I had them tossing their whips into the air and catching them, but the marionettes lacked the dexterity, I'd been forced to glue their whips to their hands so they wouldn't drop them. Controlling four men simultaneously was tricky. I accidentally dropped one and he fell in a crumpled heap, bringing Jesus down on top of him. That wasn't how the stories depicted his death.

"Let's practise the crucifixion scene then we'll take a break."

I manoeuvred Jesus to the waiting structure and attempted to lift him onto it. Whilst I got him onto the cross, getting him to stay was another matter. The puppets couldn't tie him and looping his wires was tricky.

"Maybe I could fasten you to the cross then lower you to the stage. Or would that look like you were descending from Heaven? I don't want this to look cheesy. This is a high class theatre, not Butlins."

I eventually succeeded in draping his arms over the cross's horizontal plank and secured the control bar so he wouldn't fall.

"Please," Jesus said. "Let me go."

"Puppets don't talk." I was losing it.

"Don't hurt me."

"You haven't been paying attention to the script. You don't get a happy ending. You have to die for Christianity to be born."

Opening night.

The theatre was full. People had come to see the death of my 'retirement' and the birth of my show.

The curtains rose. I watched the audience from the catwalk then raised my hands and brought my puppets to life. Jesus danced for his disciples, who followed him, pirouetting and bowing at his feet. He danced for his enemies, who cast disdainful looks and turned away. Getting him to kneel and treat the sick was tricky but thankfully, he transitioned seamlessly. The lame people jumped up and danced after him across the stage. Working multiple puppets wasn't the easiest of tasks. I was getting a better workout than I did in the gym.

Now for the crucifixion. If this went wrong, the whole musical would be ruined. I hoisted Jesus onto the cross, managing to drape his arms over it. He stayed while the other puppets reeled around him, celebrating his long and torturous death.

Shadows cloaked the stage. The audience was silent. A spotlight fell on the cross. One traitor cut Jesus down. He collapsed to the floor. I swiftly lowered the tomb around him. The dancers backed away. I dimmed the lights for a few seconds then turned them back on and moved the tomb door aside, revealing it to be empty. Jesus leapt up from behind it, dancing mid-air and flying around the stage while the other puppets fell to their knees in terror, and adulation. The audience applauded. The lights died, the curtains sweeping down to shield the stage as I hurried down to receive my applause.

The lights rose as I stepped on stage. I bowed. The audience cheered. Smiling, I bowed again. Finally, I'd discovered a way where the dance would never die.

I slipped backstage as the applause faded. I would never tire of that sound. My puppets lay where I'd dropped them. I unhooked them from the strings and carried them, one by one, to the back room. I laid Jesus on the settee.

He moaned.

"You were remarkable. You're going to be a star." I fetched the needle and bottle, syphoning more of the paralytic drug. "Only six days left."

I injected him, he stopped moaning and moving. A tear trickled down his cheek. I couldn't have my stars escaping before closing night. Dancers were easier to direct when I was controlling them. I sneaked out, locking the door behind me as my performers slept, like broken marionettes. Like Jesus, my career would be resurrected from death.

I would once again, be Lord of the Dance.

The Old Rugged Cross - Michael Noe

It was pissing rain the day I saw her out with another guy. It hadn't taken her long to replace me, and I was thankful that I had the rain to mask my tears. It wasn't an embarrassing, loud emotional breakdown. Just a small quiet kind of cry reserved for those who are near death. You can never be too sure about the stages of grief. They also apply to a busted relationship too. If I were Jesus, which one of them would be my Judas? The more I thought about it, the more I saw her as the whore of Babylon. Washing my feet, and drying them with her hair. If I were the Messiah, I don't think she would worship me. She's too selfish, too unclean. Most people are. It's all in how they're raised, what they're taught. Jennifer was supposed to love me, and only me, but things change. You can't stop time from moving on. People change, and a promise doesn't mean shit. Not like it did when we were kids.

I could be a hipster Jesus spreading the gospel of love sweet love, but I would also dole out punishment to those who sinned against me. In my life, there had been a long list of people who sinned against me. My father for leaving me with an alcoholic mother, society for lying to me about the real way the world works. Life is merely a game, some people win, some people lose. It's all rigged by something much bigger than all of them. The lies spread like flood waters over a muddy bank. The sins of the world consume us, they chip away at the pieces of our holiness. In order for me to be Jesus, I need to sacrifice myself so that I could save the world, but I don't want to do that. I'm not willing to be a beacon of hope for anyone. It takes a great deal of love to sacrifice yourself. I'm not capable of that kind of love. I don't think anyone is, and if they are, I think they're a liar. It takes a great deal of love to die for someone.

I had an uncle who was a preacher. He was a fire and brimstone type of preacher, which is the most interesting type. His sermons were always filled with warnings of hell, and the type of love that only Jesus could provide. No one loved you like the Saviour did. He was the one whom God sent to shed his blood for the sins of everyone. I often wondered what would happen if he'd said no. It was an important mission, but imagine someone tells you, you're going to be born just to die. Everything in your life is leading up to this one big event, but what if you look at everyone and say: "Fuck it, they aren't worth dying for." My uncle was big on seeing the good in people, yet he often failed because of his narrow minded views. While he preached love and harmony, there was this big reality that not everyone was going to make it to heaven. It was their sins that kept them from receiving the gift of eternal life.

As I watch them walk hand in hand I can see they're madly in love with each other. Did she ever look at me that way? This asshole wrapped a hand around her waist, pulling her closer to him. Jennifer was glowing as they made their way past shops crowded with people eager to be out of the rain. She looked like a goddess among faithless sinners. Her golden honey hair caught in the breeze and I swear I could smell it drifting. Where's his umbrella? If he were a real man wouldn't he have one? When I think of all the sins I had committed in our relationship, being inattentive wasn't one of them. There were so many bad things I could have done in our time together, but not protecting her from the rain wasn't one of them.

Here's a good question, a valid question. One that hasn't been addressed yet. Why am I following her? It's as if she's Jesus and I'm one of her disciples. I'd be the one he'd command to walk on water, but I have a moment of doubt so I begin to drown. What kind of hold does she have on me that makes me still follow her? I can tell you when we broke up down to the minute. Isn't that just a little fucked up? Who does that? Me, that's who. Let's just say two months, and just leave it at that. If I tell you how many hours it's been you'll think I'm crazy. Not you don't already. It's okay because I feel crazy as I follow her home.

I watch her new boyfriend hoping that he'll fall, or maybe he'll start convulsing in the street. This asshole is my replacement? He's not as caring as I am, he doesn't treat her the way I did. It's true, nice guys finish last. As they walk up the steps to her apartment I can hear her laugh. How often did I make her laugh? Why didn't she love me? As they disappear, I head home with water swishing around in my shoes. My jacket is waterlogged, and I silently berate myself for doing this yet again. It's not the first time I've done this, and it won't be the last.

Back home, I make myself a breakfast burrito and settle in for a night of Netflix. I've been dating a little but my wounds are still too raw to commit to a relationship. I'm still in love with Jennifer. Love, sweet love, it's the only thing that makes us human. There is hate of course, but hatred clouds your thinking, makes you do things you normally wouldn't do. I think about my uncle and how many times he's told the sermon about hate, and how it grows in a person's soul. In the end, it's all about forgiveness, turn the other cheek if you will. I know that I need to forgive her, but I just can't. I have other plans.

The rain has stopped as I walk out into my backyard. I live in a small wooded neighborhood that gives me total privacy. It's the middle of nowhere really, and I like the solitude. My parents died in a car accident five years ago, and they left me a sizable amount of cash, as well as the house I live in. I didn't kill them, so don't get your mind running off in a new direction. They were coming home from dinner and hit a patch of black ice. It was a devastating moment that left me saddened because we hadn't really spoken much since I went off into the great wide world. I was busy with my life and they were busy with theirs.

If I was going to kill anyone, it would be my uncle. He really fucked with my way of thinking about life, death, and the way the world really works as opposed to how he wanted it to work. Eventually I was able to move away from his teachings and into my own, but my parents were the full-blown sheep that he taught people to be. It's his fault there's a giant cross in my backyard. I look at it and wonder if it's going to be big enough, or if the nails will actually hold anyone . I thought about it as I built it, and wondered if gravity would just pull them downward, but then I realized that was why you nailed the feet too. It kept them from sliding down.

This was an idea I had not long after Jennifer left. I thought that she would be the one to free me from my sins. I needed absolution, and I thought Jennifer was going to give it me, but she hadn't. I thought her love would change me, and it had, but now that she's gone, I know what's going to happen. You can't run from yourself. I thought I could when I met her, and falling in love with her made me feel as if I had finally done something right in my life. It was nice to be normal for a while, to feel just like everyone else. I should've known it wouldn't last.

Her goodbye echoes in my head as I gaze upon the cross. It had taken me a couple of weeks to construct it. I felt a bit like Noah when he built the ark. I knew there was a purpose for it, but it took some time before it all came into focus. I guess I can thank my uncle for teaching me about the full mission of Christ and how his love was the redemption we never even knew we wanted. To some, he's just a symbol that people need to make their lives have some sort of meaning, to others, he's the true figure of guilt. You see him there on the cross and you know you should repent, but the world's a vile, evil place. There's no way a guy spouting hope and eternal life can be attained through a man sent by God.

It's funny how I rejected everything my uncle taught, but came back to that damn cross. The symbol of love and salvation. As I built I didn't really know why I was even doing it, but soon it came to me in a flash of brilliance. It all made sense. Every story has to have some tragic end, right? Every ending is just a beginning for another story. The cross in all its brilliance was everything I wanted and needed. The cross was seven feet tall, and six feet wide. When it was up anyone could see it, but I had solitude, and wide open spaces. No one would see while I was building, and I was thankful for that. What I was doing needed total privacy and no interruptions. This was my mission and I took it seriously.

I must tell you that I've killed quite a few people. I was the butcher of Herringbone County. My work was whispered about in a variety of newspapers, and I can tell you for a fact I was good at what I did. That's not pride, just fact. I didn't want to kill anyone, but there was this compulsion to do it. I couldn't stop even if I wanted to. Some people are just born evil, and I was one of them. Maybe that's why my uncle was so hard on me. I think he saw the evil in me, and wanted to save me somehow. Problem was, I couldn't be saved. My uncle preached at me, hoping the love of God would heal my blackened heart, but it didn't it,

Jennifer was what saved me. When I was with her, I didn't think about killing at all. The compulsion just went away. Being with her gave me the normal life I often dreamed about, it was finally my time to be happy, but it didn't last. When I asked her to marry me she said no, and then she said it was over. She didn't love me as much I loved her. She said it wasn't fair for us to be together. It was just going to end anyway. Why prolong things? I watched her leave and then I went out that night and killed a woman as she was heading into her house.

I bashed her head in with a hammer. I hit her so many times, her face was a pulpy mess. There were teeth and bits of bone scattered on her front porch. I was hoping I'd get caught, but I didn't. The next night I attacked Jennifer's neighbor. This time I gutted her and left a pile of bloody guts on Jennifer's front porch. I watched as Jennifer discovered them and the horror on her face was priceless. I should've left the heart though. It would have been the perfect symbol of our wasted love. The next night I got the idea for the cross. It was going to be redemption, the last act of a dying man. I don't mean it in the way you're thinking, this was way more literal. The cross would finally free me. I just needed to get it built.

My uncle's favorite hymn was The Old Rugged Cross. As I built mine I couldn't help but sing it. This was exactly what I needed, the cross being such a powerful symbol appealed to me. We all need symbols to keep us grounded. It keeps things in focus, doesn't it? We all need something to cling to when the storms of life threaten to take our smiles. What do you have left when you lose your smile? Life becomes unlivable, the colour drains away from everything. The Old Rugged Cross was exactly what I needed. It was an insane idea, but aren't they all?

I checked my watch and headed back toward Jennifer's place. There was a stop I needed to make first and I couldn't help but feel just a small tingle of excitement as I drove. Her boyfriend lived in a small studio apartment not far from hers. Tonight, he was playing poker with some friends, and I saw that as a sign from God himself. I needed to act quickly, or else all of my plans would fall apart. This had to be done with precision. One misstep would ruin everything, I couldn't let that happen. I worked too hard for this.

I let myself into Jennifer's apartment and headed into the darkened living room. I had given back her key, but not before I made a copy for myself. I would come here at night so I could watch her sleep. I wanted to make sure she was safe. Her new boyfriend wasn't doing it, so I felt obligated. When she was gone, I would sometimes come in just to visit and remember the way we were. We were in love, why did it have to change? Being here now made me feel close to her, as if we never ended. Tonight, I was here for something else.

I walked into her bedroom and couldn't help but smile. She was so beautiful, like an angel of grace and mercy. It was as if I were seeing her for the very first time. I shook her awake and watched as she struggled to sit, but I wouldn't allow it. I slapped a piece of tape over her mouth, and stood her upright. The knife I held against her slender throat took all the fight out of her.

"We're going for a ride," I whisper as my hands caress her back. "Don't fight. I don't want to hurt you."

She allowed me to lead her to my car but before I closed the door, I slap a pair of handcuffs to the oh shit handle and one to her wrist. She isn't going anywhere anytime soon. I can tell she's crying, and it hurts me, but she caused this. This is all her fault and now? This is happening. She's being taken against her will to my house and I bet she's wondering why. Have I suddenly lost my mind? Sane people don't do this. I allow the silence to stretch out and then I sigh.

"I've killed people. You have no idea what that's like. I don't enjoy it, if that's what you're thinking. You saved me though. Your love? It took away all my compulsions. For the first time ever I felt normal, as if I belonged somewhere. Why don't you love me?" The last words are a scream. She flinches and tries to move away from me, but I pull her close and stroke her hair. I don't think it soothes her very much, but it does wonders for me.

I'm sure a million thoughts are running through her head, but she can't voice any of them. She must be scared, I know I would be. Here we are driving to God knows where and I have yet to say a damn word about where we're going. Telling her would ruin the surprise. I want to see the look on her face when she sees the cross. I want her to wonder why it's there, and what role she's going to play in all this. The cross is massive, and I hope she's pleased with the work I put into it.

As we pull into my driveway I know she's scared. When we were dating, I had my secrets, but now? I'm free. I confessed, so now I feel free of my guilt. My burden is no longer my own. None of that matters now because we're almost at the end of the story. I realized something as I built my cross. No one was going to stop me. This was supposed to happen. My entire life has led up to this moment. I want to cry as I drag her to the back yard where the cross awaits.

"Don't fight." I whisper. She tried though and I can't blame her. There beside the cross is the hammer and nails that will go into her wrists and feet. These were often called holy nails, and it makes sense when you realise what they were used for.

I position her on the cross and feel as if I'm going to faint. My hands shake as I position the first nail, and the first swing of the hammer misses its target entirely. I try and think about something other than nailing Jennifer to the cross, but there's no way to divert your thoughts away from something like this. I once read that this was a barbaric and cruel way to execute someone, and they were right. As the first nail pounds into her hand, I feel as if I'm about to throw up. Blood pours from the wound, and the squeals hidden behind duct tape are filled with agony.

Her eyes roll back in her head as I pound the second nail in, securing her hands to the cross. The pain must be excruciating and I wonder how she's going to stay on the cross once it's hoisted up. It's the feet. Once those are nailed, there's no way to keep the nails from sliding through the flesh of the wrist. Nailing the feet relieves strain on the body by putting most of the weight on the upper body. It's the feet that I have trouble with. She stirs as I finish the task and hoist her up on her deathbed. It's a beautiful sight and I snap a few pictures just so I can relive this moment later.

I thought that she had to die to save the world from my sins, but I can see now her death will free me from my own. The crown of thorns digs into her forehead, blood pours into her eyes, drips from the nails that secure her to the cross. I feel a peace wash over me as she struggles to breath, she tries pulling herself up, but there isn't enough strength. On this cross is my saviour. I will pray to her for strength and guidance. I drop to my knees and begin to sing the song my uncle loved so dearly. I can feel the strength of the cross as I pray to Jennifer not Jesus. All my sins have been washed away and I once again feel free.

As she dies I wonder if she realises how important her death was. How necessary. It only took two hours and I watched the entire time. She took her last breath and stared directly at me. It was as if she were absolving me of my sins, telling me that all was forgiven. I pierce her side and then, I watch as the cross falls to the ground with an earth-shaking thud. It is finished. There's nothing left to do but carefully remove the nails.

Once free, I pull her body close to me and weep not with sorrow, but joy. Now I know why my uncle loved Jesus so much. It was the freedom that his death had given him. I lick the drying blood from the wounds and prepare her body for burial. I know that someday, someone will read this and they won't understand why I did this. She was just a woman, but to me she was salvation.

☐

Morning Has Broken- Matthew Cash

John opened his eyes and took in the intricate swirls and peaks of the artex ceiling. It made him think of a winter landscape, windblown waves of deep fresh snow drifting over all, giving the world that quiet cosy feeling. Either that or the Christmas cake icing from the cakes they used to have when he was a kid. Mum would always make the fruit cake and Dad would have the job of rolling out marzipan, painting it with a thin layer of marmalade and molding it to the sponge's exterior. Then he would make white icing and magic the cake into a miniature snowy wonderland. Using the ancient plastic figurines from the big jam jar with the cork lid from the cupboard above the kettle he would add life to the Christmas tradition, making the cake ornamental as well as edible. John imagined the little skiers, Victorian ice skaters and wee snowmen dotted above him on the bedroom ceiling.

What a wonderful way to start the day.

A three-inch gap between the heavy fabric of the red drapes let in a sunbeam so strong it looked solid. Birds chirped gaily, their tuneful herald to the morning whispering through the cracked open window.

For the first time in ages John felt rested, the aches and stresses of everyday life left back in the city, in the confines of his stuffy apartment, forgotten like an unimportant holiday essential.

He stretched his legs out, toes pointing to the foot of the bed, no familiar muscular twinges. He felt on top of the world.

John threw back the bed covers and rose to his feet. As he stood up the aroma of cooking bacon was just noticeable over the sweet fragrance of the flowers in the garden. A bumblebee buzzed past the window as he whisked open the curtains to greet the day. John felt like a King of old surveying his domain. The sky was a vast flawless blue, the sun already scorching hot. His parents' garden lie beneath the bedroom window, a small lawn surrounded by hundreds of varieties of floral displays. The little white painted shed half hidden by the pink bloomed clematis drapery had its door open obscuring the entrance. The distant hum of lawnmowers made him suspect that his dad was in the process of following his neighbours' lead. It was what sunny Saturday mornings were about, mowing the grass, keeping up with the Jones.

Beyond his parents garden lie rolling golden hills of wheat as far as the eye could see, with just a small silver triangle of the River Stour twinkling beneath the horizon. A red sailed yacht glided across that small snippet of water, maybe an eager competitor of that day's regatta. John tucked his hair behind his ears and smiled at the endless possibilities the day could bring.

He pushed open the window to feel the sun on his skin. Blissful, he drank in the fresh country air and went downstairs to see what his mum was cooking for breakfast.

John loitered on the hallway outside his old bedroom, marvelling at how much his parents had changed the house's interior since he lived with them. A new lease of life took hold of them when he moved out to go to university, not because their last child was moving out but because of the excitement of regaining a home for just themselves. They had fallen back in love, acted like a couple of teenagers, took on new hobbies and rekindled old desires. It was great fun coming back, to what he would always refer to as home, and hearing about his parents exploits.

The same photographs decorated the walls, enlarged pictorial memories of him and his sisters when they were young. Newer additions of his father in on the lawn outside practising yoga, something his parents had discovered a few years back. Heavy, thick bound books of yoga positions, the importance of meditation and Buddhism had joined in the ranks alongside the gritty detective dramas of his father's and the artist portfolios and prints of his mother's. He hoped that he would have as much vitality as his parents when he got to their age.

John stepped down the plush carpeted stairs, lead by the mouth-watering smell of frying bacon. He walked through the empty lounge and into the kitchen where his mother stood at the stove. His father sat at the large table, a mug of tea poised near his lips. Mum grinned at him fleetingly and used a metal spatula to jostle the contents of the deep frying pan.

"Good morning Johnny. Did you sleep well?"

John smiled at his mum, she was the only one who still called him Johnny.

"Like a log." He pulled out a chair at the table and sat down. "Morning father."

Dad sipped his tea, his face was a bit pale, John wondered whether they were on some new eating fad. "Morning son."

"You okay Dad? You look a bit peaky."

Dad smiled reassuringly and raised his mug towards his son, "Ah it's nothing a few mugs of green tea and a good yoga sesh won't cure."

John admired his father's relentless optimism.

"Too old to give his own mother a kiss in the morning now?" his mother called from the cooker.

"I would have thought you got enough kisses earlier," Dad said with a lecherous wink.

"Oh Stanley," Mum giggled with embarrassment, "not in front of John."

Dad put his tea cup down and jokingly punched his son in the shoulder, "it wasn't in front of him, he was asleep upstairs."

Conjuring up images he really didn't want John tried to change the subject. The last thing he wanted to think about was whatever amorous shenanigans his folks had been up to whilst he had been sleeping.

He stood up and walked past his father to give his mother a peck on the cheek when he stepped in something wet. He stopped and inspected the sole of his foot. It was red, dark like beetroot juice, no lighter, more like...

"Is that blood?"

Mum gasped when she spotted a few drops of red beneath her husband's chair.

"Oh Stanley," she scolded, poking the fatty spatula at him accusingly, "You're making a mess."

John frowned, still perched on one foot, unsure as to whether his Mum would tell him off if he placed it back down. His father held a bunched up tea towel to his thigh beneath the table, soaked crimson and dripping to the floor.

"Dad, what the hell?" John said pointing at his father's leg.

"Oh John I'm so sorry, here." He removed the sodden tea towel from his thigh and offered it to his son.

"Shit," his father said, as a long ribbon of claret shot from his femoral artery. He shoved the damp wad back against his leg and looked at his wife sheepishly. "Sorry Maureen."

"Oh for heaven's sake," Mum exclaimed, yanked the pan off the hob and pulled a fresh tea towel from a pile of neatly folded laundry. "I told you not to make a mess."

She threw the tea towel on the table in front of his father, her dressing gown fluttering open. John noticed her chest was bandaged. Dad swapped the tea towels and retorted with more than an air of smugness, "I told you to be careful you don't nip my femoral artery."

John looked at his mum, looked at his dad, at the thick steak of questionable origin sizzling in the pan and the bloodied carving knife in the sink.

"Err..Mum. What's going on?"

"Son," Dad started, raising himself off the chair momentarily before the pain in his thigh made him wince.

"John, sit down," Mum interrupted and ushered him back into his chair, "let me get you some juice and something to wipe that mess off you."

John slammed his hand down on the table making the cutlery jolt. "What the fuck is going on?"

Mum gasped. Dad winced again, held his palm up and looked at his wife with stern expression. "Son, allow me to explain." Dad started, keeping his eyes on Mum in case she dared butt in again. "The village has changed since you lived here. Certain," he paused and thought of a tactful way to put it, "historical artefacts have been discovered causing a resurgence of bygone, umm, ways."

"Old ways." Mum muttered setting down a mug of tea in front of her son.

"Yes," Dad agreed, "old ways."

John still looked confused. "What the hell are you going on about?"

"Son," Dad began again, searching for more words to explain an impossible situation.

"Blackbird has spoken." His mum blurted out and slapped her hands over mouth.

"What the..?"

Dad sighed, "Your mother's right John. Blackbird has spoken."

John stared at his parents like they were insane.

"I see you need further explanation," Dad said, "if you'll just let your mother eat her breakfast I'll tell you everything we know."

Father and son watched in silence as Mum got up, fetched a plate and flipped the slab of fried meat onto a plate. She sat down back in her chair and began cutting the meat with a steak knife. Detecting her son's eyes on her she pointed to the silver bread bin, "Oh John, why don't you make yourself some toast?"

He looked at his mother incredulously. How could he eat with all this insanity? His father was bleeding from a potentially fatal wound, his mum was eating something that definitely was not bacon, and they were both talking complete bollocks. The last thing on his mind was toast. "I just want to know what's going on?" He stammered in defeat.

Dad patted his son's hand sympathetically, "Okay son, okay. I'll tell you.

"You remember that pond in the dip of Bob Keeble's wheat fields, at the bottom of the hill St. Michael's sits on? The one we used to walk to when you kids were little, you used to call it the secret pond."

John nodded. The secret pond was hidden amidst a group of dense trees in the valley. The overgrown foliage made it virtually invisible to anyone who didn't know it was there. From the footpaths skirting the fields it was just a bunch of trees. But when he was a kid his parents had taken them across the field, something that was always considered taboo in the country. You just don't go walking over people's crops. But his parents had led him and his sisters along the brown furrows running between rows of golden wheat to show him the secret pond. It was thriving with ducks, coots and moorhens. They even saw a kingfisher. The tall wild flowers attracted bugs of all kinds, gigantic dragonflies zipped over the dark green water. It was magical, and he and his sisters had been enthralled. However this marvel came with its conditions: they weren't allowed to come here without their parents, under any circumstances, it was a very deep pond and if they fell in they wouldn't come out. And his parents made them promise not to tell anyone else about the pond. It was an untainted nature reserve and the fewer people that knew about it the better. It had been nigh on impossible for six year old Johnny not to tell his friends, even Matthew Goodchild his best friend. But he managed to keep that secret until his seventh birthday when he told Matthew Goodchild. It wasn't long after that when Matthew went missing and his family moved away. John now wondered if the boy had gone to investigate his six year old self's claims of a hidden paradise. He had always been gunning about the village on his own.

"Well," Dad continued, "Bob Keeble always saw that pond as an eyesore, and land that could be used for more crops. So he decided to drain it and fill it in. He found something." His father watched his mother cease chewing her food.

John suddenly knew what was coming, they found Matthew Goodchild's body, that's what his dad was about to say, he knew it.

"At first he thought it was some kind of joke, but it was obvious that the thing had been down there for years, possibly even centuries. Weighted down with chains and rocks."

John felt sick, he was responsible for his childhood friend's death, and judging by the sound of it was more than just a simple accident. Weighted down with chains and rocks. He wished his dad wouldn't refer to his dead friend as a thing though. Then his father's other words sunk in.

"Centuries?"

His father nodded, "Of course when Keeble found the numerous skeletal remains of people, mostly children, he took it more seriously."

"What? What did he find dad?"

"Blackbird," Mum said quietly, nothing but a greasy smear on her plate as she popped the last morsel of meat into her mouth.

Dad nodded, "your mother's right John, Blackbird. That's what we all call it.

"Chained and weighted down at the bottom of the pond was the skeleton of a monster. It's body was human but it's arms and legs tapered off into taloned bird feet. The remnants of gigantic wings were still fused to its shoulder blades, and its head was that of a blackbird."

John laughed without mirth.

Dad smiled sadly.

"We too laughed and mocked Keeble but that was before the dreams started."

"What dreams?"

"Visions of what once was, ancient gods, sacrifice, the end of the thing we call Blackbird. The villagers turned against it and sunk it to the bottom of the pond. A holy person, druid or whatever the equivalent was back then, did something to the water- a spell or blessing I don't know what. And that was that."

John scoffed at his parents story, it was absurd, something from an old trashy horror book. "That's ridiculous."

Not deterred by his son's mocking Dad continued.

"All of us here have had the dreams. All of us have reaped the benefits Blackbird had gifted us."

"Virility," Mum chirped up happily.

Dad nodded in agreement, "yes, yes, it's not just clean living and yoga that's given us a new lease of life."

"Fertility," Mum said overjoyed, staring with delirious affection at her husband and pressing a hand to her abdomen. "You're going to be a big brother Johnny."

"What the fuck Mum?" John spluttered, "you're seventy."

Dad scowled at him before carrying on, "we have all learned the benefits of yoga, preparing ourselves bodily as well as mentally, for the right time. When we meditate we are at one with the Blackbird, he fills us with love and light and shows us the way, makes clear our path."

"Of course there have been a few sacrifices," Mum said as she poured more tea into her cup.

"Yes," Dad continued, "it is only right that we should give back to One so generous."

Mum pointed at the greasy patch on her china plate, "I just ate a piece of your father's thigh."

John gagged and pushed himself away from the table and stared at his dad's injury. "You can't expect me to believe this?"

"Six months ago we found out your mother had breast cancer." Dad said, mournful.

"Mum, I, " John flinched.

"Oh Stanley you shouldn't have told him that." Mum scolded her husband.

"Last week I ate your mother's left breast with some beer-battered onion rings from Marks and Spencer."

Mum opened her dressing gown to show her son the flat bandaged area on her chest. "Mrs Roberts down the road stuffed her chihuahua with Paxo and the family had it for Sunday dinner."

Dad nodded excitedly, "Yes, and two weeks ago Mrs Stewart from Winchester Drive gave birth to identical twins. They didn't need both of them so.."

"Stop," John screamed grabbing fistfuls of his hair, making both of his parents gasp. "this is insane. Mass delirium. If these things people have done are true then you're all mad. You need fucking help."

Mum lowered her eyes and fastened her dressing gown up to her throat, a snooty expression of defiance took her, "well we'll find out today who's mad won't we?"

"Why?" John asked.

"Blackbird has spoken." His parents said in unison.

"What the hell does that mean?" John shouted and stumbled as a shock wave rumbled beneath the house.

His parents leapt up together, his father dropping the bloodied tea towel to the floor as they raced towards the back door.

John watched his parents run across their back garden towards the little fence backing onto the rolling hills.

Reluctant, he followed them as more rumbles in the earth sent judders through his legs.

The skies above the fields were swarming with black birds. It wasn't that unusual in the countryside, a number of things could attract flocks. But as he joined his parents at the fence he could see them shooting out of the ring of trees down in the valley of the wheat fields, where the secret pond lay. A red combine harvester stood in one of the fields, midway through harvesting a row of wheat. He could make out the small, far away figure of the farmer as he climbed on top of the machine's cabin and stood tall, his arms held aloft as though in worship.

The blackbirds swirled in the sky like an ebony hurricane, blotting out the sun.

John turned to his parents who were also raising their arms in herald to the coming of their God.

A screeching, prehistoric shriek erupted from the ring of trees clearing the last of the birds into the sky. John saw the trees being torn up and thrown aside and something huge emerge from the dip in the field. Amidst the falling trees he made out what looked like a giant blackbird's head, its orange beak as big as the combine below it, cracking open heavenwards and cawing its unholy birth cry. Thousands more blackbirds flew from its squawking throat and colossal wings beat down the last of the trapping trees.

John screamed in horrific disbelief and barely felt the sharp slice of the steak knife, still greased with the fat from his father's cooked thigh. He slapped a hand at his slit throat, his mother allowed her son a brief sympathetic smile before she dropped the knife and turned back to her rising deity.

John dropped to the ground, the air filled with black feathers, the monster's ancient crowing, and the villagers chanting.

"Blackbird has spoken."
"Blackbird has spoken."

☐

Onward Christian Soldiers - G. H. Finn

"Onward, Christian soldiers!, Marching as to war,
With the cross of Jesus, Going on before."

From the hymn written in 1865 by Rev. Sabine Baring-Gould, who, in the same year, wrote "The Book of Werewolves".

It may be true that a crucifix has power over a vampire. I do not know, for I am relieved to say I have never met one. At least, not knowingly. But the sign of the Cross has no power over a Werewolf.

I had believed, not as a hope but as an act of faith, that this Holy emblem of Christianity would protect me if I encountered such a demonic Beast. What a fool I was.

But maybe not a total fool. Perhaps, in the secret depths of my heart, my faith was somewhat lacking, for I also took other precautions.

I did not originally intend to try to find a Werewolf. I certainly did not set off thinking to track the uncanny creature to its lair. I am by nature neither a detective nor a hunter. At heart I am a scholar. My interest in the legends of lycanthropy was purely academic. I intended only to follow the trail of the Werewolf through dry and dusty tomes of folklore or, perhaps, to hear hitherto unrecorded oral accounts of such a monster from simple village folk. I never expected to find myself examining its paw-prints through a magnifying glass. And yet I was inexorably drawn into an all too physical attempt to unriddle the mysteries of the beast's diabolic reality.

I had of course researched the subject thoroughly. For some considerable time I had been privately collecting folktales and historical accounts concerning werewolves, with the intention of one day publishing a volume devoted to the subject. In France, the werewolf of Gévaudan was a notable example, and extremely well documented. The monstrous Beast that had plagued Gévaudan carried out its first recorded attack early in the summer of 1764, one-hundred-and-one years ago.

An unsuspecting girl, who was out tending to cattle in the Mercoire forest near Langogne, which lays in the eastern part of Gévaudan, was frightened beyond measure when the demonic Beast stalked her. God in his mercy was watching over her that day, for the bulls in the herd of cattle, realising the danger, had charged at the Beast and somehow kept it at bay. I do not know how many of the cattle were killed, but the accounts of the time state that the bulls eventually managed to drive the creature away. But only after it had attacked a second time. Shortly afterwards the first human victim of the Beast was slain. A poor, unfortunate fourteen-year old maiden named Janne Boulet. She was slaughtered near the village of Les Hubacs, not far from the town of Langogne. I pray that Our Father in Heaven welcomed Mademoiselle Boulet to his side. I would pray that the girl did not suffer, but some prayers cannot be answered.

The accounts of the Beast of Gévaudan were of particular interest to me for a number of reasons. These included the fact that they were relatively recent, at least fresh enough that there would still be some descendants living locally who had heard reports of the incidents from friends and relatives who had themselves witnessed the attacks first hand. In addition, the case was already exceptionally well documented. Furthermore, rather than just a couple of garbled stories told by illiterate and uneducated peasants, the existing, official, written accounts were compiled by some of the most learned members of the French aristocracy, clergy and even representatives of the Royal Court itself.

Throughout the later months of 1764, numerous attacks were reported throughout Gévaudan and many believed the slaughter to be the work of a Werewolf. Terror gripped the entire population of the region. The Beast had become as fearless as it was ferocious. It began to menace children at play, young women walking in the woods, and even able-bodied men tending their livestock in the forests. The reports I studied repeatedly stated that the monster was huge, unstoppable, and would savagely leap at its human prey, seeking to tear their throats open, snap its foul jaws around their necks and rip its victims' heads bloodily from their shoulders.

By late in the December of 1764 rumours had begun circulating throughout Gévaudan that there might be not one creature but a pair of such beasts conducting the murderous attacks. There had been so many sightings and so much slaughter in such a small amount of time, and over so great an area, that is seemed impossible that a single monster could be responsible for all of the outrages. Indeed, many of the attacks had been recorded as happening at the same time but in different locations. A few of the contemporary accounts suggest the creature had been occasionally seen with another such monster. Some witnesses thought the horrendous Beast was accompanied by its own demonic offspring.

On January 12, 1765, a little over one-hundred years ago, a man by the name of Jacques Portefaix, together with no less than seven of his friends, was set upon by the Beast. The group of men stood back-to-back and defended themselves desperately. After several attacks, the party managed to drive the monster away. This event, and particularly the fact that the Beast was so fearless in its desire to destroy human lives that it would even assault a large group of men, eventually came to the attention of his Majesty Louis XV. The King was impressed by Jacques Portefaix's bravery and awarded 300 livres to him, with a further 350 livres to be shared among his companions. Further to this, King Louis decreed that the government of France would itself now seek to locate and kill the Beast. Three weeks after hearing of the attack on Jacques Portefaix and his comrades, Louis XV dispatched two professional wolf-hunters to Gévaudan, Jean-François and his father Jean Charles Marc Antoine Vaumesle d'Enneval. The hunters arrived in Clermont-Ferrand on February 17th 1765, bringing with them a pack of bloodhounds which had been trained in wolf-hunting.

Contemporary descriptions of the Beast varied, though it was always described as looking like a wolf, yet one of massive size and monstrous nature. Most witnesses agreed that it was as big as a pony or a calf. It was said to have had a large canine head, with small straight ears, a massive chest, and a vast mouth which exposed long and wickedly sharp teeth. The Beast's fur was most often said to be of a reddish colour, though its back was streaked with black. Over the next four months the father and son hunted for wolves, disbelieving the details of most of the accounts of the monster and assuming the attacks were carried out not by a single giant Beast but rather by an entire pack of wolves. However, as the murderous onslaught continued, and as the hunters were unable to end the reign of terror by killing all the wolves they discovered in the area, the two men were replaced in the June of 1765 by François Antoine. Antoine was the King's Arquebus bearer, in effect his Majesty's Master-of-Firearms. For this royal commission François Antoine also bore the title Lieutenant of the Hunt. He arrived in Le Malzieu on June 22nd.

By September 20th, 1765 Antoine had killed his third huge grey wolf. This last wolf, which was named Le Loup de Chazes after the nearby Abbaye des Chazes, was said to have been unusually massive. At the time, Antoine officially claimed, "I declare by the present report, signed by my hand, I have never before seen so large a wolf that could it be compared to this one. That is why I believe this could be the fearsome Beast that has caused so much carnage."

The unfortunate, though no doubt deadly, Wolf of Chazes that Antoine had slain was further identified as the perpetrator of the recent monstrosities by survivors of attacks. These witnesses stated that they recognised scars on the wolf's body caused by wounds they had inflicted upon it while defending themselves.

The huge Wolf of Chazes was stuffed by a taxidermist and then sent to Versailles, where Antoine was received as a hero, being rewarded by the King with a large sum of money as well as being granted other awards and titles.

Such if is the folly and vanity of man. For later, on December 2nd 1765, The Beast of Gévaudan again attacked and grievously injured two men.

A dozen more grisly deaths are reported to have followed further ghastly attacks in the region of La Besseyre-Saint-Mary.

The Beast of Gévaudan was eventually slain, not by a royal emissary but by a local hunter named Jean Chastel, who shot and killed it during a hunt organized at the behest of a local repetition nobleman, the Marquis d'Apcher, on June 19th, 1767. Upon being slit open, the monster's stomach was shown to contain human remains.

The local folklore, based upon Chastel's own account, records that the hunter shot the creature with a silver bullet, although the term bullet is actually a misnomer. Chastel had made his unusual ammunition himself, by melting a large silver crucifix and then fashioning it into several solid silver musket-balls of a suitable size for a Charleville musket, which was the favoured firearm in France at that time. Chastel had then had the silver ammunition blessed by the local priest, before setting out to slay the Beast.

For my part, I firmly believed it was the fact Chastel had used a Crucifix, and had received a Holy Blessing upon the ammunition, which had allowed the man to finally kill the Beast. The contemporary accounts state that the monster had previously been shot and hit on numerous occasions with little or no effect. I was sure, in my faith, that it was the use of the Holy symbol of the Cross that had finally allowed the monster to be lain to rest. But, as I confessed earlier, I did acknowledge the possibility that there might be some special property in the nature of silver which may perhaps have been responsible for the Beast's demise. I never expected to find myself in a position where my theory would be tested.

I travelled to France intending to research folklore. I was of course well used to the French countryside and the ways of its people, for I had a long acquaintance with the country, its history and its customs. When I was only fifteen years old and living near Pau I had first discovered and later excavated the ruins of a Roman villa. When I was but eighteen, I wrote an article on the remains of an ancient camp near Bayonne which local antiquaries had attributed to the Romans or Saracens, yet which I was able to show, from its position in the centre of the Basque region, had in fact belonged to Basques driven by the Romans to take refuge in those mountains. I had happily returned to France looking for further evidence of legends and beliefs in Werewolves in an attempt to collate them into a coherent study. Naturally, when I was told of new reports of a Werewolf currently menacing the Gévaudan region, where a century ago the now infamous Beast of Gévaudan had been responsible for so many appalling and bloody deaths, I felt I had to investigate the accounts first-hand.

When I arrived in Gévaudan, I was enthusiastic to learn more about the supposed loup-garou, or as we would say, Were-Wolf, that was said to be currently haunting the area. While I have long had a fascination for such tales, I consider myself a rational man not prone to flights of fancy, nor one who is steeped in superstition. Stories of Werewolves and similar such monsters have come down to us across centuries if not millennia, and I had no doubt most had been distorted out of all proportion with reality. I thought than many such stories could be explained by entirely logical means, which might range from attacks by rabid wolves on the one hand to legends of battle-mad Viking berserkers on the other. Undoubtedly some lunatics were mad enough to genuinely believe themselves capable of becoming wolves, and acted accordingly. I remained sceptical yet open-minded as to whether Werewolves truly existed.

However, I was also a devout Christian and had in fact for some time been considering the possibility of one day becoming ordained as a clergyman. My sincere religious views led me to consider another possibility for the origin of the Werewolf.

If such creatures truly existed, I firmly believed the phenomenon could only be explained by demonic possession. A Hellish demon, entering into the body of a human, might readily force the unfortunate man or woman to transform into a ravening monster. But I was certain that in such an event the demon would be unable to stand against the power of the Cross. I had faith in this theory, although in truth it was mostly nothing more than idle intellectual and theological speculation. I never expected to have the opportunity to put it to the test.

I came to a village in the North of Gévaudan expecting to find a quiet, sleepy little hamlet, perhaps containing a few gullible, over-excitable peasants, or maybe a so-called witness who had seen a loup-garou in the bottom of his wine-cup. Instead I found chaos and death.

My intention to collect current accounts of folkloric belief in the loup-garou was perhaps self-indulgent. Folktales interested me. I considered their study to be an amusing and stimulating hobby.

Any amusement ended when I saw the first body.

I could not be certain a Were-Wolf had killed the child, but something had. It shredded the girl and left her half-eaten corpse as bloody proof of its merciless existence.

I prayed for the child that night. It was the night I first saw the Beast.

I came only as a scholar looking for information. I remained as a soldier for Christ, resolved to do my duty by bearing arms against the earthly emissary of the Devil himself.

I had gone to the local chapel, set on the outskirts of the village, to pray for the dead child's soul. The evening was fast approaching when I first knelt to address Our Father, and it was fully dark by the time I left the sanctity of the church and made my way outside, intending to return to my lodgings at the inn. I was walking through the cemetery when I heard a deep-throated and eerily unnatural howl in the blackness of the night. I had never realised it was actually possible for the hairs on a man's neck to stand on end. I had always assumed it was merely a picturesque expression. But when I heard that uncanny howling I swear every hair on my body stood upright. A primal fear gripped me. It was not a question of whether my courage failed me. It was something deeper than that. I was filled with an instinctive, atavistic terror that bypassed all logical thought and struck at that deep-rooted part of the brain that primitive man had relied upon to warn him of the approach of a sabre-toothed tiger, a prehistoric cave lion, or any of the other myriad horrors that menaced humanity in its infancy. For a moment I stood, unable to move. Then I gathered my senses and my resolve. I looked around me in the darkness of the graveyard and there, some thirty yards away, I saw the Beast silhouetted against the moon.

It was massive. Hideous and terrible.

At first I might have taken it to be a true wolf, albeit one of such awful size that I would have doubted it were possible had I not seen it with my own eyes. But then the Beast stood upright, poised on its two hind legs, it stood with a crooked posture, its back hunched and its forelegs raised to form misshapen arms ending in pawed hands, tipped with scimitar-like claws. It stepped deliberately forward, walking in a twisted parody of a human being. It turned its grizzled head in my direction and sniffed at me with its canine snout, while staring straight at me with eyes like saucers. Yellow orbs glowed from a cruel face covered in matted, red-black fur. Its fang-filled maw gaped wide, letting a long tongue hang out from the monstrous mouth. It grinned at me with a bestial smile. A smile that eagerly promised blood, pain and death. The Bible tells us that God made man in his own image. Upon seeing the Beast I had no doubt that Satan himself had made this creature in mockery of the divine creation. It was unnatural. Blasphemous. And terrifying.

I am ashamed to say that I stood rooted to the spot. Unable to move and equally unable to take my gaze away from the demonic horror. I think my own mouth hung open, but I made no sound. I could not move, nor speak, nor cry out. In my heart my faith in God was steadfast and unshaken, but some primal part of my brain had frozen. Had the Beast sprung at me then... I do not wish to imagine what would have happened. I believe I would have been torn asunder within moments, had not a shout suddenly broken the silent night and shattered the spell my fear had put upon me.

I heard footsteps running toward me, echoing in the quiet of the graveyard, coupled with more frantic shouts.

The Beast paused for a moment, looked once more at me with lupine eyes that held an insidious intelligence, then it casually turned away and loped off into the blackness of the night.

While Jesus is my eternal saviour from spiritual damnation, my physical saviour that night was Captain François de Marran. We did not know each other properly, having merely met and exchanged polite pleasantries earlier that day at the inn at which we were both staying, but I greeted him like a brother when he reached me and stood panting for breath. We both stared out into the darkness, scanning the surroundings for any further sight of the Werewolf. There was none. But suddenly, from out in the depths of the woods, came a loud, long drawn out, unnatural howl.

I will not describe in detail my conversations with my saviour François, who was late of the Regiment of Horse Artillery, and now on extended leave after his return home from duties in Mexico. It is enough to say that Captain de Marran and I had no doubt of the nature of the monster we had seen. Both of us were already well acquainted with the local legends of the original Beast of Gévaudan, and when I mentioned the accounts of a second creature seen in the company of the long since slain monstrosity, we speculated whether this new terror was the first Beast's offspring. I confess I was myself unsure what to think. It had been a hundred years since the death of the original Werewolf. François pointed out that even if the first Beast had indeed been seen with a demonic cub, surely that young creature would also be long dead by now? Or if not dead, then at least too aged and infirm to be a threat? I shook my head. In truth I had absolutely no idea of the life-span of a Werewolf, and besides which, I argued, it made little enough difference whether the current Beast was the mate, the child or the grandchild of the earlier terror, nor indeed if it was some wandering outcast freshly come to this region and now claiming the territory as its own devilish hunting-ground. All that truly mattered was that it was here. On that point and one other, Captain de Marran and I were in full agreement; The Beast must die.

And so I first asked Our Father for protection, and then I formed a plan. I determined we should carry the holy sign of the Cross before us, but also that we should follow the example of Monsieur Chastel in preparing our own ammunition before setting out to hunt The Beast. My belief that a crucifix would have power over a werewolf was due primarily to the accounts of the death of the original Beast of Gévaudan, although I confess I had also pondered whether the creature's weakness was in reality an allergy to silver. And so, as sinful gamblers are apt to say, I decided to hedge my bets.

The following morning, Captain de Marran enlisted the support of three retired soldiers who lived nearby the village. While they were somewhat advanced in years, none of the men were infirm, and if they felt the cold touch of fear upon their hearts at the thought of tracking a Werewolf, nevertheless they were good Christians and they stiffened their resolve to slay the monster. They needed no urging. They had all seen the mauled body of the poor girl it had slain. They had known her. And they had children and grandchildren of their own.

While François was recruiting the men, I first found the local priest, a Roman Catholic, but a good man of God despite that, and managed to persuade him to allow me to take a silver crucifix that had stood in the village church since time immemorial. I will admit the generous donation I offered in return for the item may have influenced the reverend gentleman, but I would prefer to believe he agreed for more pious reasons than money alone. I also acquired a number of wooden crosses, which were of little financial value, but which I believed would be of incalculable spiritual worth when confronting The Beast. I took the antique crucifix to the village blacksmith and asked him to melt it down and fashion it into as many bullets as he could make from the molten silver – true bullets, not simply musket balls. At first he was shocked, considering my request to be sacrilegious. But when I told him the reason for my strange request, he readily agreed and refused any payment for his time or labour. He too had known the slaughtered child.

We ran into one unexpected difficulty, in the form of the mayor of the village. Somehow he had heard about our intention to kill the Werewolf, and he forbade François and myself from trying to do any such thing. Or rather, he tried to forbid us. He insisted that attempting to hunt for the Beast would only provoke the monster and cause more deaths. Had I been alone, an Englishman abroad, I may reluctantly have been forced to obey the petty official. He was an unpleasant, pompous, red-headed man with a straggling black beard. Although I found his objections spurious and foolish, he was after all the mayor. I was but a foreigner visiting the region. But Captain de Marran turned the mayor's objections aside. François told the man that, as a commissioned army officer, he was not subject to orders from any civilian authority. The mayor insisted de Marran must obey his orders or face the consequences, telling my companion that his uncle was an army general, and if de Marran disobeyed, then he would write and persuade his uncle to have François court-martialled. The argument went on for some time and became decidedly heated, but in the end there was nothing the mayor could do to stop us. No one in the village was about to try to arrest a serving Captain solely on the mayor's say so, and besides which, their sympathies were clearly with us on the matter. Eventually, as darkness approached, the mayor stormed off, warning us we would regret ignoring him. We were glad to see the back of the officious bureaucrat, but the delay meant that it was already very late in the afternoon before we could begin our expedition.

When the time to enter the dense woods finally arrived, we all came armed. Both with prayers and with guns. The three retired soldiers each had swords in addition to pistols. François, a trained marksman, alone had the limited supply of silver ammunition, and was armed with a rifle as well as his cavalry sabre. I had no gun. I placed my faith in the sign of the cross. But I confess that I was relieved that my belief was supported with the Captain's firearm, and that it was filled with silver from the crucifix, blessed by the local priest.

That was how we found ourselves, armed as Christian soldiers, marching onward through the woods to wage war upon the unholy monster that now haunted the forest. I held an old rugged cross out before me, like a shield. My companions variously held their own crucifixes clutched in nervous fingers, or simply tucked them into their wide belts.

Night fell and still we advanced through the forest. I felt righteous, almost like a knight on a sacred quest. We lit lanterns to help us find our way through the dense woodland, and we shone these before us, seeking any trace of the Beast.

François suddenly called a halt and pointed to a patch of muddy ground. I hurried over, pulling out a magnifying glass I occasionally used for reading faded manuscripts, then bent to examine the area. I scarcely needed the glass. The wolf tracks were clear to see. But the paw-prints were massive, larger than my own boot-prints.

That was when the first man died.

There was no warning. No howls or growls. No sounds of struggle. Just a sudden, high-pitched scream from Jean-Pierre, one of the retired soldiers, cut short as his throat was savagely torn out.

I raised my lantern to shed more light and saw his mutilated body among the leaves. Or at least, I saw what was left of it.

Captain de Marran joined me, swiftly followed by Maurice, one of the other old men. We formed a circle, lifting our lanterns high and peering into the darkened forest. "Where's Jacques?" the grey-haired old soldier asked François. Alarmed, we lowered the lanterns a little to view the ground around us. And that was when we noticed Jacques' face, flayed from his skull and left resting on a fallen tree-stump. His body was no-where to be seen.

Maurice began to swear, angrily and fearfully, but de Marran hushed him. "Listen," said the Captain. "It's out there. Watching us."

We held our breaths, straining our ears to hear anything moving in the quiet of the benighted forest, then the silence was torn apart by a demonic howl. But it was not the wolf-call that chilled me to the core. It was what came after. Half-way through an echoing chorus of lupine howling the sound changed into laughter. No wolf could have made a sound like that. Nor could any human throat. The awful, half-howled laugh contained no trace, no hint, of true humanity. It was made by a thing that was neither human nor wolf but somewhere in between.

And then, without warning, it stood before us. Out lanterns illuminated the woodland just enough to see the shadowy shape of the great Beast. Its yellow eyes glinted in the pale lamplight.

I commended my soul unto God above, and stepped forward, toward the Were-Wolf. I held my crucifix high and showed it clearly to the devil-spawned monster, as I said, with the certainty of my faith, "Avaunt foul demon! In the Lord's name I cast you out. In Jesus' name, go back to the pits of Hell from which you sprang."

I watched as the Were-Wolf shook. But not with terror. With laughter. It stood before me. And then it quietly grinned. The sign of the cross held no fear for the Werewolf. None at all.

The harsh crump of a rifle-shot almost deafened me. François had fired while the Beast was distracted. The monster spun around, and disappeared into the pitch black of the forest.

"Did you hit it?" I asked the Captain. François made a typically Gallic shrug and gestured dismissively. "I don't know. Perhaps. I think so. But I am not sure. My hands were not as steady as they should have been. But I had a clear shot. I think I hit it, maybe in the shoulder."

I nodded. "In that case, if it is injured, we must find it and finish it," I said, "Heaven knows it was dangerous enough already. God alone knows what it may do if it is maddened by a wound..."

"I think I heard it moving, over that way," said Maurice, pointing to the darkest part of the forest. We spread out in a line, myself in the middle, and moved slowly forward. With my lantern in one hand, and my evidently useless crucifix still clutched in the other, I scanned the ground for any sign of blood or paw-prints. We walked on. Slowly. Cautiously. Determined to track the monster and slay the beast once and for all. Hunting our prey. I felt this was a duty I had to perform. That I had indeed become a Christian soldier, sworn to obey the commands of God and destroy evil in his name. "Do you see anything, François?" I asked. "Non. Nothing," he replied from my right hand side. "What about you Maurice? Ca va?"

Maurice, to my left, did not reply.

François and I looked at one another, then shone our lanterns behind us. In a few moments, on the ground we saw the steaming pile of bloody intestines. All that was left of Maurice. The Beast had taken the rest of him, dragging him away into the night.

François swallowed hard. It was all I could do not to me sick. "I thought we were hunting it…" I said, leaving the rest of my thought unspoken.

"We cannot fight such a monster on its own ground. We must get out of the forest." François insisted. I nodded. Partly because I could see the good military logic in his suggestion. And partly because I desperately wanted to be anywhere but in those deep, dark woods.

I don't know how long the journey back to the village took. We stumbled and half ran most of the way, stopping every so often to shine our lanterns into the darkness, or to listen, fearing to hear the diabolic Beast stalking us. Our clothes and skin were torn by brambles and thorns, but we forced our way onward. We came as Christian soldiers, but we fled like an army in terror before the Satanic horror of the Werewolf of Gévaudan.

At last we came to familiar ground. I recognised this part of the woods. We were almost within sight of the village. I breathed a heartfelt sigh of relief.

And that was when it struck.

It had been following us the whole time. Toying with us. Giving us hope, so that it would be all the more bitter when it snatched that chance away.

The Were-Wolf leapt out of the dense undergrowth. Straight at me. It raked its claws across my chest, almost playfully. It tore my clothes apart, but did not draw blood. I don't think it intended to do so. It simply wanted me to know the taste of fear.

François raised his rifle, but the Beast knocked him aside, sending the gun flying from his hands.

It turned back to me, saliva dripping from its fangs. It licked its lips hungrily with its long tongue.

I raised my crucifix, even though I now knew it held no power over the Beast. The Were-Wolf smiled wickedly. It looked at me, and the sign of my faith, the holy symbol I held before me. And then it bit the hand that held the cross.

I gasped, more in shock than pain, and the Were-Wolf chuckled that evil, bestial, laugh, the memory of which even now still chills the blood in my veins.

But its mirth was cut short as François pressed the barrel of his rifle against the Beast's back. It tried to turn, its speed was inhuman, but the Captain had already pulled the trigger. The silver bullet punched through the monster's ribs and exploded out of its chest - fired straight through the Were-Wolf's heart.

It fell to the ground. The Beast of Gévaudan was dead at long last.

Even so, we determined to take no chances.

François took his heavy cavalry sabre and, with a few hard, well placed blows, hacked the monster's shaggy head from its fallen body. "I may have this thing stuffed and mounted," he said, with grim cheerfulness, as he wrapped the bloody trophy in his jacket, and slung the bundle over his shoulder.

I felt myself shaking. I think mostly with the shock of the night's events. But also because I knew it was all finally was over. I was sure the silver bullet had killed the Werewolf. But then, I had also felt sure that my Crucifix would banish the demonic Beast, and I had nearly died because of my mistake. However, upon seeing the head removed from the monster, I was convinced that at last it had definitely and irrevocably been destroyed. I smiled, and said a prayer of thanks to God, glad that my body, my soul and my faith, had survived the long night.

The Captain and I walked on toward the village, exhausted but elated. I offered to carry the Were-Wolf's head for a while, knowing that François must be at least as tired as I was. But he said there was no need, he could manage, and besides which, if anything the head seemed lighter now than when he had first slung it over his shoulder.

I frowned when he said that. His words… bothered me. A nagging thought played at the back of my mind. A suspicion was forming.

"François, wait a moment. Let me see the Were-Wolf's head." I asked.

"My dear fellow," he replied, "We are nearly back. Let us get a drink at the inn, and there you can sit and look at it for as long as you like."

He was about to walk on when he saw the look on my face. He raised an eyebrow. "Oh, very well, see it if you must," he said, and dropped the bundle onto the ground.

I bent and unwrapped his jacket from around the severed head. We both looked at it.

We recognised the face at once. It was not that of a wolf.

It was the head of the mayor.

We buried the head, out there in the woods. And then we went back, to where we had left the decapitated body of the Werewolf, and found what had become the naked, headless corpse of a man. And then we buried that too.

François and I agreed that we would never speak of the events of that night to anyone. We knew no one would believe us. We could prove nothing. All we had to show for evidence were parts of the dead bodies of three retired soldiers, and the remains of a duly elected mayor, who by our own admission, we had ourselves had killed. There was nothing to prove he had been the Were-Wolf. And he had said his uncle was a general. François and I both decided that discretion would be the better part of valour. We would simply leave and say nothing. There would be no more Were-Wolf attacks, only some missing people. And before their scant remains were discovered, we would be long gone. Captain de Marran set off to rejoin his regiment, with a request to be assigned a position overseas, and I to return my home in England, on the first available ship.

I clasped François firmly by the hand, and he kissed me on both cheeks, after the French custom. We parted close friends, comrades in arms, and fellow Christian soldiers who together had faced a Satanic foe, and lived to fight another day.

I never saw François again.

It took me far longer to reach the French coast than I would have liked or expected, for every livery horse I hired was unduly skittish and fearful. I think perhaps it was not entirely the fault of the steeds, maybe they could sense my own nervousness and my frantic desire to leave their native land.

When I arrived back in England I determinedly did my best to forget all about the terrible events of Gévaudan. I threw myself instead into completing my book on lycanthropy. I kept my promise never to speak of what had happened. For François' sake. And my own. Neither of us would wish to defend a charge of murder. I certainly shall omit any mention of these occurrences from my book of Werewolves.

I have not lost my faith in the power of the cross, though I recognise that perhaps silver had more power over the beast in the end. But still even so, still I like to think that maybe it was the combination of both that put an end to the horror of the Beast.

Yesterday I bought myself a small silver crucifix, intending to wear it always, as a constant, silent reminder of what had happened that night in the forests of France, and how, by the Grace of God, I was lucky enough to escape unscathed, apart from the mere irritating graze where the Were-Wolf bit my hand.

But I find I cannot wear the cross against my skin. The touch of its silver burns me.

I cannot imagine why.

Unless...

The Brutality of Faith - Andrew Bell

Hartlepool, England.

The townsfolk gathered on the shore that icy day. The sea resembled undulating grey blanket, its ever-moving white surf getting closer as the day moved on. Darkness slowly crept down from the sky, and already they knew they were in for a beauty of a storm. Clouds had gathered like fishermen's wives, and they grumbled amongst themselves. Occasionally a whip of lightning would split the sky in two, filling the air with its scent of ozone. The clouds were different colours, some darker than others, like slowly healing bruises and cuts,lightning growled in the deep stomach of a few of them, the sound of angry gods ready to go to war.. After a short while they started to move, eventually they passed over; leaving a stiff breeze in their wake along Seaton Carew.

Some of the locals stamped their feet hurriedly to keep warm. It was the same every year on the fifth of November, to celebrate Guy Fawkes' night, and watch the pyrotechnics light up the sky. Sometimes a local band would accompany the festivities with their music. Sometimes it could turn into a train wreck, not always work to plan: shoddy showmanship or faulty equipment.

Dust devils sprang up and ran along the sand.

'Sarah, stay by mummy's side!' shouted Erica Stanton, for the thousandth time, or so it seemed. She already felt the first nails of the storm against her cheek. Goose bumps had covered her arms and legs; she could feel it beneath her clothes. The tiny dots of rain were hard, and her whole body shivered.

Her voice had been hoarse to begin with that day and shouting over the crowd made little help. Her teeth chattered against the brisk air that not even the surrounding crowd could shield her from. Was this whole show fucking necessary? Couldn't our local so-called magician just have booked somewhere warm? Her black leather jacket was zipped-up tightly, and her multi-coloured scarf helped to ward off the biting wind from her neck. At 34 she should be organising babysitters and going out with the girls, doing her make-up and drinking wine, listening to laughter of her best friends and pumping music; not standing here on a freezing cold beach, amongst other freezing cold people. But Sarah had wanted to come along, and when it came to her daughter she always tried her best. She knew her friends actually ate from their bins and went without of food for days because times were so hard. For instance Tracy Keenan, who had attended Brierton School with her. She caught her husband in bed with another girl. She knew hard times alright. It was one thing she could never accuse James of. He had kept his pecker in his pants, they had just grown apart. It was sad to admit, but true. And for that she was grateful that James always stuck to his word. He paid up, showed up, and was always there when she needed him. It was too bad it was over for them. Some day he would make a fabulous husband. Trouble is that, deep down, he already did.

Erica grabbed the piece of torn paper from her pocket and reread what was written in big bold letters.

The greatest show on Earth with illusionist, Reuben Turner! Do you believe?

She looked at it once more and felt a yawn in her chest, she stifled the urge and let go of the bit of paper. Maybe it would be Rueben's last effort? Lord knows, he could do with it after the stories that circulated the town about him.

As adults, they all knew that he was a charlatan. But as kids? Now that was a different matter altogether. They loved him, especially Sarah. What hung from her wall wasn't the usual chart-topping heart throb, but an image of no other than Reuben Turner. His eyes had a habit of following Erica around the room as she went about her day-to-day business. It creeped her out, but Sarah seemed to like him.

She remembered how the illusionist performed his magic at the Town Hall. It followed a very unconvincing clairvoyant act. The subject being a dead gentleman by the name of Harold Beechman. He purportedly passed away over a century ago, and through Rueben he could write down his thoughts and feelings. After a great performance that could have won Reuben a bloody Oscar, she thought, wondering why she wasted her money coming to those events, Erica, like so many of the people gathered in the audience, knew that something strange was going on here. Of course Reuben scribbled away on the piece of paper before him, and when he was finished, passed it around the audience. But later someone had really looked at the page, finding it to be fake. That person was an expert trying to debunk such magicians like Turner, and went to the local newspaper. She supposed this whole act was Turner's swan song, his last chance to redeem himself?

She ran the fingers of her right hand through her hair, pulling a long tendril from her mouth. It needed dyeing a little, she thought. With her left she felt the unopened packet of cigarettes. She knew she had a lot to live for but they were there for emergencies. Just in case. If it came to it, she would light up. But right now, after almost two months (quitting the filthy habit had been Sarah's idea for her mum's New Year resolution) she started to itch.

Erica's blonde hair was almost as long as her daughter's. It touched her shoulders, getting a little grey at the roots, but not to worry, she thought, as she tucked the rogue locks into the woollen hat she wore. A glance at her wristwatch revealed it was nearly two thirty in the afternoon. She had a hairdressers appointment later that day. Almost show-time, she thought.

Dark clouds spread across the sky. They broadcast their shadow on the people, and it looked as though the sun had been extinguished like a dying light.

Erica hadn't wanted her at the hospital but the doctors there insisted it was a common feeling. They didn't have a clue what she was experiencing, after all there wasn't one female amongst them. Even when she demanded to chat to a female nurse, it didn't work. She wanted no part in her life as a mum. Erica saw the ghost wandering the ward, occasionally holding IT, and knew the ghost had impregnated her with IT. But those feelings soon passed, the fog showing the ghost had cleared and she could see what it carried. Erica would sometimes shoo the family from the room carrying the newborn child. Birds often rejected their young entirely, they said to placate her. But she wasn't a fucking bird, was she? Ten years later, here she was. And she wouldn't give up Sarah for the world. She would die before any harm befell her little princess. Her lamb.

Sarah's father, on the other hand, thought Erica, was something else

James had Sarah for the weekends. At six foot three he towered over Erica, a petite five feet four. His hairline was starting to recede but he denied it, telling Sarah that there was no need to worry; that his eyes were falling down that's all. To which, little Sarah's brown eyes sparkled as she giggled.

It turned Erica's stomach when she thought of their divorce coming through. A part of her still loved him. Signing the bit of paper was like signing a mortgage. Till death do us part. But it was something she would have to get used to.

James was a good father. There was no denying that. He always turned up at her birthday parties bearing gifts, she would argue later that he had spent too much on Sarah, but he had no other little girls to spoil. Sarah never went without a thing; if she needed shoes, which was every month, then Erica considered it done. If Sarah wanted a new telephone, or hers' didn't quite follow the latest trend, again, Erica considered it done. They had avoided child support lawyers and went straight to a deal. They didn't want anything messy. They both just wanted out of the marriage was all.

But she called the shots.

It was her Saturday, Erica had demanded, that she was going to take little Sarah to the beach, and there was going to be no argument. Did James understand? Hell, he did. Either like it or lump it. Or face the solicitors and their pretty sharp fines. Sarah had been looking forward to it since Christmas, and she wasn't about to let her down.

Over a month had passed, she thought, and it was still blowing a gale. Although, it was winter, she kept telling herself.

'It better be worth it,' she mumbled, as more people gathered on the beach to witness what the papers had called the Greatest Show, the likes of which would astound and mystify.

Erica heard the small rumble of applause, the whistles and shouts, as Reuben Turner took his place at the PA system, set up at the edge of the peer.

Sarah wore her favourite red mac that Erica insisted had a place, and that was the bin. But no matter how many times she slipped it from under her little girl's eyes it always found its way back in the cupboard under the stairs. Alas Sarah had it loosely tied up the middle. Her long blonde hair was tied back into a ponytail, and it swung heavily as she looked from left to right. When she got home that night she'd text her friend, Jane from eight doors down. Maybe she would come out to play. Yes it was getting dark, and yes they had a curfew, but it was the weekend, she knew they were capable of twisting their parent's arms with their puppy dog eyes. She was a spitfire, alright. That's what Erica's late father always called her. Sarah just couldn't stay still. Ants in your pants was another one. She had been just three years' old when Erica lost him to cancer. Now she helps her mum jog along on school sports days in aid of the big C. She tried, anyway.

The wind seemed to get colder, and his collar was already upturned. He let go of his daughter's' hand for a few seconds whilst he tightened his collar, then grabbed a hold of it again. The sand moved with the breeze like they were one.

It was almost five o'clock, and the sun was slowly beginning to sink. Nearly time for James to say goodbye for the week, but he had to hang around, he thought. He wondered what Erica thought about that, but he didn't think it mattered much to her; after all, she didn't remind him his time was up. For that he was grateful.

The whole town had turned out, Erica thought, hardly recognizing any of the faces surrounding her. Yet bodies appeared as if from nowhere. They wore woollen hats, gloves and scarves. They beat their feet, stamping like the ground was covered in snow, not sand. Noses ran with colds, but Erica didn't think it mattered at all, as partners held on, or stood closely to each other. She heard people swear, as it got colder, and some of the towns' folk attempted to leave the beach as it was too extreme to be waiting out here, exposed to the elements. But their footsteps stopped, and they turned around as Reuben Turner spoke.

Reuben Turner's relationship with the grief- stricken had been tarnished by a certain Detective Robert Davids, when he found him to be fake.

Turner was a slightly greying forty-five year old, and he knew his craft pretty fucking well. He didn't need this ageing cretin to follow him and add to the stress. But add to it, he did. He soon learned that bugs got everywhere. That when he found the nest, he would stamp it out.

Night followed night, he'd look over his shoulder in the darkness, feel the cool breeze against his cheek, watching as a figure would move amongst other shadows, and try to blend in. And a smile would spread across his face, for he knew that there was someone there. He just wondered how much he was worth now. He knew that private detectives did not come cheap.

It had happened before. The last time had been the case of elizabeth Jennings. Fourteen years ago if not a day, he had been called over for a private séance. His name was to be found in the local newspaper, a Hartlepool number. Turner had arrived at the designated place, at his own expense (he had lied of such expenditure of course, he would make sure he included travel in the price). A black blanket bearing sigils that, he boasted, would protect them both when the dead arrived. Various crystals in a small purple velvet bag that tied at the neck with black string, a goat and a small dagger that was razor sharp. The tiny animal bit at the cage it was trapped in, but it was extremely small and would cause no bother, he hoped.

When he turned up at the house, Mrs. Jennings was not alone. The detective was there too. He claimed to be interested in what Elizabeth's dead husband had to say, but he wouldn't say what.

'The crystals do the talking, Mr. Davids,' said Turner, as though the other man had asked a question.

'I just wanted to know if he's alright over there,' said Elizabeth. Streaks of silver had appeared in her hair as if overnight. They had spoken about conversing at the funeral. It had been in poor taste, as Frederick Jennings had just passed away, yet elizabeth had been insistent.

Now the time was right, Turner had said. The lights dimmed, slowly, illuminating just the crystals. They refracted light around the table, one beam crossed with another. Then Turner sat straight in his chair.

'I hear Frederick,' said Turner. 'I can't see him, but…I hear him.'

'What do the crystals-'

'Be quiet and listen…hear that?' said Turner. His eyes were wide and unblinking.

'I hear nothin',' Davids replied, getting up from the table.

'Don't break the circle, I tell you,' said Turner, watching the detective grab his coat from his chair and smiled as he left the room. 'Now, where were we?' said Turner, returning to the crystals at hand.

Davids was a terrible private detective, thought Turner, when he came to one of his séances. He had paid like any other, but Turner knew there was something wrong when the detective refused to remove his coat. The man had been wired up with the latest machinery, he had found later. A video of the practise had been presented to him, for the detective had a hidden camera on his fake spectacles.

The séances had been convincing, thought Davids, he gave Turner that much credit. When "ectoplasm" had dribbled from the illusionist's mouth and nostrils it looked real. But it had all been fake. And at last the video was the key evidence that would put an end to put an end to the pain Turner was causing the weak.

'This is nonsense,' Turner had sneered, hearing the tape crackle as the video faded to black on the screen. He removed it from his machine and threw it at Davids, to which the detective thought fast. 'It proves nothing. You spotted a few wires here and there, but they could be anything. And I knew things about you, you probably didn't even know.'

'Wheelie bins get collected twice a month-'

'You think I'd stoop as low to find out your private life, Detective Davids?' he said smiling.

'Yes, there's one thing you got right all night,' Davids lied, standing up to leave. 'You'll hear from my client's solicitor soon.'

'Bring it, Detective,' replied the illusionist. 'By the way, we all have skeletons in our closets, don't we?'

Davids slumped behind the wheel of his Datsun Cherry and fired up the engine. He wondered what skeletons the illusionist spoke of. After all, he had nothing to hide. He took a pack of crumpled cigarettes from a pack in his glove compartment, and lit up, wondering why he did such a job.

'It's all about the money, mate,' he said, pulling away from the kerb. 'It's all about the money.'

He remembered that he had uncovered the lies last time, and he would do it again.

The PA system wasn't exactly crystal clear and it broke a few times, leaving a loud, sharp after-sound, rather like running one's' fingernails across a chalk board. The noise had that same effect. It cut through you.

'Hello, people of Hartlepool,' Reuben stammered. He adjusted the large microphone stand to his level.

At almost six feet tall and skinny some might say, he cut a fine figure of a man. Although his thinness suggested a rather outward feminine side. He had tired of confirming his sexuality years ago, and now if people didn't believe his heterosexuality, then they could do one and kiss their own ass. He had only his integrity as a serious illusionist to prove, and he didn't care about anything else.

The television and local newspaper North News were covering his story, maybe the world would see him for who he truly was? He was tired of being followed and debunked as a charlatan. The way he saw it, you win some, you lose some. That was his motto. But no matter how many clichés he used to describe his past, he didn't want illusion dismissed as garbage.

Reuben Turner was born 1977, at a hospital known as Camerons. It's rumoured that four draftsmen and a builder were killed razing the place to the ground. Spiky white hair pointed in all directions, and his father, Jonathan Turner felt all 7 lbs of him, as the nurse placed him in his arms. Their eyes met as his mother, Dorothy, slept off the horrific 17 hours it took for Reuben to arrive. He wanted to hold her hand, to be by her side when his son came into this world, but he sat smoking cigarettes, one after the other, in the "expectant fathers" room. He had heard about it so many times, so many stories. The wallpaper, pale and calming green, curved at the edges. With its well-trodden carpet, the room either made you a man, or you left. The door was always open, never locked. God knows, he watched how easy it would be to walk through the damn thing, and never look back. John stood up twice, then sat back down, lighting another cigarette. When the sparkling white uniform said she was taking a rest, he thought the baby had been born. But Dorothy was sleeping, too exhausted to go on.

John thanked the nurse, and was allowed to see his wife.

That's when he heard the scream.

He dropped the unlit cigarette. Eyes that hadn't seen sleep for almost twenty four hours stared at the room at the end of the corridor. He tried to pick up his pace, but his legs didn't feel like his own. They were made of clay and getting heavier with every step. When he reached the room, footsteps shuffled on the carpet behind him. Fingers sank into the flesh of his arms. They tried to remove him from the room.

'She's my wife-'

They held him back as the baby, covered in blood, was pulled into the world. A creature stood over Dorothy. It laughed in her face as she reddened with agony.

Over the demon's shoulder, he saw his wife's bulging eyes. They pleaded with him to have the devil out of the room, to put her child back inside of her, not to hand the baby over. To put it back. Holding his hands were nurses. Understanding, warm, careful nurses. And the doctor turned around, holding the child.

John felt the 7lbs of what was meant to be joy, only having enough strength to hold him uncomfortably. The seconds went by and he handed him over to the nurse, before stumbling, rushing to get some fresh air.

Jonathan Turner died of terror in the car park that night.

Rueben had been too young to know what his father had seen in the operating theatre, but he had what was known as instinct. He felt it, and he saw the devil, reaching for him and smiling as he came into the world.

It wasn't the old image we were used to. No slick back hair, widow's peak, red skin and pointy tail; he was loathsome, the opposite of everything. Every part of being human was reversed. His muscles and veins were on the outside, or he had been skinned, he didn't know. Humanoid in shape, even its eyes were inside out, the iris and pupil on the inside. Through its pink eyelids, the devil saw a young thing, barely breathing, a thing of beauty; everything he wasn't.

In seconds, they left. The devil walked tall, with its head held high, out of the room. Out of Reuben's life forever. One day their paths would cross again.

There was the world underneath the skin of this existence, and he wanted people to be aware of it; to open their eyes.

He knew this was his last chance.

If they could see his legs shake, how the electric shocks, rocked his every muscle, the people of Hartlepool would understand just how important today was.

Turner had everything right and double checked. He had followed them in his sleep for almost a year, and now was the time. The whole idea came one night as he had the strangest dream.

The travellers moved as one, a long black ribbon of the hungry and thirsty, following their hopes and beliefs of a better world. This life wasn't enough, nor the promise of a better world in the next; they wanted it now. No priest among them had faith strong enough to withstand this existence. Death would reveal God's face. But what if it couldn't? Nobody they knew of had returned with the secret. No, this was the only way.

After a year of travelling on foot, camping under the starless sky, losing many weak, they had reached the point beyond the veil Turner was hoping to shatter today. They couldn't see this world, but they could feel it. There was smoke between them, and it was getting thinner with every step they took. They could hear voices, and feel the rumble of feet, as they moved along. And like hounds on the scent of blood, they moved on its course. Whatever it was, maybe it was the land T'Mau, the wise one, had spoken of? The strange scent got stronger as they trudged along. They were almost through with the small leather pouches of water that they carried, and many, especially the infirm, were falling. Then they stopped to listen. A voice ahead could be heard through the swirling dust.

'Maybe this will turn out wrong, maybe you all wasted your time coming out today?' was what Reuben Turner wanted to say. But what came out, like a screech of reverb from the speakers was, 'I know you all are cold, I didn't pick the best of days.'

Marli turned to her brother, Olin, and frowned. The dust stung their cheek, and the winds continued to increase in force, but its sound had subsided.

'-but it must be today,' said Turner, looking at his wristwatch. 'In fact we have to question ourselves now.' He could see some of the people look at one another. The air fell silently as his cryptic words broke from the speakers. Some of them turned around, about to leave the beach. He could hear mumbling of voices and one or two curses.

Turner closed his eyes before speaking. He knew that the time was right, he was just afraid to blow their minds.

'Before you all return to the streets, and ultimately your lives, please put up with me for one more moment. All I ask is that you search inside to prepare you for what you are about to see.' I'm losing them, he thought, watching some of them leave the beach. He knew he had to punch this up a little-

'May I have your attention, please?'

One or two town's folk stopped on their way to the car park, and looked over their shoulders. They shouted in consternation, braying with questionable language. Some shook their hands in the air, their time had been wasted enough.

'Please,' he said into the microphone, the air heavy with the scent of burnished steel. The storm steadily approaching.

He knew that he had to just do it; there was no other way.

Then Turner closed his eyes, and clenched his fists into little hardened bullets.

It was time.

Erica remembered how Sarah had left her side. Her cheek was against her waist, and her arm had slowly snaked about her. One minute her tiny hand had moved from James's to hers, then she had gone. It was as quick and simple as that; every parent's nightmare, yet she had lost her daughter in pure daylight, in full view of the town's folk. This wasn't supposed to happen in the light of day, she thought, crazily. Where was the evil, slimy, child-catcher from that kid's movie? How come she had been surrounded by hundreds of people, and not one of them helped her? It had happened so fast. But life did have a way of moving on unstoppable. They heard Erica's screams, the shattering cry of her daughter's name as it rang out in the stillness. She saw everything in a much slower motion. As everyone held their tongues in amazement and shock, James's mouth moved open and shut, words seemed difficult also. The air seemed cleaner and everything was louder, she thought, looking about for her daughter. Yet she only saw her footsteps in the sand, how people moved aside to let her daughter's little body through.

Erica's feet shifted from their spot, as she went in search of Sarah, calling her name as loudly as she could. But the words seemed a hundred miles from where they should be. The wind picked up her voice like a fragile bone, and ran with it. She called again, her voice merely a whisper now as she made a way through the crowd. Her breath thumped in her chest, as did her heart. She didn't care where James was right now; nobody else existed but her daughter.

Turner opened his eyes and looked at the band of travellers.

Like opposite figures, without branded clothes, bewildered and tired, the travellers faced the others on the beach, and Turner wondered if they could see them? The veil had yet to be pierced, but he wanted to know…

The North Sea had disappeared, leaving a vista of golden, untouched, sand. Dunes that rolled on all the way to a sun-kissed horizon.

The town's folk stood like statues as he unveiled what indeed was beyond their understanding. In its way a band of tattered bodies, thin and dry with hunger and thirst. The travellers stood like the people of the town, staring. Silent.

'I want one of you!' said Turner, staring at the travellers with awe, and disbelief at his own power. He shouted with more confidence, his throat as arid as the beach that he saw over the scruffy heads of the people from the sand. 'Just one of you to dare, to trust your very belief, that you are seeing reality…'

Erica slipped slightly as she followed Sarah through the sand. Her feet buckled and twisted forcing her to stop for a second and regain her breath. Gasping, unable to move, her muscles as still as stone, Erica watched Sarah approach one of the travellers. Their hands touched.

When their skin met, said James much later to Erica, as they watched the doctors putting Sarah in a coma to keep her alive, something happened to the people of the town as well.

'Fuck you,' Erica whispered, as a nurse allowed her to see her daughter.

The dunes had gone on forever, or so it seemed to Olin. A cruel sun had seen many of the elderly and young of their group perish. The journey, it seemed, endless. When in fact, it had only been a couple of weeks. That's when they first spoke of the dream. It soon became a taboo subject, a dream that had been written down for the posterity of the mad and aged. They were written as scriptures, far more righteous than any Bible they knew of. But the young never forgot.

For a fifteen year old, lean and tall like his father, the great Marsela, Olin had witnessed death's face many times on the journey. He remembered the ones he had helped along the way, even lifting them upon his shoulder when the going got rough, the heat boring a hole in their head, pressing down upon their weary backs then disappearing until the next time. When they were buried in the sand, he learned quickly to forget them. It hurt, but carrying extra baggage would weigh them down. Death was just another vulture, thought Olin. Yet the bird wouldn't go away. It sat looking at you every sun-blasted day, its shoulders hunched, its piercing, black eyes looking for the next worn traveller to pick off and take back to its lair. He wondered where it had come from, trying to shade his eyes from the sun's glare. There were few trees along the dunes. The ones they came across were crooked and small, lending very little shade. One or two of them were tempted by the branches, and wondered if they were able to carry the weight of a man…but that was the last resort, and none of them were quite ready to give up. The sand was so hot at times, Olin had to move quickly like a lizard.

Every morning, as soon as he raised his head and brushed away his dreams, Olin studied the scriptures he had hid beneath his blanket. Hot parchment that grew hotter by midday, he'd read them when the others were unaware. He roved the banished writings that would surely see his head separated from his body, if he was ever caught. They spoke of a land that was beyond theirs, a place he longed to visit. Many say that God's face was there; that you only saw it when you died. Nobody could take that chance. It was a map that everyone denied existed, that some mad angel, the old ones say, had torn off its own skin and drew a picture on its pelt. With lolling tongue and rolling-mad eyes it had laughed, paranoid that their secret will be discovered, the road it imagined becoming a reality on its tattoo. It didn't tell anyone of a great paradise, or the road to Eden. It was the etchings that could spell a reason for their maddening beliefs. It was the inside of the mask that they pulled over their faces' every day. Olin knew that there was more to the skin than what was running through the others' minds. It really could guide the way, and Olin often wondered if belief was enough. They needed to experience greatness with their earthly prowess, and not just their souls.

Time was man's great enemy. It surpassed all the wealth that a life could bless a man. In the end the poor shared the soil. He was asked once by an old friend - Olin was very young at the time - If he was willing to wait until it was time to perish, until he could barely see an inch before his face, the true end. Although he was waist-height, and his mother would agree he found it hard to hold his tongue at the best of times, he fell speechless. He actually couldn't find the words.

When the others scrabbled in the sand for scraps along the way, Olin watched their desperation. It grew fiercely, and he could see it in their eyes. Hunger burned like nothing he had ever seen. Once, he had caught an elderly tribesman looking at his sister. He had seen that look before, and he had broken each and every finger on the old man's hand until he surrendered. Now that man walks with his head lowered and his hand covered up.

As the worms and spiders had run out, they started on the search for scorpions. It had been an easy lesson to learn, and if they were quick enough, and if they held them in the right place, they could count them on that night's' menu. Yet some of them had died just seconds after eating them; so the little pests were given a wide berth. Without food or drink, they had but one choice. They'd beat their fists upon the ground, then drink the blood from their bitten lips. At least their thirst was satiated, he thought. Trying to follow suit had hurt at first, and when he reached through the flesh to the blood within, it hurt. Then he had gotten used to the coppery taste. The flesh, he pretended was fruit. It grew like fire in his field where he once lived. Apples, oranges…even horse-chestnuts were rampant. How succulent it was, he thought. Now they weren't there, he still missed how they tasted. Especially against his Mother's will. He didn't really understand why fruit tasted so much sweeter beneath the stars. The gore covered his mouth and chin; it covered his cheeks too, like a scraggly beard. Soon it hardened and flaked when he touched it, crumbling beneath his ministrations, playing with his face like the decrepit and feeble-minded. He bit his lips, and his arms, until he wore the markings like tattoos. The ones around him had tasted the blood of others, and had tried tasting his, but he had kept his supply for himself. It would be there should he need it. Some would call it a selfish act, for some of them were dying of thirst. Then he moved on to his sister, who had quickly pushed him away.

'Get a hold of yourself!' she had shouted, her right hand immediately covering the bite on her left forearm. Blood dribbled down her brother's chin, drying like a blackening coin in the sand at their feet. 'That hurt!' He had slowly come to his senses and apologised later. He sat on the ground and cried. He slept on the other side of the fire that night. He had tried to move around to circulate the warmth about his body. Eventually, the right side peeled and cracked. Sleep felt no pain.

Every day was like the last. But today they were getting close.

Sarah stepped from her place amongst the flesh. Like a wall, the others stood like soldiers on parade, facing outwards. Their backs were as rigid as boards, skin as pale and cold as peat. She could smell them, although she didn't want to get too close. What if they came alive? She thought, turning around.

Stretching for miles, or so it seemed, people, as lifeless as toys, faced each other. But…what was that she could see? Sarah felt her heart lurch for a moment as vapour billowed from one of the people's nostrils. They were asleep, she surmised. Yes, their chests moved, only slightly, but they moved. Sarah turned in both directions, her throat as dry as dust now. Long lines on either side of her, stretched for as far as she could see. She turned about to see the person stood behind her.

She felt the warmth as liquid trickled between her legs. There was a floor, dark and hard, and her urine pooled about her feet. Now her skin crawled, pores rose. The girl was paler than usual, she thought. Her hair was long and blonde, it reached over her shoulders, cascaded almost. Now dark rings hung on her cheek as though recovering from an assault of some sort. Sarah wanted to reach out and touch the dark circles, wanted to take her by the shoulders and shake her awake. She knew the girl, but thought refused to register in her mind.

Sarah looked at herself in the dark corridor of faces, and she blended in among the sleepers. She thought of staying there, demanding to come awake; in her warm and cosy bed. To see the familiar shiny plastic, button-like eyes, and sticky-out ears of her soft toys, around her, once more. Sarah had never felt so alone and afraid; like a living doll among so many dead-like creatures. No matter how hard she beat her fists, and kicked and screamed, this time, sadly, she could not have her way. She could make as much noise as she wanted. She had even screamed at her own face, spittle spraying on her cheek and nose, but she stayed asleep, not noticing the pearls of phlegm on her face as it ran down her flesh. Sarah reached out, to wipe herself, but she stayed her right, shaking hand; too scared to move. Her chest rising and falling, gently, as though she didn't exist at all.

Sarah looked up and down the line, her body had taken its place between an old man, and a black boy of around her age. Satisfied that they were pretty distinctive, the old white man sported a long beard and flat, tartan cap. The black youth, a bright green track suit, his head shorn. Yes, she thought, she had no trouble finding her way back.

Sarah slowly stepped forward on the hard ground, and turned right. She looked over her shoulder, at the old man and the green, bright clothing. She wanted to see the rest of this place, even though she was scared to the bone. And as her soft face slept like an angel, she slowly looked ahead of her. One foot followed the other, face passed face. In no time at all, she came to a door.

The door had a black, metallic handle. It was cold to the touch, and her hand seemed to smoulder. For a long moment, she removed her hand, and stood still, still feeling the coldness in her fingers. The ground was hard and dusty, like the field back home, she thought. And it was real. This more than some dream, she whispered. Blotches flashed before her eyes as her heart thumped, and as she grabbed the handle, she turned it, and stepped inside the room on the other side.

Danny Wilson didn't feel too well. He had decided he'd give work a miss for tomorrow. The other lads of the group wouldn't miss his pair of hands for just one day, he thought, scratching the three days' growth on his chin, trying to control the car as he drove home from the beach. He knew that walls didn't build themselves, but his stomach growled loudly and he had needed the toilet three times since the show. He wondered if it had been the fish and chips he had scoffed down twenty minutes' ago that hadn't agreed with him. In fact the lads would probably take advantage of the situation, and get overtime pay, he smiled, shaking his head.

'Fuck it,' he muttered, stifling a yawn that grew inside, a smile spreading across his face as he soon settled into a space in the traffic. It was getting dark, and the roadside lamps had appeared. Lights, like tiny eyes, opened up along the way.

The police and other emergency services had soon descended and arrested Turner, shortly after that little girl fell down, he remembered. One minute she had been there, all strong and full of confidence, doing the opposite of what her parent's instructed: A typical child. The next moment she was lying flat upon her back, as stiff as a board. The services had arrived quickly, though. They worked as fast as the first aiders he'd seen on site once; straight in there, no messing about, pushing everyone back.

The sun still rolled over the dunes in the place the sea used to be, but that mattered no longer. Wherever the sea had vanished to, the towns' folk got themselves away from there, as quickly as possible. The hills of sand stretched before them, tiny footsteps dotted the horizon.

The strangers stood as still as stone. Maybe they knew what had happened? Who knew what they saw, maybe the girl's hand had felt like a slight weight in the stranger's hand? There one second, gone the next? In moments the little girl was on a stretcher and on her way to a waiting ambulance. Maybe they had been standing by in case anything went wrong? He'd heard stories about the police waiting in their cars or vans, at a street corner, waiting for an altercation in progress, just so they had evidence to convict. He shrugged his shoulders.

'Pigs,' he whispered, as another police van flew by, rocking the car from side to side. He took a packet of cigarettes from the glove compartment, lit one up, and drew deeply. Margaret didn't like him smoking, but drawing blood from a stone was easier.

It was a wonder he had left the damned place as quickly as he did, he thought. It must have taken almost three hours to get through the traffic. And now the sun had fallen. Beers as cold as ice waited in the fridge, that put a warm smile upon his face. Maybe he'd have that sleep in he'd promised himself for a long time?

'Always knew that magician fella would land himself in hot water one day,' he said to Margaret, but his wife was already asleep. Her face was amongst the cushions she insisted upon having for her front seat, hair a brown rat's nest, pointing in all directions. A thin sliver of drool connected her mouth to the cushion's softness. Her eyes seemed to roll around like marbles behind the closed lids, and she snored delicately.

Twenty years they had spent together, and this was the quietest time they had ever shared, he thought, smiling. He looked in the rear view mirror.

Young Cody, their five year old daughter, and Jason, their six year old son, weren't fighting. He had never known them to be settled and calm. Fighting had never begun, toys and ipods were stashed away and forgotten. Silence hovered on the air as he realised that Cody could have been like that little girl on the beach, and his smile faded. He could be holding her hand, on their way to the hospital. He thought of her parents, and his chest heaved. He was grateful… He pushed away the thought, and concentrated on the road ahead.

Danny kept his eye on the road, although the cats eyes at its centre, lit up brightly. Trees passed by, traffic eager to escape the failed illusion, now a misty blur.

He had to shout to wake them, when they arrived home. And they filed one by one from the car, like zombie extras from an old B movie. Heads were lowered, eyes half-lidded, mouths yawning. It was a shame that Danny's back couldn't hold his own five year old daughter. He spoke her name softly, at first, then shook her awake. A cool breeze swept through his prematurely greying hair as he weaved through the darkness of their front garden. He could just make out the gnomes there, and the small mound of earth he had removed for the pond he was building. Maybe he would get that up and running tomorrow? Maybe.

The Wilson's shuffled into their home like the undead, as tired as can be. Heading for the stairs, they didn't even remove their hats and coats. And they were back fast asleep as soon as their heads hit their pillows, snoring away the soundest of sleeps.

Cody wore her hat, and she had kept awake just long enough to walk the breadth of her room, not making it to the bed. She curled up on the carpet, like a cat. Swept away by sleep, she embraced its warmth.

Jason had almost fallen, Margaret's hands catching him as he fell in a heap on the ground, now hanging loosely in his mother's arms; a weight that seemed to increase per second. Margaret climbed the stairs one at a time, dropping him on the landing. The loud crashing noise went unheard, his broken and tiny body in the shadows. She thought she saw the shining of wetness around his eyes, but she was too tired, and eager to get to her bedroom. Jason curled up for a few seconds, agony coursing like a drug through his veins. Slowly he slipped into a long and fitful sleep, living and dying felt seamless.

She went to her room, the boy now a distant memory, and collapsed on the bed. Margaret was already dreaming as her feet crossed the room.

Lightning cracked, splitting the sky in two, like a whip. It was a purple slit that opened in the sky, but only for half a second or more. There was a lull, as though God's lung had inhaled for a second. Not even a bird sang. Then came the storm. Rain beat the window panes and rooftops, and the pipes inside their walls groaned as the central heating kicked into shape.

Danny watched the football, occasionally glancing up at the ceiling, seeing the field projected there. He smiled, knowing that they didn't have much, looking around the room at the random, mismatched furniture. Even the stool, he now rested his feet upon, was a different fabric than the couches cushions. Nothing matched, and it had taken the better part of two decades to really notice. But for the first time in his life, he knew what it meant to be content. The bills were paid on time (usually), the works' van was paid up and so belonged to him, the kids were doing great at school, Margaret had her courses at the college in her spare time, and the new building job was going great.

Primarily, he and the others of Middleton Co had been contracted for two months, but that had stretched to four. There was loose talk of that going on and on, but Danny didn't listen to gossip. The shopping mall had seen a lot of storms, he thought, glancing at the hard rain as it beat the window pane. Seen a lot of heavy fists. The asbestos guys had been in to do their jobs, and now it was a job for them. He'd make sure to stretch the bastard job out, he thought, smiling.

Now Tottenham Hotspurs just needed one more goal, he thought, cracking open the beer he had on the arm of the sofa, and his life would be truly complete.

Slowly, the remote control, slipped from his fingers. A small, dark shape of urine appeared at the front of his jeans, as he lost all feeling in his body. The beer can fell from his other hand as he fell into a deep sleep.

The storm continued to rage as the football match played on. He never saw the result. Spurs drew nil-nil with Middlesbrough. Then came the highlights, and finally the weather. If he wasn't sleeping he'd have seen Reuben Turner make the headline news. The uniformed officers bundled him into the back of a van and drove him away.

Then…the screen buzzed white, as Danny's chest rose and fell.

As he slept he waited. For how long, it mattered no more.

The Wilsons never woke up.

The following morning neither did the residents of Hartlepool.

☐

For Those In Peril On The Sea - Em Dehaney

We were so confident in sealing the deal, we journeyed to Paris First Class on the Eurostar. Champagne and caviar all the way. By the time we arrived in France, Renners was so plastered he could barely stand up. But it didn't matter, it was a foregone conclusion, all we had to do was take the papers to be signed and we had closed the biggest land sale in Kent history.

'Johnno,' he slurred as we wobbled out of the Gare du Nord 'We're gonna be rich. Filthy, stinking rich. Not bad for a couple of twats from Strood.'

Seven hours later, I was staring at my reflection in the black glass of a ferry window. I could feel the tension radiating from Renners. The lurch of the waves pulled at my guts. The champagne from this morning sloshed around inside, hollow and bitter. I'd told him I could take the papers, that I could handle meeting low level European royalty on my own, but he insisted on coming. Said it would look better for the firm if they didn't send a junior. I didn't want to point out that I was about to be made a partner. He had twenty years on me and had a way of looking at you, like he could turn in a second.

'I need some air'

I stood and staggered as the floor pitched. The dimly lit bar might have been sophisticated once. Now faded faux-velvet armchairs with foam poking through at the seams clustered sadly around sticky tables. Bottles clinked gently as a solitary barman stocked the fridge. Who the bottles were for, I couldn't say. I hadn't seen another soul since we boarded. This was a lorry driver's ferry, we had seen them queued up nose to tail at the port. They must keep to themselves, somewhere dank and sweaty below.

We had been due to meet our client in The Hotel de Crillon at 3pm.
3pm came and went
4pm came and went.

At half past four, I went outside for a smoke. I didn't have to, this was Paris where everyone puffed away wherever they liked, but I needed to get away from Renners constant foot-tapping and pen-clicking. He must have realised it was annoying me, because all his nervous tics had disappeared by the time I got back from chain smoking three Gauloises. Another hour passed before a slick-haired waiter appeared carrying a silver platter, bearing a single white envelope.

'From Monsieur DeVille.'

He placed the platter on the table. I leaned over to pick up the envelope, but Renners snatched it from my hands.

'My friends,' he began reading in his irritating, nasal voice. 'It is with greatest apologies that I am unable to continue with this purchase as we agreed. Due to unforeseen circumstances, I must be in London. I will meet with you tomorrow at The Albemarle Hotel in Piccadilly, where we can further discuss our business. I have made arrangements for your return journey.'

I traversed the carpeted corridor of the boat, listing to the side to keep balance. I still had yet to see another passenger. Probably all in the toilets throwing up. I knew how they felt. I pushed open a reinforced glass door against the wind and found myself out on deck, sea spray in my face. There was no moon, but I could just make out the churning water below lit by the emergency lights. Sliding about on the slick deck, being pushed along by the wind, I decided to go back inside. Sitting in silence with Renners for three hours was preferable to being out in a squall wearing only mid-priced pinstripe. Gripping onto the plastic bucket seats I managed to make my way back to the door and was just about to go inside when something swooped over my head. I looked up in time to see a black shape disappearing onto the deck above. I was sure I had seen the shape of wings, but no sea bird would be out in this weather.

At night.

My heart thudded on the inside of my now sodden shirt. Slamming the door behind me, back in the cosseting warmth of the corridor I quickly came to my senses. It was gale force out there. It was just something blowing about in the wind, some bit of cross channel junk. Feeling more rational by the second as I walked to the bar, I had almost convinced myself that I had seen some ties loose on the railings, that a life-belt had come free in the wind and a sudden gust had blown it up above my head. And that the sound I had heard over the roar of the sea was not the flap of leathery wings.

I needed a drink.

Back in the bar, I found the drinks menu printed on an A4 sheet of paper that promised 'The Finest Slovakian Wines'. I never normally drink wine, but this appeared to be all they stocked. I looked about for the barman, but even he appeared to have deserted us.

'He said to help ourselves and leave the money on the counter,' croaked Renners. He was slumped in a booth, empty wine glass in front of him, half-drunk bottle of red on the table. I grabbed one of the glasses hanging above the bar.

Renners was staring at DeVille's note.

'The deal isn't blown, don't worry,' I said, hoping to lift his spirits. 'We'll get him tomorrow.'

I plucked the note from his fingers. I had expected to see gothic handwriting, perhaps a wax seal. The signature at the bottom was executed with a flourish, but other than that it was a standard laser-print letter.

'I wonder how he knew we didn't have a return ticket for the Eurostar?'

We had wrongly assumed we would be celebrating in style, our commission from the sale being enough to fly back on a private jet if we so desired. My colleague poured me a glass and stayed silent. He left his empty. Good job too, he didn't look well.

'I think he's playing mind games with us, trying to get us to drop the price.'

'It's not about the money.' Renners' voice was tight.

'Of course it is. Everything is about the money.'

'Not for him...' Renners slapped a hand over his mouth.

I jumped back in my chair, out of the firing line in case he puked. He was pale. Sweat beads dangled off his eyebrows. The hand he had clamped firmly over his mouth looked waxy, his nails dark.

'Are you alright? You look sick.'

'I'm just hungry.'

'I'll see if I can find that barman, order us some food.'

I was glad to get out of the bar. He might have been seasick and hungover as Hell, but Renners was giving me the creeps. Back out on the empty hallways again, the constant vibration of the engines had my teeth on edge. Even if I could find someone to make us some food, I wasn't sure I would be able to keep it down. At the far end of the corridor was a door marked 'Lorry Bays'. The lorry drivers must have somewhere to get a fry-up. I opened the door and stepped onto a metal staircase, the bare walls and functional lights in stark contrast with the shabby glamour of the ferry interior. I began clanking down the steps until I got to the next level. I opened the door to Lorry Bay 1 and poked my head through. To my surprise there were no cabs, just a row of metal containers. That might explain why the ferry was so deserted. The drivers must have deposited their cargo and driven away.

We couldn't be the only passengers.

I ran down the stairs to Lorry Bay 2, and opened a door to the same scene. No trucks, just containers. The ferry lurched to its side and I had to grab hold of the metal balustrade to stop myself falling to the floor below. I heard a loud clang, and looked down to see one of the container doors swinging in rhythm with the motion of the waves.

'Hello?'

No reply.

I jumped down the steps two at a time and peered into the open container. A draught of cold air blew out, and I managed to catch the door before it swung back and hit me. The inside stank of mouldy basements and potato dirt. A solitary tea chest was pushed to the very back. I could just about make out the 'this way up' sign through the gloom. I had come this far, and even though my stomach was growling, I needed to know what was in the box. I jumped up into the container, a foetid smell filling my nostrils. A soon as I had both feet inside, the door slammed behind me with a deadly thud.

Plunged into absolute darkness, I blinked hard and put my hands out in front of me, turning slowly to face the door. I took what I thought was the two steps necessary to make contact with the cold steel, but all I felt was air. I tried to keep still and re-set my internal compass. I could now hear breathing. Surely my own, echoing off the interior of the container.

I held my breath.

Silence.

My own heartbeat in my ears.

I let my breath out. At the same time a ragged gasp came from behind me. I launched myself forward, falling through the door and back into the blinding light of the lorry bay. Scrabbling to my feet, I didn't look behind me as I clattered up the metal steps and slammed the deck door. I ran all the way back to the bar, carpet thudding dully beneath my shoes.

I burst through the swing doors, expecting to see Renners slumped over the table where I left him, but the bar appeared abandoned. A glass swayed in its hook over the bar, catching my eye.

'Renners? There was someone, in one of the containers. In the lorry bay…'

As I was saying it, I could already picture a poor Eastern European lorry driver, probably not had any sleep since he left his depot, crawling into one of his cargo containers to catch a nap before he had to resume his journey across the continent. I leaned over the bar, feeling like an idiot. Renners was on his hands and knees next to the drinks fridge.

'Have they got beers?' I said. 'I don't think I can handle any more red.'

The back of his head was twitching. I saw two pairs of legs, one kneeling with feet clad in leather loafers and another pair, stretched out underneath Renners, attached to a lifeless body. I yelped as he spun his head at an unnatural angle, piercing me with bloodshot eyes. Strings of flesh hung from his canines, now transformed into elongated sabres. Blood dribbled from his lips. Arterial spray from the dead barman beneath him covered his chalky face and splattered his shirt.

'The Master is coming!' he howled. 'And He has promised to make me immortal,' he screeched after me as I staggered backwards. 'Take what he offers you, Johnny. He will only offer it once…'

I could no longer see his head over the top of the bar, but I heard greedy crunching and slurping as I tumbled backwards through the doors.

'He speaks the truth,' drifted a voice from the corridor.

There was no-one there.

The lights flickered.

'Help, wait, help!' I babbled as I raced after the voice. Rounding the corner, the voice came again.

'A once in a lifetime offer.'

It was coming from upstairs. I ran, taking the steps two at a time, until I found myself in a small arcade, packed wall to wall with fruit machines. The only light came from the flashing cherries and golden barrels of the one arm bandits.

'Who are you? My friend…he…'

'Ahh, yes. He is my friend now, I think.' He sounded close. I could detect a slight accent. The 'r' rolled cruelly over his tongue.

'I'm calling the Police,' I yelled weakly.

'We are on the sea, yes? Who will come? You are alone in your peril. The only one who can save you is me.'

I followed the voice to the farthest corner of the room. A Castlevania game stood alone in the dark, the screen blank.

'Who are you?'

'Oh, I have many names. Some know me as Orlock. Some as Vlad Tepes. You know me as DeVille. That is not important. What is important is what I am going to offer you now.'

The shadow beside the video game unfolded itself into the shape of a man. His broad shoulders tapered to a slim waist and long legs. His face was still in darkness.

'Hear me,' DeVille whispered inside my head.

'See me.'

He stepped into the blinking light. His skin was white, made to look all the paler in contrast with his neat, black triangular beard. His eyes, ringed with violet smudges had the same bloodshot tinge that I had seen in Renners. His long hair was slicked back on his head, displaying long, thin ears. Everything about him seemed stretched and unnatural.

'I can give life to your dreams. Deliver your very heart's desire.'

I was unable to tear my eyes from his mouth. It moved at a different speed to the words coming from it, like he was caught in a satellite delay. His teeth glinted. His lips glistened. His voice was smooth and sibilant. My eyelids were heavy. My feet melted into the floor like hot glue.

Everything went black.

When I opened my eyes, I was facing a bank of dials, buttons and levers on a vast console. Lifting my head I could see the rain battering a wrap-around window. I was high up over the deck, and judging by the instruments I guessed I was on the bridge. I tried to stand, but my wrists and ankles were lashed to a chair. I twisted in my seat, causing the whole chair to spin.

I was not alone.

Another man was tied to a large leather seat next to me. His white shirt and braided epaulettes indicated he was the Captain. He saw me and his eyes widened behind metal rimmed glasses. He was gagged but began to grunt and scream, thrashing his head about against the chair.

'Calm down,' I hissed, but this just made him chuck himself about even more. His eyes were now focussed on the space above my head.

'It's him, isn't it? He's here.'

I spun the chair again, but instead of the aquiline nose and clipped beard of DeVille, there was a woman.

'Oh, thank Christ,' I panted, trying to pull my arms free. 'Some nutter has tied us up in here. Can you help?'

The woman said nothing. With a sinking heart I took in her waxy complexion, raven hair and black cherry lips. She smiled with a predatory glint in her bloodshot eyes, as two more women stepped out from behind her, flanking her on each side. Three impossibly beautiful yet strangely repulsive creatures stood before me. I could hear the Captain's terrified shrieks plunge to a resigned moan. The woman on the left of the trio had pale straw hair to match her milky skin. She fixed her watery blue eyes behind me, and before I could register, she was gone. There was the sound of ripping linen, then gargling and sucking. I tried to wrench myself out of the chair, and in an instant the right-hand woman was on me, her face inches from mine, long red hair cascading over my shoulders. Her breath stank of rancid meat. And yet, as she began to grind her hips against mine, something stirred.

'Yessss…' she whispered. 'Yessss. It's easy. So easy. That's right.'

Her tongue tickled my ear, blocking out the wheezing death throes of the Captain. I closed my eyes. Both her hands were in my hair. I felt my zip slowly being pulled down. I jerked my eyes open and saw the black-haired woman knelt between my thighs about to go to work.

'Thissss can all be yours. We can be yours forever.'

A cold hand snaked into my boxer shorts. I felt the delicate touch of a tongue, then the threatening yet exhilarating brush of teeth on skin.

'No!' I yelled and slammed by head forward, smashing the red-head in the nose. She yelped and leapt three feet in the air. Her hands became claws which buried deep into the felt covered ceiling. She clung on lizard-like, defying gravity. A drip of blood fell from her busted nose onto my face, giving me a buzz of triumph.

It was short lived.

My head jolted back as the snowy haired woman grabbed my hair and yanked. My neck was exposed to the hungry mouth of the gothic beauty between my knees and she lunged upwards. I screwed my eyes tight and braced for the slash to my throat which never came. The weight suddenly lifted from my legs, I heard a howl and a thud. I opened my eyes to see the broken body of the woman crumpled against the wall of the control room. Still conscious, despite the odd angle of her neck, she glared malevolently at me from the floor.

'Please accept my apologies. My pets are not quite house trained. A shame. They are such beauties, do you not think?'

DeVille was perched nonchalantly on the console, picking at his teeth with an exquisitely curved pinky nail. Wind and rain buffeted the glass behind him.

'What are you people?' I croaked. Blondie still had hold of the back of my head, my vocal chords like overtuned violin strings about to snap.

'We are what you could be. We are your potential. I can make you more than you are. I can give you life eternal.'

A clicking noise drew my attention away from DeVille's grand speech and back to the woman in the corner. One of her feet was on back to front and her arm was hanging down limply at her side. Unable to put weight on either, she kept slipping as she tried to stand. Her pre-Raphaelite friend scuttled down from the ceiling and took her good arm, leading her off the bridge. That left me, DeVille, the snowflake with her hands around my neck and the bloody mess that now passed for the Captain.

'If that's what immortality looks like, I think I'll pass. Thanks all the same.'

'As you wish,' DeVille nodded sagely. 'I can see you are a harder negotiator than your old friend. That is good. Money, women, eternal life, everlasting power. Name your price.'

'Price for what? The Abbey?' He was right, I was a better negotiator than Renners, and if I had to bargain my way off this ferry with my life, then so be it.

'Carfax Abbey? Yes, that is part of the deal. That, and your soul.'

A huge wave slammed against the window.

'My soul? What could you offer that would be enough to give you my soul?'

'You tell me. What is a good price for something you can't feel, can't see, hear, touch or taste?' He licked his thin lips.

'Why do you need my soul anyway? Why don't you just kill me?'

'Why do you need your soul? Answer me this, Jonathan.'

The storm outside was whipping the sea into angry pyramids of water that were crashing onto the deck. The floor was now violently rising and falling as the ferry corkscrewed over the waves. DeVille was still leaning against the control desk, as if we were drifting across a serene millpond.

I decided to make an opening offer.

'If you need the Abbey, I can make sure you get it for whatever price you like, to compensate you for not getting my soul.'

'I will have the Abbey for whatever price you like, to compensate you for the loss of your soul.'

'Whatever price I like? Anything at all?'

DeVille stood, spreading his arms wide. The grip on my throat loosened, and the pale woman appeared at his side, nuzzling around his thighs like a cat.

'Anything at all,' he whispered.

'And if I say no?'

He sighed, leaned lazily across the console and flicked a switch. Red lights began blinking all over the desk. A radio crackled. DeVille placed a finger on the receiver and the radio went dead.

DeVille shook his head.

'You had the world in your palm, Jonathan. I could have made you a God. Now you will beg me for your life. How sad for you. How disappointing for me.'

'Without me, you won't get The Abbey.'

A darkness rippled over his eyes, momentarily breaking the calm façade. He had shown his hand. The deal was mine.

'So, let's talk about price again shall we…'

The Ramsgate Herald, 18th July 2016

Demeter Ferries Disaster

The Demeter Ferry company has ceased trading with immediate effect following the ferry collision disaster at the weekend. Little is known about the full circumstances of the incident, in which the vessel steamed into the harbour wall at high speed, other than the captain is believed to have deserted his post. Meteorologists reported unseasonably bad weather in the channel for the time of year, a localised squall hitting land the same time as the ferry crash. Sources state that there was only one survivor; a Mr. R. M. Renfield, who was conveyed to a nearby hospital, and unavailable for comment at time of print. The passenger manifest left one soul unaccounted for; a Mr Jonathan Harker.

20th July 2016

Land Sale Announcement

Land registry records the sale of Carfax Abbey and attached lands to Count DeVille, of Romania, for an undisclosed sum.

Bind Us Together - Dani Brown

He walked alone beneath the trees, a lush green canopy to protect him from the clouds overhead. He was alone in the world. It wasn't a choice. Punishment for providing blissful escape to bored teens regulated to blind obedience and their bedrooms was banishment.

There were others out there, beyond the trees. Their eyes burrowed beneath his clothes and skin, searching for his heart to grasp the weight. Rumours persisted, brought to the village on the lips of those with need to venture outside the walls. That first night was always the hardest.

Cobin pulled his hood up. The diffused green light would be gone soon. He'd be plunged into darkness with only the reflection of eyes and breathing for company. There weren't any matches to be struck. They were a thing sent to live in the past and only read about in ancient books. Matches, lighters, batteries – all things that presented risk to a sheltered population.

Out in the wilds, there were no regulations. Smugglers reported hidden caches of buried treasure amongst the trees. Cobin had no hope of finding anything in the fading light. He was left with only the clothes on his back and a small bag of provisions to see him through the next few days.

Most sent into the wilds died of exposure, or so it was said. Smugglers and others having to leave the village weren't so sure. Cobin chased the thoughts away with his last reserves of the concoction he kept in a hidden location on his body and settled beneath a tree.

The village elders didn't search him thoroughly when he was booted out. It was only a rudimentary check to make sure his bag didn't contain anything past the allowed rations. He didn't want them. He knew how to hunt. The forest contained more than mushrooms beneath its canopy. Mushrooms would see him through the night.

Cobin spread out his pack on the moss that filled the forest floor. Laughter in the distance teased his trip.

"Don't sleep there, young man."

"Yeah, the toads will get you."

"Not to mention the rabbits."

Cobin's ears pricked up at that. It must be the drug fucking around in his system. He never spent a night outside, not even on the AstroTurf in the village. The artificial rain just before the globe rose in the sky was enough to put anyone apart from the most hardcore kids off.

He pulled his blankets around him and tied the strings on his hoody. The real rain was different from what fell inside the village. Harder and colder when it fell between the leaves. It had a bite. Umbrellas were another thing confined to the past.

Curfew, exceptions made for camping on the Green, meant village inhabitants only saw the rain through windows if their sleeping pills didn't work. Cobin snuck out a few times to meet his supplier's drone through the holes in the wall. The rain was sticky then. It wasn't sticky out in the forest, alone except the voices.

He looked around. Eyes stared back at him but that could have been the drug. They blinked. He blinked back and then rubbed his own. They were still there. An hallucination would be gone.

"Hello."

Cobin's own voice frightened him. Sweat poured off his forehead and dripped down the back of his hoody.

"Hello," called back.

Regardless of the heat, he pulled his blankets tighter around himself and pushed his back against the tree, hoping it would swallow him. The bark was so rough he could feel it through his hoody.

The trees that circled the wall weren't real. They were fibreglass, like everything else. He understood why the elders would ban trees upon feeling the bark scratching through his clothes. They would be torn rags by the time the sun rose. The branches hung down looking to pull his hood from his head.

The eyes blinked. A voice started to sing. Cobin couldn't work out the lyrics, not even after it was joined by a different voice.

Drumming picked up in the distance. Hazy memories tried to break through Cobin's hallucinations. Drumming was to be feared because it was something the Village elders couldn't block out.

Synaesthesia kicked in with the words and drums dancing on the air. A rudimentary guitar sound fell across them all. Guitars were another thing confined to the past. Real guitars were a little icon on a tablet screen.

Cobin shivered. His sweat turned cold but that didn't stop it soaking through his clothes.

The bass on the air was a mist covering the ground in blue fog. The drums shone through in fireworks of reds, oranges and yellows to contrast with the cool colours on the forest floor. The chanting was purple, the words hovered before his face. Cobin rubbed his eyes. He didn't want to see the guitar.

Something crawled through his blankets and onto his lap. He screamed. That would have been visible too if only he'd open his eyes. The chanting stopped.

"It's a toad man, lick it."

"Yeah, lick it."

Cobin was too frightened to disobey.

"Was I this bad when I was chucked out alone?"

"Yes. We all were."

Another toad hopped into his blankets.

"With the rains, come the toads. And the locusts. Don't forget the goddamn locusts."

Cobin didn't know what locusts were but he had seen images of toads on his tablet screen, always flashed up with the messages that licking them would result in a horrible death by falling from the sixth-floor window in a high rise with the false notion of belief in human flight. It was displayed through pictograms, as reading had been outlawed by the elders when the Village was first wrapped in a cotton wool wall.

Cobin knew how to read. His father taught him before he himself was banished.

"Open your eyes. Enjoy your trip."

The chanting started again. Each word made the leaves curl into themselves.

"Come, dance with us."

Cobin was pulled to his feet, still with his eyes shut. He wouldn't be able to hear footsteps across the moss, it wasn't like the grey concrete covering the Village wherever there wasn't AstroTurf. Cobin found himself sucked into the rhythm.

"You need to drink."

His dance partner sucked water right from the leaves. Cobin copied. It tasted so fresh and earthy but that could have been the toad and shrooms. Everything in the Village included strange unnatural undertones.

He remembered his father bringing home something from the forest one night. It melted in his mouth. Then his father was gone. Driven out by the elders to die of exposure. It occurred to Cobin, the people taking his hands and dancing might know of his father's fate.

"Hey, how long have you guys been out here?"

"Us?"

"Long enough to know who you are, Cobin."

"How do you know me?"

Banishments were common in the Village. Cobin didn't attend every one, it would be impossible. Once a person was banished, all memory of them was wiped from the Village hard drives.

"We don't expect you to remember. We remember what things were like."

"It is better out in the wilds."

"Yeah."

"Do you know my father?"

"Of course we do."

"It is too dangerous to travel at night with the wolves and wild cats lurking about. We're taking you to the settlement at sunrise."

"Enjoy the night, for tomorrow, we have a journey ahead of us. Then work."

Fear ground through Cobin's trip. Work was not a word he liked the sound of. It was always something useless and pointless set by the elders.

"It is different out there. Everything has a purpose."

"Yeah man, we were part of the work programme too. That wasn't work. That was lining the pockets of the elders while doing damage control."

A toad landed on Cobin's head, breaking the intensity of the conversation with laughter and more dancing.

"It rains hallucinogenic toads out here. How cool is that?"

"Wait 'til you try the chilli."

Cobin didn't know what chilli was but if it could make him trip balls, he'd be cool with that. His stomach seized up.

"Into the trees, man, into the trees."

He fell to his knees, earning himself a scab on something sharp that lurked beneath the moss. The moss hugged him and didn't injure in the same way a concrete floor did. It kissed his knee where it allowed one of its secrets to hurt him. His new friends touched his back.

"That's it, get it all out. We have to start walking soon."

The drum beats no longer danced on the air but he did puke in rhythm with them. A toad landed in his lake of sick. It was the last one to fall from the sky.

A faint green shimmer hung on the air. It wasn't brought on by the memory of the trip. It was real. Morning had come. It was earlier than it was in the Village. The elders had control over that too. A flask of sweet liquid was handed to him.

"Drink."

Cobin obeyed and felt better with immediate effect. His bag had been packed. They were ready to set off. His new friends handed him some food.

"It isn't fresh. It was baked the day before yesterday."

It was the best thing he tasted. Better even than the sweet liquid from the flask. It was the first time he felt natural sunlight on his skin. Even bliss suppliers never left the Village, unless they were caught and forced out. Cobin noticed the bow and arrow slung over the shoulder of one of his companions.

"What's that for?"

"Rabid animals."

The answer was so no-nonsense, Cobin found it unnerving.

"Here, we bought you a gun. Your father said you could shoot."

Cobin accepted it. It was a small handgun, not the air rifle he was used to wielding in the secret forest his father built in a hidden room before he was sent out into the wilds. The grass was AstroTurf and the mushrooms fibreglass down there. Out in the wilds, reality lurked, not even the taint of licking toads and swallowing back shrooms could take it away.

The trees became thinner and the light brighter as Cobin was led away from the forest. Things lurked around the trees but Cobin didn't see anything. His eyes and mind were accustomed to the bad things being brought to him by the Village elders for the sake of their personal amusement.

A smell like the most potent skunk weed drifted across his nostrils.

"Shh."

"What is it," Cobin mouthed.

"Skunk. They shouldn't be out this early."

Cobin smelled the reason people were exiled without ever having touched skunk weed. The stink was pretty difficult to miss.

"An actual animal made that smell," he mouthed.

The man next to him pointed to the gun. Cobin cocked it ready to fire. They were away from the scent before the skunk appeared.

"Shoot it."

Cobin did right away, blowing its little body apart. For such a little creature, they were drenched in gore. The odour caught up with them.

"Ugh, eau de skunk. Tomato juice baths for all of us."

Cobin raised his eyebrows.

"Tomato juice gets the smell out. Unfortunately, we won't be at the settlement until the day after tomorrow."

"Is there a river or something?"

"It won't get rid of the stink."

They walked on in silence, Cobin hoping no more wildlife found them. The trees gave way to grasslands.

The sun beat on Cobin's back. At first it was pleasant after a lifetime kept beneath artificial lamps but it soon became uncomfortable. Its trail across the horizon seemed to take forever.

They had water but Cobin wasn't used to walking so far. Frequent rest stops were the course of the day. As the sky turned pink, they set up camp for the night. Sweat made the encounter with the skunk worse.

After a night of tripping followed by a day of walking, Cobin was asleep before dinner had been cooked on the campfire. He ate it cold the next morning as the sun came up.

The day passed in the same way as the day before it, minus skunks. The only animal encounters were with those meant to be out in daylight. By the time camp was set for the night, Cobin found himself once again exhausted.

He didn't have the energy to stay awake and listen to stories of the settlement. He drifted off on a story of how they were going to rise up and knock the Village elders off their perches. The next morning, he ate his cold dinner before they set off.

"We'll be arriving just as the sun sets."

Nervous excitement coursed through Cobin's system. His legs could use a rest and vibrating chair. They weren't used to that much exercise. The land began to climb. Rocks and pottery, broken pieces of concrete and glass made the terrain difficult.

"It used to be a great city. Our archaeologists have found the library."

Cobin's companion said this with a great sense of pride.

"Is that why the settlement is so far away from the Village?"

He had so many questions.

"Yes, we used materials from the city to build our settlement and learn from the past. The elders want everyone to remain in the dark and filled with hate. Without a connection to each other and nature, the most dominant repulsive personalities will be at the top of the heap. It wiped out civilisation before and it'll do it again, if the elders aren't taken care of."

"What about the drums?"

"Settlers go out for months at a time to mess with the elders. It is a rite of passage for those born out here."

"Why hasn't the Village been brought to its knees yet?"

"We've been waiting for you?"

"For me?"

Cobin was puzzled. There wasn't anything he could offer the outcasts. He still had a mother and brother trapped inside.

"For you."

Cobin wanted more of an explanation but he didn't think he was going to get it out in the ruins of the former city.

"There's a road."

Cobin's companions led him to a bit of straight flat land where the grass was well-worn. They met more people for the first time clearing chunks of concrete from the road.

"This is real work, making the way safe."

Toads sat in aquariums every few yards, to be licked at will. They were sheltered by sun umbrellas.

Cobin looked around at the people actually doing stuff that was constructive rather than pointless. He felt something indescribable well inside him. One of those emotions the elders thought they could do something about if all trace of their existence was denied. There were no elders in the wilderness. They wouldn't survive long without antiseptic and hand-sanitising gel.

"Want a toad?"

"Sure."

"Keep hold of it, these ones have more than one lick in them."

He licked it. His tongue was greeted by a sweetness he hadn't known before.

"Even the mushrooms taste nice here. And they won't make you sick."

Cobin walked on in silence, licking his toad and trying to take everything in. Hallucinogens helped his mind from blowing out.

There was so much activity. There must be exiles from other Villages. It was no wonder travelling post masters were related to elders. They would have reported back to the population about the world outside. It wasn't the end of civilisation, but the beginning.

And everybody was singing. It seemed that even the blades of grass and rocks sang in praise to the magical toads, as if the world outside the Village was bound together by them somehow.

Eventually they came to buildings that were clearly inhabited. All had toads painted on them in the colours of the rainbow.

Cobin couldn't resist another lick of the toad. It was too much to take in. As they walked on, the buildings became smaller and closer together.

"Farms are on the other side of the settlement."

Cobin strained his eyes to the horizon.

"They're like the farms of old. Everything is planted directly into the earth."

After the high-rise green houses, Cobin couldn't imagine what they looked like. Those sorts of pictures were banned from his tablet.

In the towers, they grew in a liquid solution and everything was clean and sterile. Fruit and vegetables had plastic balls attached around the flowers so everything would grow to the exact same size and shape. To do it any other way was considered primitive and outright illegal. He walked on, licking his toad in silence.

People walked towards him and his companions showing no signs of stepping around. Their arms were outstretched. Memories teased Cobin. He squinted his eyes. And then dropped his toad and broke into a run. His father broke away from his group and ran to meet him.

Tearful and still tripping slightly they didn't say anything. Cobin's father wrapped his arm around him like a long lost friend and walked towards the settlement. The smell of sweat and stale skunk spray didn't seem to trouble his father.

After a bath in tomato juice followed by a shower and some fresh clothes, he was brought into the hall where his father waited. Plans for taking out the Village were rolled across pushed together tables.

"Everything was made by hand. It offers a great satisfaction denied to the population by the elders."

Cobin paused to pretend to take in and admire the carpentry skills. Trouble was, the admiration for something so beautiful made by hand was so intense, he couldn't comprehend.

"Look over here son."

Cobin followed his father's finger to the papers on the table.

"You make paper?"

"Actually we found this, but yes, we have the skills to make paper."

Cobin was more impressed by the second. Each thing brought with it new amazements. It was no wonder the outcasts sang.

"Now you're here, we ride out tomorrow."

"What about mother and my brother?"

"We'll save them. Don't worry."

Cobin wasn't filled in on the details. Food was brought out. It had all been grown around the settlement and cooked on-sight. These were concepts Cobin only heard rumours about.

After the feast, psychedelic tea harvested from tree bark was brought out with hash brownies. Cobin was tucked into a bed. There were soft beds back in the Village but nothing compared to what he found himself waking up in.

The sounds of the settlement didn't keep him awake that night. There were sounds, of wolves howling in the distance and big cats hissing at each other. It was relaxing, especially when the only comparison was the trek to the settlement and the nocturnal arguments of the Village.

They set out on horseback when the sun was at its highest with carts full of toads and supplies. Extra toads were loaded into carts to fling at the Village. The plan was to bring down the Village with light and love to wash away all the fear and hate.

They had to go around the forest because the catapults wouldn't fit between the trees. Going was quicker than on foot despite the trees attempts at taking over without anyone around to cut them down.

Villages didn't expand outwards, they expanded up. The glistening towers could be seen even above the top of the highest trees. The forest hugged it on all sides. The carts had to be left and the catapult taken apart to fit around them but that didn't matter because it could be put back together again.

There were enough soldiers from the settlement. Only the old and frail stayed behind to tend to the farms while war was waged. They didn't start singing until toads were flying through the air.

The toad was king. Voices rose about the benefits of licking the king like a lollipop. Subliminal messages about opening the gate were put in with the overt messages of the benefits of toad licking.

The gate rattled open, pushed by a large group of teenagers. Their voices joined that of the settlers. More villagers stepped into the forest with king toads in their hands, voices raised about the glory of the little green gods.

Every last villager stepped out and filled the forest. There were plenty of toads to go around.

Cobin's father handed him a lit torch.

"You'll need explosives son, but I want you to light the first fire."

Cobin ran into the Village, not sure if his mother and brother were outside. There weren't any wooden structures but fibre glass could melt. He eyed a nearby tree.

The elders were nowhere to be seen. They could have escaped disguised as refugees but that seemed unlikely. They liked where they were and had a not-so-secret fallout shelter buried beneath the highest tower of them all.

Cobin smoked them out with the noxious fumes released from melting fibreglass being forced into their air vents. They were as high as everyone else but in the worst possible way. Plastic was not the best thing to get intoxicated from, second only to a combination of cleaning chemicals and cough syrup.

They came out scratching their bodies, convinced bugs were crawling under their skin. They were bound together with extra-itch hemp twine and their clothing ripped away. The last remnants of an ancient itching powder was puffed all over them and their hands tied behind their backs.

The settlers sang as they blew up the Village. Nothing was preserved except the pet turtles. They couldn't be let free into the river due to snapping turtles wanting to feed on their succulent flesh. The children of the settlers picked them up and put them in their pockets. They didn't want to hurt living creatures. Village children saw what they were doing and did likewise, even if they didn't yet understand the reasons.

The elders were chained behind a cart and not offered a lick of a toad. The gallows waited for them. It was to be the first and only executions in the settlement. Bonds of hallucinogens and light couldn't be broken except by the negativity brought by controlling freaks. Their families were offered the chance of redemption. They were just happy to be free.

And everybody sang as the settlement grew up around the trees fuelled only by vertical farming, love and LSD.

☐

Lord of the Harvest - Mark Lumby

"YOU heard 'bout that Collingham kid, didn't you?"

"Yeah, sure. Dan Collinghams son. Fifth biggest farm in the County, I hear. Ain't that a tragedy." They shared a large brown bottle of homebrew. "I'd say it's the metal plate in his head that does it, though. Screaming out madness all over Silverton. Must be damaging his brain," Richards said as he past the bottle back to Ewan.

"It's there to protect his brain, Pa. To protect what happened before he had it put in.

"We live in a farming community, son. Accidents happen all the time."

"Not in Silverton they don't."

"Yeah, well, maybe you're right on that."

"I am right Pa," Ewan said, wiping the top of the bottle and passing it back. "But that kid ain't right. After his pa reversed that tractor into him, had that plate put in, he ain't been right since. Shouting things all over town, seeing things that other people can't see. It ain't right. People are scared of him, about what he claims to see."

"But it's just the plate making him say those things," he assured. "Nothing else. And as for seeing what he sees, we just gotta accept that the kid got brain damage. It's tragic, but there it is."

"I know, Pa. I know. But that's the point I'm trying to make. He had an accident. He is the way he is because of it. That's his excuse. But, Pa—and don't shout back at me—" Ewan pushed back his chair, stood up and nervously tucked in his shirt. He could feel a storm brewing.

Richards leaned back in his chair, frowning, and peered at Ewan through squinted eyes. He placed the bottle on the kitchen table.

"But Pa, people are scared of you, too. You don't wanna know what they say about you in Silverton."

"Oh—what do they say, boy." He sounded puzzled and annoyed that the people of this town were whispering behind his back.

"Well, Pa. You've been talking, haven't you."

"Talking? I've been saying nothing."

"But that's not the truth, is it?"

Richards lowered his head, chin on his chest like a child sulking. "I—I gotta tell people, Ewan," he said softly. "They have a right to know."

"You're scaring them, and at the same time, they're laughing at you."

He raised his head with a jerk. "Who's laughing at me!"

Ewan held his palm in surrender. "Doesn't matter, Pa. I'm not going to be naming names or nothing."

"I bet it was Abraham Jones. I know I told him. Or Grace Elland from the mini market."

"But the whole town knows. I wish you could've been more secretive about it."

"They deserve to be warned. Although, right now I'm not too sure. But I suppose they need to know what coming to them—well, what may be coming, anyhow."

"But you're scaring them with your lies, Pa."

Richards slammed his fist onto the table. "Don't you ever accuse me of being a liar in my own home."

"I'm sorry, Pa, but that's what they're thinking."

"What they think?" His face contorted like he had just sampled the sourest of sweets. "But it scares them, so I guess they must believe me too. How do you explain that, boy," he said smugly.

"They're afraid—"

"Of what I say is the truth? That's why they're afraid," he put in.

"No Pa. The Collingham kid got an excuse. The town people know that. But now they compare you to him. They talk about you—not in a bad way—but they're worried. They respect you, Pa."

Richards started to laugh, reached for the bottle and drank the remainder, sliding it across the table. "They won't listen to me, Ewan. But my own son? Flesh and blood. We have the same grit under our fingernails." He stared at him, shook his head, then allowed the fading light of the window to distract him.

"But pa, it's the farm. We'll lose everything." When Richards never gave him an answer, Ewan went over to the pantry and collected another bottle of homebrew. He unscrewed the top and took the first swig before passing it to his pa. But he scoffed at the gesture, his arms remained folded. "Pa," Ewan eventually said, "Mandi is expecting. She's three months in."

Richards didn't even react. Still as a corpse.

"We hope to move from the apartment. It'll start to get cramped around there," he chuckled.

Richards was motionless, though his eyes fluttered momentarily Ewan's way. "What I'm trying to get at, pa, is that I've got responsibilities now. I gotta make a good safe home. I gotta make things secure."

Richards unfolded his arms, and without turning to Ewan, without looking at him either, he extended his hand. "Congratulations, son. That's—well, that's good news, I suppose."

"You're gonna be a grandpa." He took his hand.

"Ain't that the truth," he said without so much as a glance. He just watched the window as though something was coming and he could smell it in the air like rain.

Ewan took another mouthful of beer, leaving the bottle on the table for Richards. "To the baby," he toasted. But his pa never touched the bottle, never shared his sentiment. In fact, he looked sad, as though a cloud even darker than before hovered over him. His arms were folded again. Ewan looked out the window too. He watched the corn field rustling in the warm evening breeze. "It's time Pa."

Richards was thinking about what the town folk had been saying about him. He thought of the baby. He looked at Ewan, who was already expectantly watching his Pa. Richards joined his son at the window, acknowledged the corn field with a nod. "Father Johnson blessed the field with his own hands, showering that holy water on the crop, so he must've seen something to do that. Seen what I seen. He don't think I'm crazy."

"Father Johnson is a kind man."

"What you say, boy?"

"I'm saying he's a kind man. Don't wanna hurt no one."

He glanced at him. "Are you—are you suggesting he's laughing at me? Mocking at my request to bless this field, and now he's choking himself up in that cosy parish of his, laughing at my expense?"

"He told you what you needed to hear."

Richards was silent, toying with the words in his mind, wondering if Ewan was right. Surely, not Father Johnson. Surely he had seen what lived in the corn, too, and Richards wasn't all alone. Finally, with a feeling of abandonment, he said, "Well, I can't stop you, son. But if you do this, I won't be around to see what's coming," Richards protested, but it sounded like a warning. He ran the tap, filled a glass from his left and drank it empty. He watched the corn field like he was searching for something.

"What's coming, Pa?" Ewan's patience was being stretched. He already knew, but he was sick of hearing the same argument. That's all they ever seemed to talk about nowadays. And now the whole town knew. "Old age is turning your wisdom into mush; you're making no sense. The town folk think you're sick as the Collingham kid."

"I don't need to make sense! This is my farm," Richards said, slamming the glass down onto the draining board. "And I'm telling you that death is coming from that field." He thumbed over his shoulder with stabbing motions at the field.

"Pa," his voice strained and desperate, "the harvest will die if we don't cut it now. We lose that, we'll lose the farm. Surely you can see that!"

Richards went over to him. He shrugged, and explained softly, "We have other corn fields." And he sighed away from his son because he was exhausted of justifying himself just as Ewan was tired listening. He couldn't make him understand. Why should he? Ewan hadn't witnessed the things his pa had. If he had seen what he had seen then maybe he would see it differently.

Maybe.

Ewan snubbed his chin in the air, hands on hips. "What's so different about this one, Pa?" He sounded irritated, his voice higher strung than his Pa's. "Looks the same as the rest of them."

"But it ain't!" Richards spat. "I've told you all this, damn it! Don't you ever listen to me? You can do want you want with the corn, Ewan." Richards pointed out the window. "But I'm telling ya. You Goddamn leave that field alone! The rest of them are all yours. I don't want them. I don't want any of it. Burn them for all I care. But that field there," he reminded him, "that corn is my corn."

"Sounds like a threat, Pa," he said.

"It does, don't it? Maybe it is, but don't test me, son, because I don't wanna show you the darker side to your Pa."

"What will you do? You're an old goat, and sooner or later, this will be my farm—my inheritance."

"And I won't deny you of that! But in the here and the now, the farm is mine. Cut any part of that corn out there in my field, and I swear as God is my witness, I will take you down with the same tool you'll use to do the cutting."

They both fell silent as though a bomb had gone off and they wouldn't be heard anyway through the noise. Ewan disappeared out the room, went to the bathroom, not because he wanted to, but because he needed to distance himself. When he returned they were both silent for a while longer.

"We cut it now and death will come," Richards eventually warned him, staring at him with such intensity, so much rage, that he might as well have been shaking a clenched fisted in front of Ewan's face. "I'm God of this land, son. I am the Lord! And I shall protect all who will perish if I do not." He wiped spittle off his chin with the back of his hand.

"Sounds to me, Pa, that you've made up your mind already."

"I suppose I have, son. I suppose I have."

"So—you just gonna let it die?"

Lips tight, he nodded proudly. "And if I do, then we'll all be saved." He held his head high. "Saved from the evil that hides in that corn, like a plague."

"I don't get it! I just don't. How will letting the crop die solve anything?" It was a question asked quietly, as though he had almost given up in trying to persuade his pa otherwise.

Richards shrugged. Ewan was still talking when he walked over and opened the kitchen door. But Richards had stopped listening. He had made up his mind, just like he had yesterday and the day before. Last week and the week before that. Just like the first time he had ever laid eyes on them and he knew what must be done. Ewan's voice an irrelevant murmur from behind, Richards leaned against the doorway and rested his eyes momentarily, breathing in the warm scent of corn and a reminder to him that the land would be lost to the bank because of that one field. He opened his eyes and sighed. They would lose everything.

The tops of the corn rustled like a plea for help not to let them die. The breeze from the field struck Richards on the face. The smell was pleasant, but it reminded him of flesh burning and of rotten meat. And everything unholy. It offended him.

Ewan watched his pa, saw the strain in the creases of his eyes.

"I just know," Richards replied, remembering the last question he had heard Ewan ask. He grimaced at the fields, because only he could hear the screams that mocked him. Only he could see the yellow eyes that peered through the shadows of the crop, staring back at him like a thousand blood thirsty fireflies, wanting to use their razor sharp claws to strip away his skin. He could imagine that they would do it to him slowly like peeling a banana, fascinated by his skin turning to raw flesh, sore and juicy. Another slice would take away his flesh, muscles and veins wrapped around old bones. He would hope that by this time, maybe the shock and the pain would have already taken away his life, steal him away from the guilt that was left behind.

For now, they were waiting. They looked at him with both hatred and hunger. With a patience that was unsettling. They could wait forever. Richards knew that if they did ever escape, then he would be the first to die, the first to know how it would feel to have his stomach ripped out. And then they would turn to Ewan. He would know by now that his pa was right all along. Though there was no consolation in being right. Because everyone would be dead.

"You have to trust me, son," His eyes were moist and raw around the rim. "Trust your old Pa one last time." He was calm as if he was calling a truce. He had one eye on the fields. Always checking like a warden in a prison. Making sure the cells are locked.

They still watched him fiercely.

Eyes yellow and as lost as all the souls they had stolen.

Watched him as they prepared to steal more.

The day had left a sour taste in Ewan's mouth, not even made better by the ten empty bottles of Coors he had carelessly tossed on the dirt. The last light to Richards house had been put out. Ewan slid off the rusty hood of his weathered brown pickup truck, nipping the eleventh bottle by the neck. He downed the last mouthful of froth before he threw it into the corn field.

"Why you so special," he called out to it as if it were a living, breathing thing. He caught the spittle down his chin with his palm. Richards was prepared to let the farm go for the sake of one damn field. And why? Because of a plague?

A plague, for Christ sake! The old man had lost his mind.

Ewan stared at his Pa's house with bitterness he thought he would never feel. He resented him. They had always been close, and even more so after his Ma had died three years since. But now, their relationship was at the crossroads. And all because of that one field, its corn swaying in the breezy shadows like many hands waving back at him, waving goodbye to his inheritance.

"I'll open your goddamn eyes, Pa," and raised another bottle as if toasting the house. He sauntered across the dirt, kicking out at loose stone and saying out aloud, "I'll show you the frickin' plague, pa." He wanted his pa outside. He didn't care if he was comfortable and tired and old. He wanted to see him now. He crouched down to pick up a hand full of gravel, stood unsteadily back up and tossed the handful at the house, scattering them like a cluster bomb, striking the wood, skimming across the porch and smashing the windows. "You get your ass out here, Pa!" he screamed, took another swig from the bottle. He had a wide smile when a light came on. Ewan whistled at his Pa, and shouted, "Yeah, thats right. You come on out here!" He threw the bottle at the house just as Richards came out the door.

Glass and alcohol splattered around his bare feet, but Richards showed no anger. "What's all this about, boy? Come on in—we'll talk," he lifted his arm as though it was over the shoulders of an invisible man. He watched Ewan sway where he stood, could smell the alcohol from the puddle now being absorbed into the wooden floorboards. He felt sorry for his son. Although what Richards was doing could be misunderstood as madness, he did have good excuse to exercise such a decision. Ewan might not understand that yet, may never understand. But Richards would have to live with his choice, regardless. And he feared he would lose a son in the process.

Ewan spat at the ground. He wiped the his mouth, but spittle still clung from his chin in a single glutinous strand. His eyes were bloodshot. He swayed away from his pa, staggered toward the corn field, muttering to himself, "I'll show the old bastard!" He faced the field, leering at his pa from over his shoulder. Goddamn plague. I'll make you see.

Richards saw what he was doing and his heart leaped into his throat. He wasn't calm anymore. He considered reaching for his walking stick, which he'd left leaning against the doorway. But instead, he went back inside, appearing seconds later with his hunting rifle. Slowly he climbed down the steps using the rifle to steady himself. "Ewan! You step away from that corn, now."

He glanced at him, shaking his head in short fast motions. "I'm gonna make you see, Pa. And when I do, first thing tomorrow, we gonna strip this field bare."

"Ewan, please. Come on inside—let's talks." He was off the steps and was walking across a patch of grass where he could still make out the chalk lines from a miniature baseball field he had mapped out for Ewan when he was nine. But he would need to pace the equivalent length of a real sized baseball field if he were to reach Ewan in time. Richards hobbled a few steps closer, and although not giving up, would never be able to catch his son. "Stop! Stop right there!" he pleaded. He waved the rifle in the air as though he was stabbing at bugs. "You're making a mistake, son! Please don't go any further."

Ewan stopped right on the verge of the field, caressing his hand through the corn, testing it expertly. "It's ready to be harvested, Pa," he quietly said, but never turned around.

"You don't understand, son," he pleaded. "We can't! They will—"

"Why not, Pa? The plague?" he laughed as though it was the funniest joke he had heard, and twisted around on his heel, ripping a handful of corn with him. He showed it to Richards, who was now standing twenty yards away from him, and lifting the corn to his nose, inhaled the smell with a deep satisfied breath. His back was touching the giant growth of corn as he continued to sway. The corn danced with him.

"Step away, son," Richards urged. "Just walk forwards." He extended his hand, but far out of reach to touch.

"And we'll talk, pa?" He shouted, mocking him.

"Yeah, we'll talk!" For a moment, Richards thought he was getting through to him.

"But it ain't gonna change a damn thing." His arms raised at either side of him, he let go of the corn.

Richard looked past his son and into the field. He could see their yellow eyes peering back at him, twitching and blinking. Their eyes became larger, shinier. Richards could feel them approaching. Saw their hands with razor sharp claws part the tall lengths of corn. Richards reached out his arm, flapping his hand eagerly, ushering for his son to step away. "Come, Ewan!" He was angry. He took another few steps forward, a bit hastier. "Please, Ewan—son!" his voice crumbling apart in his throat, like grains of sand disappearing through fingers. He struggled as he became incapable of speech, claws attached to long arm-like tentacles reaching out through the corn. Reaching for Ewan.

Richards moved as fast as his ailing body would take him, his bones cracking and joints protesting at every step. Not far away from him now.

Lifted his rifle.

He could smell this—thing lurking inside the corn like warm, rotten meat. He feared it would take his son. And if it did, Ewan would know nothing but life and then death.

There would be no in between.

No pain.

Or that was the very least Richards could hope for. But— no. He would not allow it to steal away his son. He aimed the gun at the field.

Ewan's eyes widened at his crazy pa. He staggered to the left, trying to move aside of the rifle's aim, but unknowingly avoiding the thing in the corn as its claws cut through the air and for his neck. If Ewan had not been so drunk, he would've been dead. With his hands, Ewan protected his face from the rifle shot as Richards took aim and fired. He was sure his aim was accurate, and even though his hands were trembling, he had the creature in his sight, yellow eyes staring right back at him.

Ewan's white t-shirt was scorched by the shot on the shoulder, deep red absorbed into his top like a sun rise over the horizon. Ewan clutched at the wound. "Pa, what you doing?" he shrieked, then twisted his shoulder to get a good eye on the wound. "What in God's name!" He never saw the creature reaching out for him.

"Move your goddamn ass!" Richards yelled, not realising he had shot him in the first place and raising the rifle a second time. He struck Ewan at the side of his head, stripping away the top of his ear. Crimson showered the corn, disappearing moments later as if the field was devouring his blood. But still, Ewan was unaware of all this.

They would be able to smell the blood, was all Richards could think.

Ewan stumbled to the right, but he was also stepping backwards into the corn. Another claw reached from the crop and swiped out again, narrowly missing Ewan's leg. But he had already fallen. Surely, he was theirs for the taking. He was in their domain and unless he got a move on, they would smell his blood, feel his fear. It wouldn't take them long to pounce. Richards was surprised they didn't have him already.

And through the tall lengths of the corn, the shadows were made brighter by yellow fireflies. The corn shook in the distance, getting closer to Ewan, attracted by his scent, seduced by opportunity.

Richards could see the beast was even closer, ready to steal him for himself.

Ewan struggled to stand, but he wasn't in any rush. He had no idea that death was all over him.

He dabbed the side of his head with his fingers, noticed at the blood, felt the tip of his ear was missing, and showed his fingers to his Pa.

"Look! Look what you did—asshole!" Ewan screamed, unaware of the smell of rotten meat that was getting closer to him—waiting, and the many that were scuttling through the corn, starved monsters who hadn't eaten in a long time.

Their feast was so close.

Richard crouched to one knee and started to drag Ewan away from the corn, aiming the rifle into the field just in case they pounced. Although, he had never shot one before so he wasn't sure whether bullets would harm them. He grabbed his son by his collar, and as Ewan tried to find his feet, Richards kept on dragging. He never knew he had the strength, but from somewhere deep inside it had shown itself. And at the same time, Richards shot another warning into the corn.

They were both still way too close to the crop, but far enough not to be touched by those things. And as long as the crop remained uncut, those things that were born in there would never be set free.

The tops of the corn stopped trembling, the yellow fireflies bright and illuminating, had now faded to a dim glow—and then nothing.

"You see, boy!" Richards said to Ewan. "You see why? What I'm protecting you against. Protecting everyone!"

Ewan stared at the field, dabbed at the wound on his head, touched the shrivelled skin on his ear. He finally found his feet, though unsteady and disorientated, his left ear whistling. He tried gulping like you would to help your ears pop from high altitude. Dazed, he stared out into the field. He looked shocked when he turned to Richards, still cupping his ear. His eyes were wide, penetrating into Richards as if by staring at him with all that intensity would burn him. "You blew it off!" he yelled.

Richards acknowledged as though he had shot him on purpose. That was the plan. Truth was, his aim was shaky, and he had been aiming for the creature. "It was for your own good," he admitted in a direct voice. He held his head up proudly. "I needed to get you away."

"Goddamn Pa! But you shot me. Twice! I'm bleeding."

"There's some Band-aid in the house," he stared to walk past him. "Let's get you sorted, you big baby. Nasty little shits, aren't they. Got quite a bite."

Ewan swayed into him as he passed, accidentally pushing him to the ground. He wanted to say sorry, but he was angry with him. Still more stories of these things. "What you on about, Pa? You shot me, that's all I know."

"In the field—they nearly had you! If it hadn't been for your Pa, you'd be dead by now," he said as if he thought his son should be thinking him instead of being so angry. "I could see them, son. They nearly—"

"Who?"

Richards frowned. "Them!" He poked his rifle in the direction of the corn, then used it to heave himself to his feet.

Ewan looked out at the field, shook his head. "Ain't nothing there but yellow money, pa."

"Yellow money? Please, not this again, son. I told you. Not that field. The rest of them—yes. But just leave that one alone."

Ewan hadn't stopped shaking his head. He started laughing. "You really think there's something living in there?"

"You saw it, Ewan. I tried to get you away from it—from them."

"I seen nothing, Pa. I seen nothing but a crazy old fool. You cut my head. Damn blew my ear off."

"But I'm telling you, son. They're in there. Vicious and smelly, evil crawling over their skin like mites. They damn nearly killed you, separated your head from the rest of your body."

Ewan checked his neck and slapped the side of his own head. "It's here, Pa. All here, all mine."

"Yes!" He pointed at the air. "Because I stopped them. I pulled you out before they could get you."

"There's nothing, Pa. Look—let me prove it." He pushed passed Richard, halting at the perimeter to the corn field. He peered through the corn, parting it curiously with his hand, not because he expected monsters with huge teeth to leap out at him, but because it was dark and anything wild could jump out. He squinted into the darkness. Eventually though, Ewan turned around to look at his Pa.

"Don't be stupid, son. Just come back."

"Nothing in there, Pa," and he took a step back into the corn, walked backwards through several yards, his eyes never leaving his pa. He lifted his arms wide at either side, like wings, and grinned. "See! Nothing." And he started to snigger, toying with his pa, erupting into an improvised sing song. "Come and get me! Come and get me! Anybody there?" he sang out, swaying to his little tune. "Kill me. Eat me—"

Yellow fireflies began to glow.

"Ewan, stop this. You don't know what you're doing."

"Just having fun, Pa." He stopped dancing and walked slowly towards Richards. Only, for his pa, it wasn't fast enough. Richards was getting agitated and ushered him to speed up.

The fireflies shifted between the stems, getting larger, becoming closer. The corn shook.

"Quick, son. Just come on out. You're scaring me." The knot tightened in his stomach, pulling and stretching against his supper, making him feel sick.

"See, pa," Ewan said again. "Nothing to be scared of," he grinned and finally stepped out from the corn, walked past Richards with a confident look on his face and headed for the house.

Richards kept on watching the field, yellow eyes in their masses looking back at him. They showed their long thin faces, pale grey and covered in soil, a jaw that stayed open, teeth as long as fingers protruding from cracked lips. "He really didn't see you," he said to them, "even when it was nearly too late for him, he didn't even know you existed. But I promise you this—you will not leave your prison."

They snarled back at him.

"You're bound. I will not let you leave."

Behind him, the door to the house slammed shut.

Richards was still sleeping when Ewan had arrived back at the farm. It was early morning. The warm glow of the sun had yet to rise from behind the fields. But you could see the light ready to explode into day, scorching the house with its heat. He had only been at his apartment for a few hours. Couldn't sleep though. He thought about his pa, wondered if he was going crazy, seeing the things he said he saw. Ewan had wondered whether he too had seen what his pa claimed was hiding in the corn. Because for him, to believe in his pa would have made it simpler. But he had seen nothing. Richards idea that the corn imprisoned some kind of plague was ludicrous. It was impossible. A crazy idea from a crazy old fool. It was just a corn field. One corn field. No different than the others. It contained nothing but crop, and soon, just like the rest of the fields, it would be stripped bare.

Yellow money.

Ewan climbed into the harvester and sat in silence looking out at the field. He stared intently at the corn, trying to confirm what his pa had seen, give him some excuse to believe in him. He even willed the corn to move as though it harboured life. He didn't like betraying him. He had respected him all these years for the dignified man he was. And, although he had been brought up better and shouldn't be doubtful over him, he felt no plausible reason to allow the crop to die. He sure felt ashamed with himself for his actions. But the truth was obvious. Wasn't it? There could be no plague. It was stupid— impossible.

Ewan held the steering wheel tight. Last night he had slipped the keys into his pocket before Richards came into the house after him. Sat in the harvester he slowly inserted them into the ignition. He tried to be quiet, but every jingle and bang seemed amplified ten fold. And when the engine roared and the harvester began to move, he knew that his pa would hear it from inside the house. The floors would hum like a Tibetan monk meditating, the pictures on the walls trembling, the cups rattling in the cupboards. Ewan looked at the house, and in a way, he wanted his pa to storm out, to climb into the harvester and drag him from his seat. At least then he would have an excuse to not defy Richards. And he wondered if falling out with his pa was worth keeping the farm going. Or whether he should just support his pa's madness, their relationship staying strong.

Ewan turned the key to the first click, illuminating the huge head lamps over a field that was seduced by the early light of the sun. Then he turned the key to its second position, sparking the harvester into life, engine roaring and protesting against his actions, a mechanical dinosaur, its rotary teeth turning like a corkscrew as the machine slowly moved forward and into the corn field.

There was no method in the direction Ewan was taking. He just ploughed right in, teeth chomping greedily at the corn, cutting and consuming the crop, spitting it out into the trailer behind. He drove towards dawn, which was creeping over the horizon, the tops of the corn turning orange. They shook as the harvester drove through them and sucked them into its digestive system, the machine moaning satisfyingly as it ate everything. But in the distance, where the sun had started to shine on the corn, the tops of the stems also trembled, for no reason. From the left and right, from straight ahead the crop vibrated, and rippling not unlike a wave, the vibrations were coming in a 'v' shape towards the harvester. Something was moving within the crop. Something, which was not the harvester, was causing the corn the shake.

Ewan saw the pattern the movement created, noticed the 'v' shape heading straight for the harvester.

For him.

And as the harvester munched even closer to the wave in the crop, so did the ripple come ever so closer to Ewan. He glanced back at the house whilst continuing to go forward, then turned back to the movement in the field. His left leg started to twitch. He had never seen anything like this before. Although, it was possible it was some animal that had gotten loose. But what he saw wasn't just one animal; there were many and they moved with intellectual purpose.

They were coming for him.

The harvester came to a stop. Ewan's breathing became deeper. His eyes widened and his mouth became dry. If he got out now, whatever was out there, with the speed they were going would catch up with him in a blink. And if he decided to stay inside the harvester, he would be trapped.

In an instinctive decision for survival, he snapped the handle open, fell out of the door and crashed to his knees on a shallow path of cut stems. He could hear them now, the grunts and growls of hungry animals. But now he was on the ground and too low to see the tops of the corn shiver. He couldn't see them coming, could only hear them. He scrambled to his feet, stumbled then got up again and ran down the path the harvester had just made. He could see the house. The lights were still off, which was surprising. It would've felt like an earth tremor in that house, and Richards couldn't even sleep through the sound of crickets.

The growls were louder and didn't sound like an animal anymore. Didn't sound human either. But Ewan continued to stumble through the flattened corn stems, screaming for his pa to come out with the rifle and blast his pursuers brains out the other side of its heads.

"Pa!!" he screamed as he felt his pursuer growling close behind. He could sense how close it was. The heat from its body. Although the sound of stems snapping and feet scrambling through the field did put the thought in the front of his head that he was in trouble. He didn't have the courage to turn around and see for himself. The smell got stronger, rotten meat and faeces. Ammonia and iron. It was suffocating. He was suffocating. He remembered Charlie Stinger from high school, suffocating from an asthma attack in the changing room. He had been all alone, until someone had found him dead on the cold tiles. This is how Ewan had felt, choking for air. Sweat poured from his head, stinging his eyes as the air continued to thicken. Ewan could taste metal as though it was in the air. It was so pungent that, for a second, he thought he had bitten into his tongue. As he exited the corn field, he covered his nose with his arm. But even though he had stepped over the threshold, against his Pa's instructions, the corn had been cut. The creatures, tall and thin and naked, their pale skin matted from the dirt in which they had lived, were now free from the field. And when the smell intensified and the air grew warmer and thicker, stale and harder to breathe, he knew there were more. It was pointless trying to run. He looked up at the house, which only seemed to get further away the faster he ran towards it. It was still too far away and they would surely catch up with him anyway. Ewan slowed and stopped. He looked at the house praying that the lights would shine. They didn't.

He slowly turned around as the creatures had also stopped running, their stale breath warming Ewan's scalp. He could reach out and touch them. Frightened, he stepped back and looked up at one of the creatures. It was absent of any hair, neither head nor body. He looked head height at its chest, strong but skinny, covered in dark veins that pulsed and moved around his torso like long thin snakes. Ewan took another step back. There were more of them standing around him and emerging from the field, scrambling out like ants from a hole. They never seemed to stop, crawling and climbing over piles of their own to escape from the corn. Their bodies matted with mud, glistening in sweat, shimmering in a morning glow that was fast appearing. Ewan hoped that the sunlight would burn their skin, send them back to where they came from. But God wasn't showing mercy.

Pa was right.

Ewan noticed that some held younger versions of themselves, welded to their sides like a deformed growths, umbilical cords swinging in the dirt as the creatures ran from the corn. The babies were as grey as their mothers, eyes sleeping, looking dead.

The tall creature looked down on him, still and as grey as a statue. Its long teeth escaping from its elongated jaw, dripping with saliva, chest heaving from the chase. Ewan lowered his head. He knew what came next wouldn't be good. He could feel it throughout his body like an oppressive electrical current, cold and tingly.

Why hadn't I believed in you, Pa? Crazy old fool.

The creature reached its thin fingers over the top of Ewan's scalp, its claws digging deep and drawing blood from the rear of his head. Ewan shook with fear, not pain. He couldn't feel the pain, even though he knew it should be like knives slicing into his skin. He bowed lower, lamenting the realisation of his fate.

Richards had heard the harvester come to life like a roar of thunder in an imminent storm, and the humming sound it made as it jerked forward. Knowing what this would mean, he hid himself under the sheets, away from the inevitable. He tried to make himself invisible as if it wasn't happening. He screwed his eyes. Maybe he would go to sleep and wake up where the sun shines through the curtains and Ewan bursts through the front door and starts brewing the coffee. Or else, not wake up at all. Just take him while he slept. He would never know.

There was nothing he could do now. He was old and slow and by the time he had reached the front door—he couldn't bear to imagine.

He could see them in his mind, he didn't know how, maybe because he was the only one who could see them altogether. He imagined something pale squatting over Ewan's body. The sun was creeping over the horizon flooding a sea of warm haze over the corn. The creature's body, grey and sick looking, seemed to get paler and more diseased as the light bounced off its skin. This beast was over his son, eating from his stomach, ripping out stringy intestines, consuming them like spaghetti in a ravenous feast as the others stood patiently watching. He saw it crack open Ewan's chest with a single swipe of its left claw, and delve inside, retrieving his heart. Its long sharp teeth sank into the dead organ, consuming on something so taboo. Then it stopped, and turned as though it knew it was being watched. But there was no one else there. Richards wondered if it could sense him. Just as he could see this creature in his mind, could the creature also see Richards.

The thing screamed at something invisible, glutinous blood caked over its long jaw, red dripping from teeth that looked even longer now its mouth was wide open, and inside of it's mouth Richard could see smaller teeth at the rear of its throat, pushing out and retracting like something else breathing inside. Slowly it stood, a tall hunched figure, thin yet its muscles pulsed under pale coloured skin, covered in deep cuts, bloodless wounds that went down to the bone. Wounds from torture. From hell.

Yellow eyes stared at the house, searching for its next feed.
Searching for Richards.

It threw its claws to the dirt and ran in huge leaps on hands and feet, abandoning Ewan for the other to feast. It jumped right past where Richards was watching, not even sensing he was there. Only sensing where he laid, cowering under the covers, smelling his fear, feeling him tremble as it ripped through the front door, a high pitched call as though alerting others of its kind.

And the others followed, close behind, grunting and sniffing their way through the door. They sniffed every part of the kitchen, the pantry, through the hallway, and the bathroom, searching for their feed. And all the time, their leader stood tall at the door, calm and collected. It closed its yellow eyes as though it was searching for something from within, and it snarled, Ewan's blood drying on its long jaw. It knew where Richards was hiding; they never had to hunt him down like a pack of wolves.

It knew.

More were bursting through the door, pushing past their leader. And the field continued to give birth to these creatures, these monsters of the corn.

Tens of them. One hundred. And still they grew strong, infecting a world of a plague not of disease, but consumption.

As they searched for their next feed, the leader yelled out, a call for them to stop; and it walked through them, knowing exactly where to look for Richards. It could see him, whimpering for his lost son.

It opened the door to Richards bedroom. Walked through silently, saluting the others to wait, growling and snapping their teeth, and went towards the bed.

Richard cried inwardly because he knew he had failed. He screwed his eyes even tighter, praying he could fall deeper into his mind and not feel the pain; keeping quiet but knowing the creature was there, beside his bed, looking down on him, Ewan's blood dripping onto his sheet. Soon his blood will be on the sheets, too. As Richards distanced his mind from the creature to some happier place, his jaw clenched, tooth grating into tooth, chipping away at the enamel.

It peeled away the covers, removing them delicately—slowly. Richards was shielding his head with his arms. He dared to part his elbows and peer at the monster. Shock stripped the tears from him and all he could do was sob. He couldn't make it to his happier place. His eyes bulged as he stared the creature in the face. His mouth was open, dry lips quivering but no sound. He couldn't speak. His hand reached out for the bed frame and he started to pull away, trying to escape, his nails tearing at the ends as he gripped into the wood, coming away from the soft skin underneath and snapping.

Its eyes embedded themselves into Richards, paralysing and numbing him like an anaesthetic. Whether fear was the reason he could no longer move, couldn't feel the dampness of the sheets beneath him or smell the warm urine in the mattress, Richards never knew. Was it showing sympathy towards its prey?

Unlikely. There was no compassion behind those eyes.

But he would never know. And as the creature flipped him onto his back, Richards stared into its eyes, yellow and demonic and dead, and he imagined the plague spreading across the Country like a Mexican wave.

Across the world.

Mandi.

He wondered what they would have called the baby. He had hoped Lucy after his wife or Stuart after his grandpa. But no point thinking about that now. In time, they too would be a food to the creatures. An extra added treat when they cut open her stomach.

Before it launched its left claw into Richards chest and its right into his pelvis, Richard whispered in a voice all broken, "Yellow money," as if he was talking to the creature. "Should've just left it alone, boy." And for one blissful moment, through wet eyes, above all the sadness that was to fall, he had a smile on his face, his mind clear, swimming in song. Because, for Richards, this was the end.

☐

☐

Olaf Lily-Rose - G. H. Finn

This story is inspired by Ólafur Liljurós ("Olaf Lily Rose"), an Icelandic folk song from the 14th century, which is still traditionally sung around the so-called "elf bonfires" on Þrettándinn, the last night of Christmas, "Twelfth Night" (6th January)

Olaf rode along the cliffs, his eyes wary. A gentle breeze stroked his skin. Brooding shadows spread over the rocky land, making him uneasy. This was a dangerous, unfamiliar place. Iceland was not as civilised as his native Norway, and he held a deep mistrust for these barren wilds. His small, shaggy pony was used to the rough ground but it could still stumble and break a leg, or unseat him and run off. Leaving him alone, far from the nearest farm.

But Olaf was less worried about falling from his horse than about other, less tangible, threats.

Both to his body... and to his soul.

The young man crossed himself and muttered a quick yet devout prayer; fingering the silver crucifix he wore, asking that Jesus and all the Saints would protect him.

This was a godless place. Or, rather, the gods it belonged to were not his own. Iceland had been a Christian country for only a very short time, and Olaf knew only too well that for many of its inhabitants it was 'Christian' in name only.

Half of the people here showed nothing more than a sham of Christian faith. Pretending to accept the teachings of the Gospels when in public, while nurturing their true beliefs in the Old Ways the moment your back was turned. If they even bothered to wait that long. Many of the families still worshipped before carved wooden idols. Sacrilegious depictions of their ancestral gods. Odin. Thor. Frey. Ull. Heimdall. And so many others. They even prayed to goddesses. Frigg. Freya. Skathi. And more he didn't even wish to think about. The people still believed in their old gods and goddesses. The only thing that had changed was that now they worshipped them behind closed doors.

It was all too common. Olaf knew for a fact that all of the seamen on the ship that brought him to Iceland went to church each week. Every Sunday each man knelt before the cross as they said their prayers to Jesus.

But then, the moment they set sail, the same men made the sign of the hammer as they prayed to Thor. They thought that when it came to gods, it was better not to take chances on offending any of them.

Most of the families on the Icelandic farms he had visited were even worse. In private, half of them made no attempt to hide the horgs, the heathen altars, they had set up inside their homes. Here they made offerings of bread and mead to their pagan gods.

Even those who claimed to be good Christians would regularly leave out offerings to spirits. Some left food and drink for the dead who dwelt within their burial mounds, continuing to watch over the farms that had once belonged to them. Others offered milk and butter to the Vættir, Land-spirits, asking for fertility and a good harvest. And worst of all, some even held Blóts – sacrifices – to honour the Elves.

Olaf would have liked to have all such pagans executed, for in his eyes they were nothing more than Devil-worshippers. He thought heathens should be offered the chance of accepting the merciful love of the true God, and if they refused then they should be put to death. Brutally. As an example to others. That was what his namesake, Saint Olaf, had done in Norway.

But Olaf knew he could only pray for God's just retribution on the Icelandic heathens, who surely would all burn in the fires of hell. There was nothing else Olaf could do. As long as they carried out their worship privately, the heathens were protected by law. It was part of the compromise the Icelanders had struck with the Pope when they agreed, at least nominally, to be converted.

Most of the Icelanders felt it was far easier to agree to call themselves Christians than to fight their neighbours, or to find themselves unable to trade with Christian countries to the south.

It had taken many dire threats to persuade them to accept God's love. They would probably have held out against fire or the sword, preferring a swift death to renouncing their worship of the Æsir, the Vanir, their ancestors, and the spirits of nature. What finally persuaded most of them was fear their families and their children would starve if the Pope carried out his threat and banned all Christian countries from trading with them.

And so, in name at least, the Icelanders accepted the righteous salvation offered by the church. But in reality many did so grudgingly, if at all.

Olaf himself was very different. He had been brought up all his life as a Christian. His faith was firm and he accepted the teachings of the church without question.

In Norway he was a popular young man, much praised for both his bookish scholarship and his good looks. Olaf's pale white skin and vibrant red hair had earned him the nickname "Lily-Rose". Many girls made eyes at him, calling him handsome, although quite a few men made disparaging remarks about his almost feminine beauty. One man, Erik Wolftooth, even said that Olaf was so fair of face that he must have had Elves among his ancestors.

That taunt got under Olaf's skin far more than anything else. To dare to suggest that one of his forebears had bred with a damned Elf! Everyone knew that Elves were morally corrupt. Evil seducers of the innocent. Beautiful to look at but foul in their black hearts. Inhuman monsters that were denied the grace of God. Soulless.

Olaf wasn't a particularly violent man, but when that insult was thrown at him he had challenged Erik to the Holmgang – a duel. Olaf had won, and done so without actually killing Erik, perhaps as much by luck as anything else. While custom dictated honour was served and the matter was now over, Olaf was privately advised that it might be wise to make a journey abroad until everyone's tempers had cooled. There were many who had sympathy for Erik.

And so, reluctantly, Olaf had sailed to visit his distant kin in Iceland. At least they were Christians.

Olaf realised his mind had been wandering. Lost in thoughts about Norway as he rode along the cliffs, he had somehow missed the cairn which marked the turn he needed to take to find his way to the farm of his second cousin, Ingvar Bjornsson, called by many Ingvar Christ-Priest.

Olaf scolded himself, but it was no use regretting his lack of care. He looked around and saw no familiar sight. Nothing at all to guide him. He had gone astray and was now lost.

Olaf brought the pony to a halt and stilled himself, trying to decide what he should do.

Night came quickly this far north. It would soon be as black as pitch. At least there was only a gentle breeze and not a howling gale blowing at him.

On a clear night there might be moonlight enough to ride by, perhaps he might even navigate by the stars, but the sky was filled with clouds and not enough wind to clear them. When darkness came he would not be able to see his own hand in front of his face, let alone find his way back to Ingvar's farm.

Olaf knew he could simply stop here until morning, but Iceland had almost no trees. Without wood he would be unable to build a fire, and it would be a very cold night wrapped only in his cloak.

Worse than that was the thought of what might lurk in the darkness.

Trolls were said to haunt these cliffs.

And... other things.

He could turn around and retrace his steps but with the twilight making the landscape seem even stranger than before, it would be a miracle if he could find the way.

Olaf fingered his crucifix nervously. Might there be another farm nearby? Somewhere he could beg shelter for a night?

A Christian farm would be sure to offer him food and a bed.

In fairness, so too would a heathen settlement, for hospitality was held to be almost sacred amongst the followers of the Old Ways. Not even the poorest hovel would turn away a traveller, lost and wandering in the night.

Olaf didn't relish the thought of sleeping in a house that held an idol of that one-eyed devil, Odin but even that would be better than becoming food for a hungry troll.

Or to be attacked by an undead draug

Olaf's keen eyes scanned the horizon. And then he saw it. A huge stone, too great for human hands to have lifted, set upright on top of a grass-covered mound.

He caught a glint of firelight. A flare of red. Perhaps from a cooking fire? It looked too bright to be a fish-oil lamp.

Whatever it was, at least it meant he was not alone.

Olaf kicked his pony forward, turning it away from the edge of the cliff, to head toward the ancient stone, standing stark upon the dark mound.

Long before he reached the stone he clearly saw the fire burning before it. A gentle wind fanned the flames. He wondered if someone had collected driftwood, washed ashore on the rocky beach beneath the cliffs. Or perhaps it was made by burning dried turf, as they did in the isles of Orkney.

Dusk had turned to night as he reached the mound. Then suddenly he was not alone.

A girl stood before him. He hadn't seen where she'd appeared from. It was as though she had walked straight out of the ancient, stone. Olaf snorted. She must have been behind it and had simply walked around the huge boulder, hidden in the darkness until she came close to the firelight. He stared at her.

He had never seen any woman who could come close to matching her unearthly beauty. Olaf gazed at her. She was enchanting. Not merely desirable but inhumanly glamorous. Her skin, pale as the moon, seemed almost luminous. Her long red-gold hair coiled in tresses and hung unfettered, reaching to her tiny waist. Her legs were long and lithe, almost deer like. She moved effortlessly, like grass stirred by the soft breeze walking barefoot. Her face was delicate, with a pointed chin and high cheek-bones that for some reason reminded Olaf of a cat. She wore a green and yellow dress, barely showing the subtle yet complex knot work design hidden within the skillful weave of its thin fabric. Her large eyes twinkled like starlight and captured his own as she smiled her red lips parting sensuously.

"Greetings Olaf Lily-Rose," she said in a voice bubbling with some dark merry joy that Olaf could not guess at.

"Well met in Jesus' name," Olaf replied.

The girl frowned, and again Olaf was reminded of a cat. One that might turn in a moment from a soft purring delight into a snarling beast with vicious teeth and claws.

"Greet me not with that name," she said, coldly. "But be welcome all the same. Warm yourself by our fire."

Olaf was dismayed. The beautiful woman was clearly not a Christian. It saddened him to think she would therefore be damned to hell for all eternity. But, he reflected, it would be no more than she deserved, for refusing to heed the word of the Lord. It was a pity that such beauty would burn in the Devil's pits, but such was God's way and it was not his place to question it. He wrestled for a moment with his conscience, wondering if he should simply turn away and ride into the night, but the lure of the fire, and, if he were honest with himself, the girl's beauty was too much of a temptation. He dismounted from the pony and moved to stand in the glow of the fire's light. With an effort he stilled his troubled mind and stood with the sea breeze wafting through his unkempt hair.

Then a thought struck him. She had called him by name! How could she have recognised him? They had never met. Olaf could never have forgotten seeing anyone as fair as this girl. Was she a Völva, a witch? He swiftly put a hand on the hilt of his sword. But he controlled his fear. There were not so many people living in Iceland that strangers riding in the night were an everyday occurrence, and news travelled fast in a small community. Probably one of the farm-hands had told neighbours that Olaf was visiting Ingvar, and by now half the country would have heard. The girl might simply be making a clever guess. He relaxed, but still asked, "I don't know how you know my name. I am new to these shores and I don't know yours. How do you come to know me, fair maiden? We have not met before; I could never have forgotten one as pretty as you."

The woman laughed like ice breaking on a frost-covered morning.

"Fair maiden am I? You speak as though you were at the mead-bench in a hall, and I was a serving-girl who caught your eye! But no matter, for I think you don't mean it as empty flattery, so I shall take it as a compliment. As to how I know your name, there is little that is hidden from my folk and a lot that we know. I know much about you. If you would be our guest, then be welcome here. You shall be offered the best we have to eat and drink, with a place at the head of the table and a warm bed to sleep in."

The woman paused, pouting slightly as she added, "And you are somewhat handsome, so you might not necessarily sleep alone."
Olaf was shocked. He had heard that heathens were often free with their love, but the brazenness of the woman still surprised him. He was also puzzled. He decided to be polite.

"I thank you for your offer of hospitality, and I would be grateful for food and somewhere to sleep. Though I would prefer to be alone, so that I may say my prayers. But I do not understand. Is there a farm nearby? Where do you and your kin live?"
The woman smiled softly as she answered, "We live here of course. Within the hollow hill. Beneath the stone, deep within the mound. It is a fair place, where we dwell. Few are asked to visit us. We do not usually welcome guests. Many would consider it an honour."
A terrible suspicion dawned on him, Olaf recoiled in horror.
"What manner of woman are you? Who are your people? Who… What are you?"
The beautiful woman smiled again, her face calm and at once both young and ancient, then she asked, "Can you really be so blind that you do not recognise one of the Álfar when she is speaking to you?"
Olaf spluttered, "You are an Álf-kona, an Elf-woman?" The young man fingered his sword-hilt.
"Naturally," the woman replied. "I have made you an offer of hospitality. Would you be so rude as to refuse it?"

"I will not dwell with Hell-spawned beings such as you." Olaf answered with a snarl. Then as the night wind fanned the blood-red flame which burnt upon the mound, he paused to think for a moment, before saying, "Everyone knows that your kind do not have souls. Without a soul you cannot go to Heaven and are thus damned. But will you now repent your wicked ways, forego all evil and accept Jesus as your saviour?"

The Elf-woman's eyes widened, then she answered, "Does this pass for courtesy among your people? I have bade you welcome and invited you to be a guest. I have offered you food and drink and lodging. I have said you would be welcome to dwell with us and asked nothing of you in return. And what is your reply? You offer only insults. Yet I shall show you that we elves have manners that are better than your own. I repeat my offer. Come and be with us. Forget this prattle about religions. Be welcome, not in the name of any God, but as an act of kindness."

Olaf shook his head. "Not unless you will first accept the Lord Jesus as your saviour." Once again he fingered his sword.

The Elf-woman's beautiful face creased into a frown of distaste. "I know of your beliefs. I have heard the words of the Christ-priests who came to convert the men and women of this land.

"You tell people that they should have faith in your God. That they should worship him and that if they do not, when they die they will cast be into a burning pit?"

"Yes," said Olaf, "Only the righteous who believe in God shall be saved."

The Elf shook her beautiful head, saying, "For all their faults, the Æsir and the Vanir make no such threats. They can be arrogant enough at times but they have never been so childish as to punish those who do not believe in them. They do not even ask to be worshipped, let alone demand it. You call your God 'Father' and say he offers 'salvation'? Salvation from what? From the threat he himself menaces them with? Your God insists people should bend their knees to him, and if they do not, he will have his Devil torture them for all eternity. And why? Because you claim that once, at the dawn of time, a woman ate an apple, and for that all humans are damned unless they accept Jesus as their Lord and Master?"

Olaf smiled, "Yes. All sinners shall be punished in the fires of Hell. It is only right and proper. Questioning the ways of Our Lord is a blasphemy. I suppose I was being too generous to you. You are soulless. A demon such as you is bound to revel in the lies of her master, Satan. There can be no salvation for one such as you. You cannot be saved."

The Elf laughed, coldly.

"I'm told that your God was nailed to a cross. Thor has a hammer. I know which one I would sooner call on to save me."

"But as for Satan being my master. That is feeble-minded silliness. I am an Elf. We acknowledge no God's authority over us. We would hardly serve a Devil. How poorly you know us.

"I will ask you only one more time, in the name of hospitality and in the hope of a better understanding between us, come and live among the Elves a while. Perhaps then you will like us better."

The fire burned upon the mound. Olaf said a prayer. And then he drew his sword.

The soft breeze blew through the night, fanning the red-flames and casting a baleful light on Olaf's face. He wore an ugly expression as he snarled, "I do not wish to know your people or your ways. I would rather believe in my Christ. I have offered you a chance to put aside your evil and to ask God for forgiveness of your sins. You have spurned that offer. That is an insult to God. And for such an insult to God you must die. I have heard that iron holds a terror for unclean spirits. If you will not accept the love of God then you may feel his wrath through the cold iron of my sword."

Olaf swung the blade at the Elf-Woman's head. He was well trained in the arts of war and his blow would have cleaved a man from skull to hip.

But the Elf was not in the path of the blade.

He hadn't seen her move. He barely felt her gentle touch upon his hand as she took it and twisted his wrist sharply. He let go of the sword in pain. The Elf-woman took it and stabbed the weapon into his side. The keen blade pierced through his ribs. His chest erupted in a fountain of blood, splattering the ground with scarlet. The Elf drove the sword on, twisting it inside the wound. Olaf tried to cry out but his mouth filled with blood and he produced only a spray of crimson. He fell to his knees in shock.

The Elf bent her beautiful head, close, to whisper in Olaf's ear,

"Three times I offered you hospitality. You replied only with insults, and then you tried to kill me. You could have been a friend to the Elves, and that would have gained you much. But now you have found only death. If I were kind I would slay you now. But who ever said the Elves were merciful? Instead I will tell you something, kinsman. Did you not wonder when so few men ever meet an Elf, even fleetingly, why I should be so kind as to invite you to dwell with us? Did you not think it odd that I would overlook your lack of respect and make the offer again, and yet again?"

Olaf spat out a mouthful of blood and managed to croak, "You were trying to lure me from the path of righteousness…"

"No," said the Elf, "I was being polite to a relative, albeit a distant one. Your great-grandmother once had a tryst with a cousin of mine, in the dark forests of Norway. We share the same blood, you and I, although it has thinned a lot in your veins. Even so, I would have welcomed you as kin."

"You lie!" Olaf spat, his body arching in pain.

"Elves rarely lie," replied the Elf-woman, "We don't feel the need. Especially not when truth brings more pain. I will leave you now, to make your peace with your petty God, even if he is unworthy of the loyalty you have shown him."

Olaf set his mouth grimly, then he stilled himself and said, "I will gladly accept death, for I have served my Lord, and he will reward me in Heaven."

The Elf-woman looked down on him. No pity showed in her dark eyes as she said,

"Your God would reward you? For trying to kill one of your own kin? For doing your best to murder an unarmed woman?" She shook her head, then muttered,

"Maybe he would. I do not know. I know nothing of your God. Odin would feed you to his wolves if you came before him after doing such as this. But maybe the Christian God is different."

"I will beg God for forgiveness of my sins," Olaf whispered.

The Elf-woman's sharp ears caught the words and said, "He can only forgive what is his to forgive. You insulted me. You tried to murder me. And I do not forgive you."

Olaf's body shuddered. He knew he did not have long to live. With an effort he said, "All the same, I shall ask God to forgive me. I put my soul in his keeping."

The Elf smiled, saying, "But kinsman, I have told you. You have Elven ancestry. We share the same blood. And the same spirit." She shook her head as she bent close to his ear and whispered, "What makes you think that you have a soul?

"Perhaps you should pray that you are wrong in your beliefs.

"If not, send your Devil my regards when you see him."

Bring In The Children - Betty Breen

Bring in the children, O bring them today;
Speak to them gently, and show them the way;
Careless they wander, and thoughtless they roam;
Bring in the children, for here is their home.

"It's me mummy," Barry called, closing the front door and putting on the latch. He slipped off his black rubber shoes and placed them neatly on the mat. He knew better than to walk them through the house. He had been born in this house, and he loved it although he cherished his mother more than anything. She was the only thing he ever allowed himself to think about, apart from God.

"I know it's late, the service ran over." Barry hung up his plain black rain coat onto the hook above his shoes. Carefully he did up every button and slid his hands down the sleeves to get out any possible creases. He took off his trousers and folding them he placed them on the wooden bench. Next his jumper, shirt and tie. Lying neatly in a pile were the clothes he had removed before leaving that morning. The hallway was where all outdoor items remained. His house was clean, free from any germs from the outside world.

"I'm just going to clean myself up."

Barry walked up the stairs, carefully avoiding the banister and the wall. He needed to scrub himself down and wipe away the dirt and grime that was trying to crawl its way into his skin. Barry wasn't concerned with his physical appearance, those worldly things would only cloud your mind and he knew God didn't concern himself with such matters. Barry, at around five foot eight, had the physique of a young boy. Never worried about correct nutrition or muscle building like his peers, he lived off simple meals. His hair was dark and thin, fashioned in the same simple bowl cut that his mother gave him as a young boy. His nails were cut short, no whites ever grew, he couldn't bear the thought of any dirt nesting there. He scrubbed himself daily. 'Squeaky clean Barry' was his nickname. He had considered it a compliment until the kids at school started going 'squeak squeak' whenever he walked past. 'Dirty hands do the devil's work' his mother would remind him daily.

As he stood in his hotter than normal shower, his mind went over the morning's events. Today had gone well. He had been asked to talk to the children about repenting and changing their sinful behaviours. He was pleased at how well it had gone. Most of the children had sat quietly, apart from a small group of sinners at the back. He had seen their mocking faces, laughing at him. 'Spoilt little brats' his mother called them. Barry scrubbed his hands harder at the memory of their taunting giggles.

"They will see the light," he said aloud to himself. "Little devils that need a good beating, mummy says."

Barry turned the shower off and stood there to drip dry. Stepping out, he dressed himself in the neatly pressed clothes that hung in the cupboard. Seven matching outfits. All labelled with the day they must be worn, a cross stitched onto the top pockets. Barry was proud of his faith. His mother had always taught him that to hide his faith from the world was a sin. She had caught him once saying he didn't believe in a 'silly god'. After washing his mouth out with oven cleaner, she locked him in a cupboard for three days. Barry smiled, licking his lips at the fond memory of his mother's discipline.

"Mummy, is it okay to invite some of my flock around after church next Sunday?" His mother had always told him that he needed to do God's work, that he was the chosen one. God had given him the task of saving his children. Since then God had visited him in his dreams, telling him exactly what he needed to do.

"Thanks mummy. We won't disturb you I promise." Barry leaned over and kissed her cold cheek. "I'm going to bed. Shall we pray together?" Barry dropped to his knees, placing his hands in prayer. Above them hung the image of Jesus nailed to the cross his mother had painted when she was a little girl. This was to be a constant reminder of the pain and suffering he had endured.

"O my Divine Saviour, transform me into yourself. May my hands be the hands of Jesus. May my tongue be the tongue of Jesus. Grant that I may live but in you and for you, and that I may truly say with St. Paul: 'I live, now not I, but Christ lives in me'. Amen."

> Bring, O bring the children,
> O bring them today,
> O bring them today;

Bring, O bring the children,
O bring them in today.

Barry ran through the trees. They were taller and wider than he had ever witnessed. His breath quickened as he tried to run faster, desperately avoiding the fallen branches. Quick glances behind showed him that he was not gaining any distance. The creature was quicker than him, its senses were sharper. It was able to avoid the never-ending trees with ease. Barry's chest tightened as the world seemed to close in around him. Suddenly he stopped. His stalker was now in front of him. His breath came out in thick clouds, his lips dripped with foaming saliva.

"Why do you run child?" The creature's voice boomed, echoing through the trees.

"I'm sorry, please forgive me." Barry felt a warm wet patch between his legs.

"Are you not the chosen one?"

"Yes, yes, please forgive me." Barry's voice was pathetic as he pleaded.

"Maybe we have chosen wrong, you show nothing but idleness, why should we believe you are a worthy servant?"

"Please, I beg you," Barry, sobbing, fell to the wet rotting ground.

"Get off your knees, you pitiful creature. Have you not heard our commands? Bring in the children."

The shadow snarled, stepping closer to Barry.

"Bring in the children. Rid them of their sins."

"Yes, I will. I promise. Please forgive me. I will do as you ask."

"Good. Now be gone."

Barry woke shivering. He gasped for air as he felt the tightness release in his chest. He ran to the bathroom, turned on the shower and got in. With a metal scourer he scrubbed the salty layer from his skin. He had disappointed God, and for that he must be punished.

Barry didn't sleep much after his midnight awakening. He tossed and turned, going over his plans. Suddenly he remembered his mother. He ran down the stairs calling out:

"I'm so sorry mummy, I'm coming."

Barry entered the front room where his mother sat in her arm chair. He collected some warm water and got to work. He washed her down, delicately using a sweet-smelling soap; he changed her clothes then lit the candles. Her favourite scent filled the room.

"Ahh cinnamon and orange mummy, you like that don't you." Barry gave her a kiss and turned her chair to face the mantel, where Jesus could look down upon her. He prayed with her before blowing out the candles and returning to his morning routine. Important things needed to be done and lateness was never acceptable. He rubbed across the scars on his wrists, previous punishments flashed into his mind. This morning there were extra chores to be done. He laid the dining table, in preparation for his afternoon guests. A name card sitting in every place, with him at the head. Each place had a small piece of paper with a hand-written prayer on it. In the centre of the table lay the Holy book. A King James version that his mother had used her whole life. He closed the adjoining door that lead to the front room. His guests would not disturb his mother.

Just before he was about to leave he went back into the front room.

"I'll pop the radio on mummy so you can listen to the service. And don't forget I'll be bringing home some friends later. Today is the day of cleansing." His kissed his mother's cheek and left.

> Bring in the children, O seek them abroad;
> Win them from evil, and train them for god;
> Gladly our mission, O let us fulfil;
> Knowing that Jesus will be with us still.

"Great talk Barry, I really think you are starting to speak to the children." The pastor patted him on the shoulder and gave him a friendly smile.

"Thank you sir. I've invited some of the flock for lunch, they seem really eager to hear more." Barry counted to ten in his head, trying to forget about all those invisible germs festering on his jacket.

"Lovely idea Barry. Jesus will have many crowns waiting for you in heaven." At this Barry beamed. "How is your mother keeping?"

"Okay, thank you. She misses coming."

"Well, give her my best. God bless you Barry."

Barry picked up his satchel and walked over to the group of teenagers that he had invited back to his.

"So, Squeaky, you got some booze at yours?" the boy named Tom said.

"Yes. I have some wine that has been blessed for us to share."

"And you gonna pay us, right?" This time it was the blonde named Charlene that spoke.

"Let us go, shall we?" Barry led the way. Tom, Charlene, Tammy and Rich following close behind. Barry could hear them whispering, laughing and cursing.

"Please I would ask you to mind your language when we get to my home. My house is a sin free place and my mother would be most upset to hear such blasphemy."

"Sure, whatever Squeaky," Tom laughed.

Barry's face began to burn, he hated that name. Painful memories taunted his thoughts, 'squeak squeak, there goes the freak!'

"Please, don't call me that."

Dirty, filthy animals. Why would God want such disgusting little brats in his house? Barry thought to himself. I mustn't question you, I'm sorry lord. Barry tried to look ahead; they were nearly at his house. If it were up to me I would free this world of their ignorance. As they entered his street the excitement started to bubble inside him. Suddenly he was unaware of their whispers.

"Please if you wouldn't mind removing your shoes and placing on the feet covers. The blue ones just there. Mother doesn't like shoes in the house." Barry entered first, stopping anyone from getting through before him.

"Everyone thought your mum had kicked the bucket Squeaky!" Tom said flicking off his trainers without a care.

"I heard you'd eaten her," Rich chipped in, just loud enough for Barry to hear. "Squeak the freak likes the taste of meat."

Barry's mind twitched.

You don't deserve to be spoken to like that, not by them. Show them who's boss.

Barry took in a long breath. "I thank you for your concerns but my mother is still here with us." Barry led the way down the hall, towards the back of the house. The teenagers followed him snickering.

Stay focused now. After today they will show us the respect we deserve.

"Wow, your house is really dull mate," Tom said.

See, no respect! Don't let them speak to you like that.

Shut up. We must follow God's plan. No more rolling over Barry, you are in control.

We are in control.

Quiet! Enough.

"I don't need things, it is what is in your heart that matters," Barry said indicating for them to sit down.

"So, when we gonna have that drink?" Tammy said popping some sort of grotesque pink gum in her mouth.

"I thought we could share a small glass of wine first. Then we will pray and eat. Once that is over we can drink more in celebration." Barry stood at the head of the table and smiled down at his flock. He sat holding a gold goblet filled with red liquid. He passed it to Tammy who sat by his side.

There you are you dirty bitch, drink up.

Quiet.

His head rushed with anticipation, his heart beat faster and louder, pumping with adrenaline.

"In front of you you'll find a piece of paper. On it is a prayer. I thought we could all read it together." Barry picked up his paper with shaking hands.

"Whatever, if it gets us to the end of this freak show." Charlene said opening her paper.

We are not freaks. Squeak squeak the freak.

SHUT UP.

Together they began: "Dear lord Jesus, I believe that, you are the son of god. I believe that you died on the cross for my sins, and you rose again from the dead, and you are the right hand of the Father. I accept you, and confess you as my …,"

"What the fuck is this shit man?" Tammy said.

"Please don't swear or inter…"

"I will fucking interrupt. I ain't here for this bloody shit. You told us there would be booze." Tammy started to get up, screwing up the paper before throwing it at Barry.

"Jesus, have you read this Tom?" Rich spoke over the table.

"Please, stop blaspheming," Barry's face turned red.

We're losing them Barry. Keep it together now.

"Yeah dude seriously, if all this weird Godly shit is your thing then that's fine, but we seriously ain't digging it." Tom spoke politely, although his face was agitated.

"Please, let us finish the prayer."

You're losing control. Command their respect.

Tammy continued to walk away. No longer able to keep in his frustration, Barry slammed his hand down on the table. "Have you not been listening to us…to me…?" Barry blushed, "I told you, you need to repent, to be cleansed!"

"Fuck off. Come one Char," Tammy carried on towards the door.

"SIT THE FUCK DOWN YOU STUPID CUNT!" Barry screamed.

"Whoa dude, take it easy. Hey Tam, sit the fuck down yeah. Let's just say the words; you don't have to mean it." Tom was calm but the room was filled with a tangible intensity.

"HOLY FUCK"

In all the commotion Barry had not noticed that Rich had walked into the front room.

"Holy Jesus, holy mother of God. Tom get your ass over here," Tom stopped staring at Barry and ran into his friend.

Barry had lost control.

It's not our fault.

These kids were beyond saving. They were pure evil.

They did not deserve to walk on our God's beautiful earth.

Tammy ran in after Tom. Rich was standing in the corner, throwing up. In the chair underneath the mantel piece was Barry's mother. Well what was left of her. Her eye sockets were empty and the skin on her face was black. The smell of rotting flesh engulfed them. Resting on the arms of the chair were her skeleton fingers, stripped of skin. A fly, cleaning itself, rested on her mouth. There was no tongue inside the toothless orifice which was wide open as if in a dying scream. The fly, startled by the commotion flew inside, then out of her ear and away.

Tammy went over to Rich and started to pull him back. Charlene and Tom were standing by the door. Charlene ran out retching. Tom went after her.

"You sick fuck," Tom shrieked.

He was close enough for Barry to almost taste the cigarettes on his breath.

"Let us out now man or I swear," Tom said making himself tall.

"You swear what? You'll tell your mummies? HA! You think they'll believe you over me, a respected member of the community? Squeaky clean Barry?" He began to grin. All the memories of torment were suddenly rising to the surface of his mind. He was angry, his eyes crazed. "You are not leaving here until the Lord's work is done."

Charlene screamed. "The front door, it's locked. I can't open it."

"Open the door mate. Please. We won't tell anyone. Just let us go and that will be it." Tom sounded suddenly defensive.

Calmly, Barry seated himself. "I think you'll find it would be preferable for you all to sit now. Your insatiable need for the Devil's nectar will be your downfall." Barry said.

"Tam, I don't feel so good," Charlene stumbled to the floor.

"You see, we knew you would not cooperate. The Lord thinks you can be saved. But we know the truth. He can't save you. You're foul, repulsive, nothing can save you." Barry's grin spread high up his cheeks. "Only Death."

> Bring in the children, so friendless and poor;
> Joy to their hearts will the Saviour restore;
> Bring in the children, compel them to come;
> Jesus invites them, and yet there is room.

"Squeaky squeak, here comes the freak, watch your tongue, he'll eat the meat," Barry sang merrily. No need to be quiet now.

"I think we did an admirable job, don't you mummy?"

We did a splendid job.

In front of Barry lay four naked bodies. It was hard to tell who was who, so he had placed the handwritten name cards above each one.

Pathetic predictable bastards, we knew you'd drink it.

Once they had all passed out he laid them down and tied them up. He hadn't realised how strong his malnourished body was. Living off only his mother's flesh and potatoes had proven to be nutritious.

From the golden goblet he had used serve to the wine, Barry poured battery acid over the four dirty teenagers. Starting with their faces, he moved slowly down, making sure all flesh was covered. He had waited for them all to wake, watching them squirm, listening to them plead for their lives. It was pitiful. It had almost made Barry hard. He had not experienced that for a long time. Not since the last and final beating his mother had inflicted upon him.

They told him they would change. It's funny the things you will say when you have lost control. When someone else holds your life in their hands. "Jesus never begged," Barry told them. "Accept your fate gracefully, for you have chosen to walk the sinful path."

Their deaths were beautiful. The acid bubbled on their skin, burning slowly like a scented candle. Their screams, loud and piercing at first had faded quicker than expected.

Maybe the Lord had mercy on them and their suffering.

We doubt it. God is not gracious, he is fierce and unforgiving. We have the scars to prove that.

"For the wrath of God is revealed from heaven against all ungodliness and wickedness of men, who by their unrighteousness suppress the truth. Romans one, verse eighteen. Our favourite." Barry whispered with a smile.

☐

Take My Life And Let It Be - Lucy Myatt

Nick awoke with his head throbbing and his mouth dry. The worst hangover in history had taken effect. He carefully opened one eye and surveyed his surroundings. He was in his living room.

"At least I made it home," he thought to himself as he summoned all his energy to sit up on the couch. Holding his forehead he looked over to the coffee table where he could see an almost empty bottle of whiskey and a crumpled pack of cigarettes, which would explain the dry mouth and headache. He looked to the other side of the room to see a set of divorce papers, which would explain the drinking.

Nick sat in silence as he retraced his steps from the night before. He remembered heading straight to the bar after his wife had dropped off the papers whilst picking up their son. After the first couple of shots of whiskey, the rest turned into a hazy blur of anger, tears and regret. Flashes of last night attacked him as he tried to stand and dragged himself to the bathroom to brush his teeth.

"She doesn't want anyone else, she just doesn't want me," he remembered whining to the barman.

"Fuck you bitch," he had screamed at the family photos hanging on the walls. With the toothbrush hanging from his mouth, he made his way back into the living room, retracing his steps. Upon inspecting the photo frames he could see that they were all broken with shards of glass scattered about the floor. Shame surged through him. He was embarrassed to think what he may have done or said whilst in public.

He looked at the clock on the wall. 10:30 am. He was late for work. Nick cursed himself, looking at his dishevelled appearance and trying to find his phone so he could ring work and explain. He looked under the coffee table and to his horror he stared at broken shards of plastic, a bent motherboard and a smashed phone screen. He picked up the plastic shrapnel as a new memory played out in his mind. Last night, after he had stumbled through the doorway, after drinking more alcohol than he knew he could handle, he had picked up his phone and downloaded the app 'Let it be.'

"I ordered a fucking assisted suicide?" He remembered how he had struggled to see with double vision and it had taken multiple attempts to use the phone when nothing seemed to make sense. After finally installing the app he had smashed the device up. Demonstrating his dedication to his own death, as you can cancel the 'appointment' if you change your mind. He desperately tried to work out the time he ordered the kill. He roughly remembered seeing the clock face read 4am so it had to be after that. After you request to die via a suicide app, someone would come and take your life within the next 24 hours. The opportunity to cancel this has been removed as he would need a phone that was intact to do that. He currently had no more than 17 hours to live.

Nick's stomach turned as the sound of someone knocking on the front door echoed through the house. Through instinct, he dropped to the floor, paralysed with fear, worried that somehow, the person on the other side of the door would have x-ray vision.

"I requested the hit for here?" He was naïve to this app but did know that you could have them track you through GPS and 'surprise you' or you could request a specific location and simply wait for them. Which had he done?

"It could be Jen. She could be coming back to say sorry." He knew deep down it was not.

"It could be Jack." This was more possible.

"It could be someone to kill me." Fear convinced him. This was the right answer. Death was at his door.

He needed to leave. Now. His arms & legs moved. It was a miracle. Escape; but how? The kitchen door. It opened into the back garden. Distance. He needed distance between him and death. Between him and the other side of that door. Sweat ran down his face. Stealth was never his strength. But now his life depended on it. Out into the garden, the bright sunshine hit him. His head throbbed. His stomach lurched. He wanted to be sick. No time for that. He glanced ahead. The garden gate. Freedom. The front garden. You could see the front garden from the alleyway. You could see the alleyway from the front garden. Only a sliver. The tiniest of views. But too much of a risk. It would all be over if they saw him. He couldn't take the chance. He heard the banging on the door again. Louder this time. Adrenaline coursed through him. The fence. He threw himself at the 6ft fence. His arms dragging him over. Legs scrabbling frantically. Another fence. Then another. Heart racing. He stopped, breathless. Hidden in an alley in a neighbouring street, he slumped to the floor, catching his breath.

He did not live too far away from the high street, it was not an impossible mission to make his way there, buy a new phone and cancel the transaction. A cold sweat took hold of his body as he clutched the jacket he woke up in and almost passed out with relief as he felt the wallet in his pocket.

Paranoid and vulnerable, he chose to avoid main roads and public transport. Instead he kept to every back alley he could see, with his back against to the walls and fences whenever he could. Whilst on his way, he cursed the app even existed. Five years ago, assisted suicides became a legal and profitable business opportunity. They believed giving people the right to kill would remove any illegal murders. It did not, but suicide was on the rise and no company was going to make the moral decision over profit. So apps like 'Take my life' and 'let it be' were now an everyday feature on the news.

Pain shot through him as his bare foot rested its full weight onto something sharp. Pulling what turned out to be a glass shard, blood began to drip and then gush. It was going to get infected but he had no time to find a way to clean or cover the wound. He scolded himself for not grabbing his shoes as he ran out of the house but footwear had not been his main priority when a potential hitman was at the door. He argued that maybe he could have spoken to the 'suicide assistant.' Explain that it had been a mistake but he had never ordered one before, he did not know how they worked. He had heard of jobs going wrong before, the assistant not confirming the target or the details being wrong and another person getting killed instead. No programme is without flaws and Nick was not about to take any more risks.

"What have I become?" A year ago he was a proud, successful father and husband. Career driven and comfortably able to support his family if needed. Now he was a pathetic sack of skin draped over bones and suffocated in filthy rags.

Another memory of the night before played out in his mind. He was hunched over the bar, barely sitting on his stool, still in the same clothes as now. Preaching to the clearly uncomfortable barman.

"Pete, can I call you Pete? There is nothing left for me Pete. She doesn't want me. Doesn't love me. Probably never did. Slut. No. She's not. But she doesn't love me. I wonder if she ever did. Maybe she loves someone else and he doesn't want her. I wondered if the kid was even mine once. Jack doesn't even look like me. Got a DNA test done behind her back. He is. But she found out and that's where she claimed it began to fall apart for her. Apparently I was too jealous. Too paranoid. She didn't seem to understand I just loved her. Passion is not paranoia. Stupid bitch couldn't tell the difference."

He stopped in his tracks as doubt danced around inside his head.

"Have I always been a mess? To not trust my wife as much as I have done? Is that why she left?" Truth was, he still did not know why. Maybe he never would. He saw nothing as broken. He saw nothing to fix.

Nick stopped to catch his breath. The reality of the situation mixed with a litre of whiskey followed by an adrenaline chaser finally caught up to him. His stomach hardened then contracted. He hunched over and rejected what seemed to be everything inside of him. As vomit splattered over the floor, parts of it sprayed onto his bare feet and lower legs. He stared at the contents on the floor, not completely sure if he could continue. Then he thought of his son, hearing how his dad had died in in a puddle of his own sick in the back streets of his home town and for the first time, he found true courage to go on. With a throbbing head, blurring vision and bleeding feet, he tried to focus his brain to look out for more harmful objects on the floor as he limped closer to the high street. Whenever someone passed, he would flinch and clench his fists in preparation. They were never who he expected them to be. His most pitiful moment was a mother pushing her baby in a pram that had turned the corner and surprised him. Giving him such a fright he whimpered and squeaked 'No please.' The look of confusion and fear in the mother's face made his head swim in shame.

His behaviour was only part of what contributed to the shocked and wary faces of the people who passed him. His bare, bloodstained feet matched the dirty and creased trousers he had slept in. His whiskey stained shirt even fashioned a cigarette burn near his breast pocket. An aroma of ash, vomit and alcohol radiated from him. He once took such pride in his appearance. The outfit was a well fitted suit to represent his success in his career. Now the jacket flapped loosely over his frame, giving him the appearance of a sickly boy wearing his father's clothes. The desperate look was finished off with a gaunt, sick face and matted hair.

The walk should have only taken twenty minutes but his paranoid mind had followed a much quieter route which resulted in him having to walk for an entire hour. His feet were so cut up by this point that every step left a bloodied footprint. By the time he reached the high street, he practically fell into the store and searched for any smart phone he could see. Ignoring the concerned faces of the staff he demanded a new phone. The young, confused boy hesitated for a second deliberating whether to serve him or not but Nick was grabbing his wallet and shoving money into his hand whilst slamming his bank card on the counter. Taking it as a very large tip, the young man ran to the back to get the device trying to hide the look of disgust. This image would occupy the boys head for the rest of the day. Questioning why someone with so much money would dress, act and smell the way he had. He wondered if the card had been stolen but rationalised that he had known the pin. He also pondered if he would ever receive a £45 tip again just for serving someone but eventually he would finally drift off that night and sleep away the questions and never think of Nick again. The luxury most people have when they are not living in horror. Nick ran out of the shop clutching his only chance of survival, in search for a safe place to stop and set up the phone. Distraught and exhausted he spotted a public toilet sign and ran for it. Once inside he threw himself into a cubicle and locked the door. He sat on the toilet, giving himself a second to breathe. His breaths coming shallow and fast he ripped open the cellophane around the box with his teeth. Once the phone started to power up he impatiently set it up as quickly as the device would him allow him.

To his horror, so close to safety, he dropped his new phone. Unable to react he watched it bounce into the other cubicle. Even without the app installed yet, could the 'assistant' find him? He needed the phone back. He dropped to the floor to see if he could reach the phone from underneath the dividers. Stretching his arm across, he was just out of reach as it had slid two stalls over. Nick's arm almost dislocated as someone bursting into the room made him jump violently. Was it his killer? Had he found him already? Maybe he was only minutes behind him the whole time. He stepped on top of the toilet seat to hide his bloodied feet. He was not even aware that he was crying. He had no plan left other than to beg for his own life before the assistant could react.

He heard someone relieving themselves at the urinals.

"It's a ruse; they just want me to feel I can come out." The mystery man zipped up their pants, and left, without washing their hands. Nick was frozen. Feeling more unsafe than ever and convinced his killer was outside waiting for him. He needed that phone back. He stepped off the toilet and counted slowly to three. He fumbled at the locks, opened the door and rushed to his phone, locked that door behind him and sat still for a second. Praising himself on the surviving another minute. His fingers shook as he installed the app and let it sync with the details on his phone. They had become the sync generation. Nothing was a stand-alone piece of information or technology anymore and your phone was the heart of it. Holding his breath he opened 'Let it be' and went to click on cancel suicide.

There are no requested suicides with this device.

He stared at the screen in disbelief. Had he imaged the whole thing? Had he truly been so paranoid and self-loathing to let himself fall so far?

After checking every bit of data on his phone he finally accepted his life had never been in danger. He must have been so drunk he passed out and dreamt the whole thing. Maybe the reason the phone was smashed was because he had dropped it, or even thrown it. He remembered being so angry last night.

Standing up he realised it was time to make his way back home. He had become very aware of how terrible he looked. He had been angry for much longer than just last night. He had been angry for years. When his wife wanted a divorce he blamed her, saw himself as the victim. He refused to accept he was ever at fault. He had to accept he was a walking joke. He was the reason they were getting divorced. His anger, his lack of understanding, his adamant refusal to ever listen to her.

But today would be the birth of a new man. He saw his life for what it truly was and what it could be. His life was not over, not even close and he could still have the happy ending he had always wanted. Walking on his blistered feet did not seem to hurt so much as he got closer to home, smiling at everyone like a crazed man. He walked past the local bar he drank himself almost blind in the night before.

"Nick, mate. Didn't expect to be seeing you today." Nick looked up to the see the barman standing in the doorway.

"Oh, no. Just walking home." The barman's grin fell from his face as he stared at Nick's horrific appearance.

"Well, anyway mate, you forgot something. Wait there." Quite clearly not wanting Nick to follow him into the bar and scare the people inside. He popped out holding something and pushed it into his hand. "You left your phone here; it's been ringing all morning. Don't know how the battery has lasted so long."

Nick stared at his phone in silence. It looked like it was the same model. He remembered struggling to be able to read and make sense of a phone last night in a living room? Had he dreamed that too?

Staring at the screen he had sixteen missed calls and four voice messages.

He dialled his voicemail and the civil tone of his wife spoke on the other end. "Hi Nick, our son has left his phone at yours, I'm in work so he's going round before college to pick it up."

The next message played.

"Nick, if you're ignoring me because I dropped off the papers yesterday then that's pathetic, I thought we would at least be able to talk about our own child."

His hand shook as the next message played.

"I haven't heard from Jack. I haven't heard from you, what's going on?"

"Nick, where is our son? He's not answering, you're not answering. I'm getting worried. Are you listening to me?! You're scaring me."

Frozen in fear, he tried to piece everything together but nothing seemed to fit.

He remembered ordering a suicide. But there was nothing on his phone.

He had smashed his phone but here he was holding it.

The app syncs with the details on that person's phone.

It would have been Nick's bank details but everything else on the phone was Jack's.

Ice ran through his veins and ignoring the dirt filled open wounds on his feet he ran towards his house.

"It's ok. I dreamt it. It wouldn't have worked. It was my bank details. It's fine."

He ran faster and faster and the closer he got to the house the safer he felt. Comforting himself repeatedly in his head whilst praying to any God that would listen.

"The suicide assistants notify the authorities after the act has been carried out. I see no sirens. I see no lights. Please God, let him be ok."

He reached home just as the ambulance was pulling up outside it. His knees began to buckle. He looked to his front door, it was ajar.

Two paramedics left the ambulance one pulling the stretcher whilst the other carried the black bag and entered Nick's home.

Colour drained from the world. He could not hear anything, as if someone pressed mute. As the paramedics moved in slow motion, he looked down to the phone in his hand. He could not take his eyes off the app he had just tried to save himself from.

The phone bleeped, an ominous notification, the apps logo flashed up on the screen, a receipt for the next of kin.

Aum - J.G Clay

Aum....

The word. The first word, uttered in the primal chaos of the Universe's spawning. Or so that Doctor had said. The Badmarsh closed his eyes, relishing the cool of the air conditioning, the firmness of the plush chair supporting his thin expensively dressed frame. The round pleasant face of Doctor Digvijay Kaun floated against the dark of his closed eyelids, thick lips moving rapidly, eyes magnified by thick milk-bottle bottomed glasses.

For an academic, Doctor Kaun had been pleasant enough. Killing the man brought The Badmarsh little joy. But, that was what he was being paid for; very handsomely paid for. Professor Brubaker had not hired The Badmarsh for his looks, pleasing though they were. Amongst Delhi's criminal fraternity, he was a legend, feared and respected in almost equal measure. The Badmarsh – The Hooligan - was the killer's killer, a consummate professional known for taking pleasure in his work. His meticulous nature and eye for detail ensured no trails lead back to him. Even the police respected him. The job he had done on the Deputy Commissioner earned that respect.

Aum....

That word again. The Doctor had chanted it, never wavering even as the stiletto blade parted skin and muscle, grinding through his sternum before puncturing the heart that had beat a steady sixty year old rhythm. As blood spilled over Doctor Kaun's prodigious lips, his final breath had delivered the word.

Aum...

The Badmarsh's heart skipped a beat. The word had been louder this time, more insistent. His eyes snapped open, darting back and forth, inspecting the tiny apartment he used as his Delhi base. A more lavish palace awaited him in the wilds of Haryana, away from the prying eyes of the Government. Keeping a low profile in the city ensured survival and freedom.

Aum...

It rang out again, more breathless and excited this time, caressing his ears. The hairs on his arm and neck rose in salute. Alert, The Badmarsh pushed his right foot forward, opening and balancing his stance in readiness.

Someone was here with him.

He knew the apartment well, attuned to its atmosphere. There was an unmistakable heaviness in the air, the presence of another body sharing his space.

Aum....

He pivoted swiftly, hands outstretched ready to chop down the intruder. A shape moved in the periphery of his vision; melting away into the shadows before he could get a good look. It looked like a column of smoke topped with the bleached white bone of an animal skull. Rigid, he peered into the gloom.

The shadow creature had gone.

Breathing heavily, The Badmarsh lowered his guard.

Aum....

The word melted into the dark, along with the smoky apparition.

It would return. The Badmarsh knew this.

The telephone rang, eliciting a surprised wince from the killer.

As he turned to answer it, a wisp of smoke danced past him, caressing his cheek with an arctic touch. The Badmarsh inhaled sharply, shivering despite the humid air of the Delhi night.

Aum...

Dana Brubaker scowled, almost slamming the receiver of the antiquated phone down in frustration. Digging her fingernails into her palm, she closed her eyes, counting to ten and focusing on the pain. Pain was a friend, an instructor, a way of life. The Saviour had endured so much pain; a crown of thorns, beatings, whippings, and the icy feel of nails hammered through his own flesh. If the Messiah endured, then so could she? But then, the Messiah had never been to India, despite the myths being peddled about his time in Kashmir. Propaganda. Propaganda and bullshit.

A hand closed on her shoulder, a familiar grip infused with warmth and an unwelcome feeling that loosened the tops of her thighs.

"Trouble, Dana?" She turned a half smile-half scowl on her face.

"That fucking Hooligan!"

"Language, Dana. We may live amongst the heathen but we do not need to stoop to their level." Eyes – crystalline blue and cold – bored into her own brown ones. There was little warmth to be found in that gaze. Pastor Avery was stern, even for a Man of God. He gave the impression of solidity, of having been carved from granite rather than being born and brought up in the bayou. It was that solidity that she had found alluring, terrifying and comforting at the same time. It was reliability backed by the Word of the Lord. Casting her eyes down in shame, she spoke softly. "My apologies, Pastor. This country gets to me."

Avery nodded, his expression fatherly. "I understand. Both your distaste and your reservations. But remember, we are here to do the Lord's bidding. The treasures buried beneath the soil of this Godless land will help us bring God's Kingdom to this world. Bear the discomfort a little longer. We're almost done."

Dana nodded, looking up at the Pastor once more.

"Will our friend return for the interrogation?"

"He said he would."

The Pastor clasped his hands together in delight. "It'll take him about a half hour. Why don't we have a little drink? Our guest can wait."

Dana nodded, gratefully. A drink would be good. Three or four would be better.

Aum....

Louder this time, the noise seemed to envelop him. Sweat sprouted from his forehead, dripping down the end of his nose. His skin prickled at the acidic liquid coating him. Wiping his face with a free hand, The Badmarsh turned up the air con, weaving through the evening traffic with one free hand.

Aum, Hleem Bagaalamukhi....

The car swerved, his arms going into spasm as the force of the chant hit him. Honks and hoots filled the air, railing at the expensive bronze car weaving across the motorway. Panic began to well up in within him, an unwelcome feeling for Delhi's number one killer. Pulling the car to one side, he screeched to a halt, unsure of whether he had come to a stop in a safe place. Car and lorries rushed by in a haze of diesel and horns.

The Badmarsh leaned forward, resting his head on the steering wheel, his breath shuddering in and out.

What was that…?

Aum, Hleem, Bagaalamukhi, Sarva Dushtanam Vaacham…..

His stomach roiled at the sound of those words, his tongue slick with a foul taste.

Stop it…

Aum, Hleem, Bagaalamukhi

Stop

Sarva…

"Stop!" He sat bolt upright, a frustrated roar escaping from his lips. A black anger surged through the Badmarsh's torso. Lashing out, he pummelled the steering wheel, relishing the crunch of knuckle on plastic as the pain drove the strange words back into the recesses of his consciousness. The agony swelled to the point of being unbearable. Breathing hard, the Badmarsh sat back, grimacing at the feel of sweat stained cotton. He glimpsed into the rear-view mirror, heart stopping in an instant. The bone headed column of smoke stood behind his car, its nebulous arms outstretched.

With his good hand, he slammed the Mercedes into first gear and roared off, unmindful of the curses and horns.

The Sadhu sat cross legged, his bearded face slack in a beatific expression. He smiled at the sight of the two Americans, beckoning them into the dank basement as if they were honoured guests. Pastor Avery strode forward, his block face impassive. His eyes glittered with malice. Dana followed, almost timidly. Her head bowed a little, lush locks of black hair falling across her pale full face. The Sadhu twisted his hand in a quixotically Indian gesture, raising his eyebrows in an expression of mirth.

"The Doctor told you nothing, I presume?" Dana started a little, working hard to cover her reaction at the holy man's clipped English tones. A sly wink informed her of her lack of success. This man – benign, venerable and impossibly British – missed nothing. Folding his huge stubby hands before him, Avery glowered down at the Sadhu.

"A setback, nothing more. The Doctor turned out to be more stubborn than he looked. Unusual for an Indian." The jibe did nothing to shake the Sadhu's composure. He relaxed a little more, regarding his captors with amused satisfaction.

"Mr Avery…"

"Pastor…"

"Forgive me. Pastor Avery. You and your delightful Professor here have combed the length and breadth of Bharat, snatching up ancient tomes, kidnapping men of knowledge, digging into the heart of our dear mother. And for what?" He paused in reflection, his brown eyes becoming a little misty. "The Arabs, The Turks, the Mongols, the British. They all came here with the same purpose as yours. Better disguised, of course. For the Arabs, their intentions were cloaked with religion and bloodlust. The British named it as 'trade'. Beneath the lies and the murder, there was a different purpose was there not?"

Avery tensed, his heartbeat increasing a few notches.

Dana looked away, unable to stand the holy man's scrutiny. His gaze seemed to strip her bare, tearing through the careful academic façade she presented to the world; Professor Dana Brubaker, renowned Indologist, buster of myths, presenter of an alternative history that would turn Indian society upon its head. The controversy had been a smokescreen. The Sadhu could see the pretence. The shame burned her, balanced by fervour, to bring the secrets of this land to the feet of the Messiah. In doing so, no one would be able to stand against the Second Coming. No one. Finding courage and her voice, she sneered.

"What did you Indians do? Nothing. You let yourself be invaded and slaughtered. The power you had was for nothing."

The Sadhu threw his head back, his laugh full-throated and hearty.

"Oh, my child. How little you understand? Do you really think we would have revealed our secrets to the Mleccha – the Unclean – of the West? Be they Arabs or English, you are not mature enough yet. When an opposing force is uncivilised, the best protection is yielding. And that is what we have been doing. Supplicant. Saving our knowledge for a time when it will be necessary, not to be used in the manner of a spoilt fat child throwing a tantrum."

Avery stepped forward, his hand clenched.

"Violence is unnecessary, Pastor. You want the secret of the Ninth Harmonic. The key to the First Word. I will not give it to you. Shanti, my dear Pastor. Shanti."

Without warning, Avery struck the sitting man across the cheek. The Sadhu's head whipped to the left, the meaty slap filling the stale air of the basement. Dana gave a shocked gasp at the sudden strike.

"You sonovabitch. Look what you made me do." The big man's voice quavered with a twang of Tennessee that only crept in with his rage, "I can only hope that Jesus forgives me."

The Sadhu smiled, his teeth stained with blood. "I'm sure she will."

Footsteps from behind interrupted them.

"You're gonna wish you talked to me, you shitskin muthafucka. This man here'll make you wish you'd never been reborn." The Sadhu's smile grew even further.

The Badmarsh entered the room.

His head and jaw throbbed intensely. The drive from his apartment to the smart diplomatic district had been an ordeal. The strange chant returned, whispered this time but no less intense. The words seemed to seep into his bones, his very cells, imbuing them with a nauseating energy, making his body alien to him. As he entered the house, he saw black smoke rising from his pores. Squeezing his eyes shut, he dismissed it as a hallucination, brought on by fatigue and too many killings. His very soul felt sickened.

Offering a cursory nod to Professor Brubaker, his eyes alighted on Avery. The stout American glowered at him.

"You look like shit, my friend. You been drinking?"

Unable to reply, his tongue too big for his mouth, The Badmarsh shook his head, wincing as the motion brought fresh agony to his strained system. Avery nodded, seemingly satisfied. He motioned to a table at the far end of the room.

"All the tools you need are over there. Get his tongue wagging." Jabbing a finger at the holy man, Avery turned.

"Will you not stay awhile, Pastor? Professor? Your friend here is quite the artist when it comes to pain. He has learned to harness it and channel it. Surely this is too good an opportunity to be missed."

The Badmarsh glanced down at his would-be victim. Tears filled his eyes regret, sadness, he could not tell. The pain in his jaw grew, the muscles knitting and twisting. The Sadhu smiled at him tearing his heart even further. A voice seemed to whisper. "Pitch, harmonics, intent. The first word of the Universe is the first word of the Bagaalamukhi Mantra. The intent was planted. Now it is time to release."

The Badmarsh began to tremble. Agony flared as his mouth yawned open of its own accord. His eyes rolled from side to side in terror as a column of black smoke coalesced before him. From the folds of the mist, a white skull grinned at him. The voice continued to whisper. Doctor Kaun planted the seed within you. The seed of his vengeance. The seed of our safety. The seed of Sound and the First Word. Sound can heal or kill. The words are mere window dressing.

A heat – thick and horrid – pulsed at the centre of his chest, blooming and radiating outwards and upwards. He tried to howl in anguish as the Bagaalamukhi Mantra liquefied him internally. Organs tore free from their moorings, cast into a soup of blood and melted tissue.

Black smoke and white bone filled his vision as his vocal chords twitched into life.

"Aum, Hleem, Bagaalamukhi, Sarva Dushtanam Vaacham, Padam Stambhaya Jivhaam, Kilaya, Vinashaya Hleem, Aum Phat Swaaha."

The Badmarsh turned to Avery. His mouth, stretched impossibly wide, leaked a thick soup of red punctuated with blacks and purples. Yet the words powerful, deep, otherworldly – rumbled from his throat, unobstructed by the fountain of gore. Numb, the Pastor stepped backwards, his lips moving in a soundless litany of Christian prayer. As if in response, the chant grew louder.

Aum, Hleem, Bagaalamukhi…
The Lord is My Shepherd…
Sarva Dushtanam Vaacham
I….shall…not…want

He faltered as the keening cadence of the mantra cored into his brain. Blooms of light – green, red, other colours profound yet never seen before – exploded in his vision. He screamed the Lord's name as the colours faded into black. A high-pitched whining assailed his ears, growing in pressure. The last thing Avery would ever hear was the popping of his own eardrums and the rushing of blood filling the cavity. Yet the mantra continued to ring in his head unabated.

As he opened his mouth to bellow out his sorrow, his tongue tore free, oozing from between his lips. It hit the stone floor of the basement with a satisfying splat that he would never hear. The agony drove him to his knees, his mind teetering on the brink as he realised that this was his cell; trapped within his own body with no sight, no means to communicate and no sound save that of the mantra echoing throughout.

Dana froze, unable to comprehend what she was seeing. The Badmarsh continued spewing both viscera and mantra, colouring the room with an unpleasant sound and a coppery odour. Avery - eyeless and tongueless - pitched forward, lying still. Whether he was dead or alive was she did not know.

The Sadhu still sat cross-legged, regarding her with the same fascination he had shown previously. He held a hand up, a ragged slash bifurcating the beige palm.

"Bas, Badmarsh. Bas karo."

Abruptly, the mantra ceased, leaving an unpleasant ringing in her ears and mind. Silence crashed down on the meaty smelling basement.

Dana swallowed, her legs jittering. Her heart pounded against her sternum.

"You may be wondering what you have witnessed?" He allowed her a moment to answer before continuing. "That was the power of Sound. The power of Aum, the first word of the Universe. It may well be the final one. That was the power you sought, to elevate your own false concept of the Gods above all others. Sound has many uses, Professor. Healer, comforter, torturer, destroyer. It all depends on the harmonics. Take the Bagaalamukhi Mantra, the one our dear friend Doctor Kaun implanted into your murderous friend here. If sung in the Fourth Harmonic, it becomes a means of self-cleansing and self-knowledge. Switch the key to the Ninth Harmonic and it renders your enemy deaf, blind and mute. If you are daring enough to use the Thirty-First Harmonic Variant, you could destroy a world. Not wise, if you have no means of escape."

Seemingly exhausted, the holy man wilted a little. Dana had not moved. A puddle formed around her feet, acrid and ammonia smelling. Her eyes were glazed, staring at a point into the distance. Her mind fragile from a life of indoctrination and playacting – snapped, her personality cast into a howling void, filled with fragments of prayer; some known, others arcane.

He laughed, a sad sound, a different Harmonic.

Exhaling, the Sadhu flexed his hand, the gash in his palm widening as a ferocious unblinking eye pushed its way through webs of flesh and tendon to stare at the carnage. Pointing his palm at the catatonic woman before him, he began to chant softly.

"Aum…..Aum……Aum…….."

☐

This Little Light Of Mine - Edward Breen

Not a man to normally sweat, he could feel it now dripping from his armpits and down along his sides, soaking into his clothes. Uncertain whether it was fear or the sudden effort of sprinting after years of inactivity that caused the sudden extreme diaphoresis, it crossed Patrick's mind that he should be thinking about more important things. Like what the hell that light was and why it was chasing him?

At eight am that morning his eyes shot open as if a bugle had been blown into his ear. He was out of bed before he remembered that he didn't need to be, not anymore, not for the last ten years. It hadn't taken them long to tell him he probably shouldn't be leading a congregation after getting charged with drunk driving for the fifth time. Not to mention the swearing from the pulpit, which in hindsight—sober hindsight that is—he had to admit was probably a mistake.

Of course he had always been fond of a drink, what with being of Irish extraction. Why else would he have chosen the church as his vocation, he used to joke when it was still funny to joke about such things. The heavy drinking started after the accident, which happened about a year before his ignominious sacking by the Bishop.

That morning was special for more reasons than being God's day off, though. That day would have been his little boy's eighteenth birthday. Every year it gets easier, or at least that's what well-wishers and his councillors would have him believe. But it never did. Every year was the same as the year before. He would wonder what his son would look like now that he was eleven or twelve or whatever age he would have been that year. While he sat down to his habitual two boiled eggs and soldiers the revelation that it would have been Thomas' eighteenth birthday today hit him. An adult today. What would he have given him as a present? A little car to call his own? Money? A Walkman or iPod or whatever kids had now? His indecision made him think of his wife and the tears finally came blurring his vision and soaking his cheeks.

Life rambling on and strict routine helped Patrick with his grief and ongoing battle with alcoholism, so he was there when the local supermarket opened at ten am to get his weekly shop. He didn't go to church anymore; too many awkward looks and comments whispered behind hands for his liking. And the new reverend was an asshole with his sanctimonious sermons and dramatic inflections. So he shopped on a Sunday now, 'worshipping at the altar of consumerism,' he would joke with anyone who would listen.

Pushing his trolley along the harshly-lit aisles his thoughts wandered again to his wife and son. Never anything too deep just how she liked coffee as he picked up his tea, or how she liked low fat yoghurt while he picked up the full fat tub. How Thomas used to love cars and how every week they would be duped into buying him a new one with big saucer eyes and cuddles that melted their hearts. It took all his power not to drown the place in tears when the cashier asked him how he was. Such an innocent and meaningless sentiment usually. Not that morning.

He drove the shopping home and splashed some water on his face. God he needed a drink. Just a bottle or two to get him through the day and then…the cold water shocked him back to sense and he quickly put the cold things in the fridge and got out of the house to continue with his routine, lest he be tempted. Not that he had anything stronger than mouthwash in the house, but even that had started to look appealing.

The gym was always his next stop on a Sunday. Exercise was his Saviour. Without it he would never have finally kicked the drink, of that he was convinced. When he was on the treadmill his mind was blank. He supposed it was a form of meditation, or prayer he should probably say. He smiled his first smile of the day at the thought of that quip as he stepped into the gym, only for it to fall away when he saw who had got there before him: Gladys and Cindy. Two octogenarians who always managed to get two treadmills side by side and walked on them at slithering pace for well over the supposed fifteen-minute-maximum-on-any-machine-during-busy-times rule. Walking past their lycra-encased, saggy arses he found to his mingled delight and dismay that there was a free one right beside them that morning, and he had forgotten his headphones. Great.

He set the machine at six miles an hour so he could get warmed up. It was an easy jog for him and he usually kept at that pace for five minutes before upping it to seven and a half for the last ten. That way he worked up a good sweat and his mind could focus on little apart from his legs. The noise from the machine was almost enough to drown the two crones beside him out, but not quite. Especially when they increased their volume to compensate.

'…and she told me somebody saw it last night.'

'You're kidding.'

'I'm not. How could I? You know my Bob was killed by the beast the last time anyone saw it.'

'I remember. You poor dear, how are you holding up?'

'Oh, you know. Alright. It was almost ten years ago. I've moved on.'

'So I've heard. How is Julio?'

Patrick decided to turn the speed up before he heard anymore about Julio and whichever one of them it was that had 'moved on' with him. Thankfully the sound of machine drowned them out and he could relax into his run. But he couldn't stop thinking about what they had said. He vaguely remembered seeing a newspaper heading in the supermarket earlier that said something about a monster. Now he realised what it was about. He remembered the last time it happened. It was one of his last weeks as a Vicar. In fact he was sure it was one of the reasons he lost his job. The rumours were so ridiculous that he had lost his temper at the pulpit one Sunday. Some old drunk, obviously Bob, had fallen into the lake and drowned. The people had somehow revived some old story about a monster that would come out of the lake and devour the unjust. The last known sighting had been in pagan times. A history buff had unearthed it and the people latched onto it. Some of the idiots had even claimed to have seen it with their own eyes.

The tightness in his chest rose to a crescendo before he realised, with not a little relief, that it wasn't his problem anymore. They were not his problem anymore. He was Patrick the ex-alcoholic ex-Vicar now. No one cared what he had to say about any monsters. Nor was it his place to lecture them about it. The second smile of the day blossomed as he finished his run with that thought rising above all others.

After a shower Patrick went straight to the Hog's Head for Sunday lunch. It was a tradition that his family had which he kept up since the accident. Most weeks he went and thought about the good times: the laughs they shared in the pub, the wonderful and sometimes frankly terrible food they had eaten as the place changed hands. It had been pretty good since the last people bought it, though.

'Afternoon Rev.' it was Andy, one of the only things that had managed to cling on throughout all the buy-outs. He was nice enough, just a bit weird. He had an unusually good memory and Patrick supposed it made people feel special when he spoke to them about things they had told him only once. It made it seem like he cared.

As Patrick approached the old fashioned maître d lectern, another of the fixtures of the place over the years, Andy leaned close and whispered—although there was no one close enough to hear—'how are you holding up Rev?'

It took Patrick by surprise. So much so that he answered, 'okay, thank you Andy,' without even thinking.

'I'm sorry, I don't mean to be forward, Rev, but…they never found him did they, the driver of the other car?'

Still a little shocked, but starting to get annoyed, Patrick answered, 'It was a hit and run Andy. You would have read about it in the papers if they had been caught wouldn't you?'

'But the car went in the lake didn't it?' Andy asked, not sensing Patrick's annoyance in the slightest.

'Yes, Andy it did. Now if you wouldn't mind I would like my usual table and to sit in peace and enjoy a nice Sunday Lunch with my thoughts.'

Andy got the message this time and Patrick instantly regretted his tone. The poor man's face was full of hurt when he brought him to the table and left the menu. Then he turned his back and left Patrick alone, just like he had asked. He thought how his wife would have told him off for being unkind to Andy, she would have told him how Andy was one of God's special creatures and as a Vicar he should know that and be more sympathetic. The thought caused a sharp pain in his ribs, a physical symptom of remorse he was so familiar with. Poor Andy was only trying to be nice. He made up his mind to apologise when he was leaving.

The stale beer and gravy smell of the place drew forth the memory of one of the last times all three of them had been there. It had been Thomas' seventh birthday. Patrick and his wife had tried to organise a party at the house with all of his friends, but his son had insisted that they went to the pub for lunch. Just like always. They had bought him a miner's helmet that year for his present. The boy had just found out that his grandfather had been a collier and become obsessed with coal mining. He was so happy with it; Patrick could still see his face now, his smile brighter than the lamp that he kept shining in people's eyes. He'd worn that thing until the day he died. In fact he died wearing it. When the recovery operation—that's what they called it when everyone was dead, rather than a rescue operation—was done they found him with the chin strap still tied. Patrick insisted on it being buried with him. Not exactly a Christian thought, but he couldn't bear to take it from his son when he was alive, so how could he now that he was dead.

He barely registered the meal but remembered to find Andy before he left.

'Look, I'm sorry. It's been a bit of a tough one Andy. I had no right to snap at you. Please accept my apology,' he said.

'I was just thinking, it's weird isn't it. The monster showed up around the same time, and now on his birthday here it is again,' Andy said.

Patrick was shocked at Andy's complete lack of understanding but swallowed his anger. There was obviously no helping it. Andy didn't realise what he was saying was hurtful. He was just trying to be nice.

'Yes. A coincidence indeed. See you next week Andy,' Patrick said.

While he wouldn't let it make him feel animosity toward Andy, the comment had got him thinking about the beast again. Why was it that every place in the country seemed obsessed with beasts and boogey men? Bodmin had its Beast, Loch Ness had its Monster, Norfolk had its Black Shuck and now they had their…Lake Thing. Pathetic, Patrick though, it didn't even have a name and yet it had been blamed for drowning a man.

His head hurt when he got indoors. Wishing for the day to just end, he decided to cheer himself up with some old photographs. He opened the attic and pulled down the ladder. He liked to keep them up there so that he wouldn't be tempted to look at them all day, every day. But on special occasions he allowed himself the luxury of happy grief. It wasn't sadness he felt when he looked at photos of his family. The holiday snaps, birthday pictures even silly every day images of Thomas covered in flour while baking a cake made him feel as though he was feeding his heart.

The first album was from a holiday they had decided to spend around the local area. They went to the rubbish fairground with its rickety roller coaster and rusty merry-go-round, his wife hated all that stuff so all of the photos were of him and his son grinning and laughing.

There was no beach nearby so they had gone to the lake with their deck chairs and swimming trunks. It had been extremely hot that summer. They could have been in Spain or the Canaries if they closed their eyes and imagined the smell of mud that dominated the area around the lake was actually seaweed. He could still smell it now, all these years later, looking at the photographs of those happy times. A tear ran down his cheek and he had a double take at one of the pictures. The photographic paper had been bleached in one spot, almost completely white. He cleared his eyes and looked closer and saw that there was a little pair of feet visible underneath the bright flare. Then he remembered his son had been wearing his mining helmet even then and supposed it must have reflected some sun into the camera. Looking closer it seemed like it was above his son's head, like it was coming from behind him. He hadn't noticed that before.

The daylight was growing dim when he looked up from his album. It was getting late and he needed to go for his walk. It was one of the other things that kept him sober. Part of his routine. He did the same walk every evening: down the road a mile to the lake, another mile along the water's edge and a diagonal of just under a mile and a half home in a rough triangle. It would take him the best part of an hour, because the ground was uneven. He made sure to take a torch, just in case evening caught up on him before he met the boggy ground of his way home.

He was glad of the torch because it was getting dark when he reached the lake. It was an especially poignant place to go this day for a walk. It was here, after all, his wife and son had died. The official report was that they were driving home from school on the road that borders the edge of the lake. A speeding lorry with a broken headlight—reportedly seen by another motorist the same night at a similar time—ran them off the road and into the water. The coroner said they were likely alive when they hit the water because of the water in their lungs. Patrick always wished he hadn't known that. He would have felt better thinking that they had died in the impact. The car was wrecked. It looked like it had been crushed in the centre, but the police said that can happen when hit side-on by a heavy vehicle. The lorry was never found and nobody ever convicted. That was ten years ago and he had never been able to get over it. Maybe, he thought, if he could have said goodbye or at least if they had caught the driver.

The light appeared in the water just as he was walking along the last hundred meters of his planned route along the lake. At first, he thought it was a reflection of the setting sun. It grew brighter as it seemed to rise through the water and he realised that it was an actual light. It was bright, almost too bright to look at, but he couldn't look away. Hadn't he seen it before somewhere, that shape, the colour. It broke the surface as the sun went beyond the horizon and suddenly it was truly too bright to look at. The loud splashing that accompanied its coming startled him, and he started to run.

He didn't know why it was chasing him, or why he ran. But he did and it was. He didn't have to look behind to know that it was catching up. His shadow was growing shorter with every step he took as the light approached from behind. He didn't need his torch anymore; the darkness was being turned into an analogue of day by the light behind him. He chucked it over his shoulder, hoping to hit whatever the light was, but it didn't slow. The boggy ground was tough going and he started wheezing. There was no way he could run, not this this fast, for a mile and a half.

He stumbled awkwardly and fell with his foot in a soft hole in the ground.

Then it hit him: it couldn't be. But it must be. Why else would the light be following him? It had to be his son. Or at least his spirit. Patrick didn't know if he should believe in such things, his erstwhile faith battled with it. But he wanted to so much. He wanted to say goodbye. That would be all. He could say goodbye and tell him he still loved him and his mother. If his spirit was there so must hers be.

The light was almost on him now. He became more sure than ever. The pressure of grief and longing lifted from his chest. It was time to let it all go and say goodbye. Then he could sleep properly again, stop treating every day like a ritual. Everything was going to be okay. Everything was—

The light appeared to be floating. No it was attached to something, like at the end of a stick. As it moved over his head beyond his field of vision he followed the stick back, it was bowed under the weight of the light.

The eyes made him scream. They were as big as footballs and lidless, one on either side of the massive flat head. The smiling mouth was next, with three rows of triangular teeth, glistening in the light of the lamp. The smell made him gag on his scream. It was like a swimming pool full of rotting fish and sewage. He had seen something like this before with its protruding jaw and the lamp on the end of its head, but wasn't it a fish and usually smaller than a salmon? He couldn't remember the name now, but it didn't matter. The thing was clearly not just a fish. Behind it writhing tentacles pushed against the soft ground, carrying the fish thing with the light just above the ground.

Patrick felt his bowels turn to water but barely noticed. The smell was already more than he could bear and he was soaked through from lying in the bog. Also the teeth were getting closer to his legs and despite its appearance Patrick was sure it would be faster than him.

'Is that you?' he said without really meaning to. 'Son? It's Dad. Don't you remember?'

The thing stopped its advance and turned slightly so that one huge eye was pointing directly at Patrick. He thought he saw in it a flicker of recognition, of love.

His leg was gone before he realised the thing had moved. It happened all wrong. First the realisation, then the pain, then the movement. The leg jerked slowly back into the things throat. Patrick found his scream again and was making no sense. He could see his life leaking from the stump just below his torso. The pain was gone, replaced by coldness. This time it happened in the right order; he saw the movement of the thing, toward his head, then an instant of pain, then he didn't feel anything at all.

The People That In Darkness Sat - Pippa Bailey

Sam was on the floor before he heard the slap. Lying in the pool of water from his now empty glass, he reached around for anything to help him get his bearings. The soft plush of his mother's stockings stroked his hand, as she kicked it away.

"You disgust me boy, you did that on purpose," she said, as she threw a cloth at him. "You better clean that up properly, or you'll get another one."

"But I I…" Sam was defeated once again. His face stinging, yet another new bruise to match the others. He pushed the cloth around, attempting to soak up as much of the water as he could. Her footsteps meandered behind him, before she eventually left the room, taking his sisters with her.

Sam sat on the floor of the back room, he wasn't allowed in the parlour with his sisters. He was too much of a bad influence, according to his mother. The television echoed through the wall, as they sat and watched Harold Howser preaching about sin. Sam waited for them to come and get him; it was the same every night. His father would beat him for any transgressions throughout the day, followed by an hour of prayer and repentance.

Howser was a big promoter of beating away the sin, any child can be reformed he said. Though day after day, his father could never beat away his curse. Sam knew he was a cursed child, damned by God they told him.

When the front door opened in the mornings, Sam could hear other children laughing in the street outside as his father left for work, swiftly followed by his mother taking his sisters to school. Sam was returned to his place on the floor in the back room, and instructed not to move. With the house empty he could finally relax, in his short twelve years of life these were the rare moments of peace from the daily punishment he received.

Sam lay on the floor listening to the bird's joyful chirping through the window, before it was abruptly stopped by a knocking at the door. He jumped to his feet, no one ever came to their house, he was too much of an embarrassment for his parents to ever let anyone see him. The knocking continued in a fast-paced rhythm. Leaning around the door into the hall, he listened to the vigorous drumming.

"Hey. Hey kid, I can see you," said a gruff voice, from outside the house, "are your parents' home?"

"I...I can't talk to you," said Sam, as he turned to go back to his spot on the floor, "sorry Mr."

"Kid, I just want to use your phone. My car broke down, and you're the first house with someone in," he pounded his fist into the door frame, "come on kid! I just want to use the phone; you won't get in any trouble."

"I'm not supposed to talk to anyone." Sam wrung his hands together, he knew he shouldn't have left his spot on the floor, this was the first time he had spoken to anyone but his family in years. "I don't know how to open the door."

"What d'you mean, don't you go out?" The man asked, impatiently.

Sam gripped the door frame, "Not allowed to go out." He ran his hand along the wall, as he stepped towards the front door. Fondling the locks, he found a latch that twisted, and the door slowly clicked open.

"Ahh thanks, kid. Where's that phone?" Said the man, as he stepped inside patting Sam on the top of his head, before looking down at him. "What the hell! Oh kid, I'm sorry, I didn't know."

Sam looked up at him; his empty eye sockets hung open slightly as he raised his head. Turning away, he walked slowly back to his spot on the floor and sat down, listening to the man calling for help with his car. As he placed the phone back onto the receiver with a sharp snap, Sam's mother walked in the door.

"Who are you, how did you get in here?" She angrily approached the man. "GET OUT. Get out of my house!" She screamed at him, as she pushed him out the door, letting it click behind him.

Sam was shaking as he heard her walking towards the doorway, her shoes shuffling on the carpet. Putting her hand atop his head, she tore at his hair, dragging him along the floor into the hallway.

"You let a stranger in this house? You let someone see you, you disgust me boy." She threw him hard against the stairs. Despite being tall for his age, he was powerless to defend himself. "Just you wait until your father gets home. You're done for boy, no amount of beatings will remove your sins, you're a curse on this family. We should have drowned you the day we set eyes on you."

Sam bolted for the door, he remembered where the latch had been, and took off running. The sounds of birds in the trees whipped around him, as he ran towards the woods. His mother on her knees in the doorway, screaming so hard she retched. Sam continued to run.

He let his back slide slowly down against the rough brickwork, his stick clattering loudly as it fell. Thumbing the ragged hole in his shirt Sam grimaced, it no longer offered the same shelter it once did. Shivering, he wrapped his hands around his legs, resting his head on his knees.

"Get going kid, no panhandling here." The whiskey scented man grabbed him under the arm, yanking him upright. Months on the street had left Sam's childlike features hidden. He had always been big for his age, looking closer to fifteen, or sixteen than his meagre twelve. He was lucky to pick up his stick, whilst being forced back out of the alleyway again. It has been days since he last got a meal, and rainwater could only do so much to quench his thirst.

He pushed onward, the road becoming more rugged as he walked. The bustle of the town sounded so far behind him now, his stick catching on the dirt ground, sending him stumbling every few steps. Sam could feel the furious sun beating down on him, the ground sizzled from the last of yesterday's rain evaporating. He needed to find shelter, or risk ending up sizzling along with it. There was no such luck, the further he walked, the more punishing the sun became. His face now raw from the heat, each salty droplet of sweat stung like acid. Sam's stick caught against a rock in the dirt path, propelling him abruptly forward onto the ground. He lay bleeding; dry empty sobs came in waves, before there was only black.

The Man in Black watched, as the boy walked slowly down the path. He followed at a distance, his life leaving him with every tortured step. The cross roads loomed ahead, the sandy ground shining like diamonds in the sun. With each wave of his hand the boys stick would jerk, sending him stumbling. A toothless smile crossed the man's lips, as he drew ever closer. Watching him reach the crossing, a single gesture sent a rock catapulting towards the boy's feet. Upon colliding with his stick, the boy fell hard, his head abruptly smashed against the ground. The Man in Black continued his slow swagger towards the unconscious boy, standing over him he snapped his fingers, a dark leather bound book, and quill appeared in his hands. With a few quick scratches from the quill, he then pulled a page from the book. To any outside observer this scene would have been rather bizarre, but with no eyes on the road, The Man in Black could go about his work undisturbed.

"My son, why are you here?" Asked the man, as he stroked his long fingertips across Sam's bloodstained face, "sit and talk with me a while."

The fiery touch woke him with a jolt, his head throbbing and echoing with pained voices. The man's words cut through the din.

"Your time is growing short, the stench of death encroaching upon you. If I take my leave of you here, you will be gone before the sun has faded."

"Please, please sir don't leave me here. I have nothing," said Sam, shaking as he pulled himself up. "I am cursed. I am a curse; God wouldn't give me eyes, like everyone else."

He lifted his head towards the man. Without his eyes he could not see the way the man shimmered from one plain to the next, like static as he moved. His bare feet left not a print on the ground; he appeared to merely float across the surface.

"My boy, you are cursed. For your sins, you have no eyes. Before you were even born, you were a corruption of life." A sly smile crossed his thin lips, pulling tight against his toothless gums. "But there is something I can do for you."

"Really sir?" Sam reached out his hand to the man, he let it list in the air for a few seconds, before exhaustion once again left him slumped on the ground.

"I have a deal for you, a bargain. I can give you what you want. Your life, your sight, a chance to live like everyone else." Once again with a click of the man's fingers the quill appeared, along with the single sheet of paper torn from his book.

Sam's head lolled against his chest, "A deal?"

"Yes my boy, a deal just for you. All that I ask is that you bring me something, and I will give you what you desire." He rolled the pen between his spindly fingers.

"W…what is it that you want from me? I have nothing to give s…sir." His voice barely a whisper.

"An eye for an eye my dear boy. I will release you from your seat of darkness; you will bring me the eyes of others. I will grant you one year of life for every pair you bring me, but I want only the eyes of the living," he said with a shrill cackle.

"I…I can't do that! How can I bring you eyes?" He shook as the man drew closer to him, the intoxicating waves of heat made him dizzier. "I don't want to hurt anyone."

"Ah, well this is a onetime deal, boy. When I take my leave of this place you will not see me again, unless you agree to this bargain." He slowly uncurled his fingers from around the pen, stroking the nib sharply across the wound on Sam's forehead, before sliding it slowly into his hand. "My boy just sign here and I will give you everything you want. I ask so little of you, and offer so much. Sign my boy, and you will be free, free of your curse, free of your old life. Sign… Sign and change your fate. What has God had to offer you, but suffering?"

The Man in Black thrust his crumbling page at Sam, watching carefully as he finally surrendered, leaving a blood red scrawl across the paper. With a flourishing turn the man vanished, leaving Sam alone once more, prostrate on the ground. The excruciating pain of death crippling his body, dry sobs drowned the sound of the approaching car.

"Open your eyes son," said the doctor, tapping Sam on the arm. His body now strewn with wires, a rhythmical drip of fluids feeding into him from the unit by his bed. Instinctively he fluttered his eyes open and the light flooded in, sending him into a screaming panic. The new sensation of a blinding brightness was too much for him to comprehend. Flailing his arms and clawing at his face, he pulled his drip out, leaving a trail of blood across his bare chest. Sam was quickly restrained and sedated.

The lights were dim when he regained consciousness; he let his fingertips play across his eyelids, the smooth curve of his eyeballs beneath them, the slightest pressure making his head throb. Sliding his fingers away he opened them slightly, the light was less harsh, filtering in gently. Colour, Sam had never experienced colour before. His head was awash with these new sensations, the whiteness of his bedding, the pink of his skin against them, he wiggled his fingers.

"Ah, you're awake," said the doctor, peering into the room, "you had us worried before, bit of a panic there."

Sam nodded, "Where am I?" he let his eyes follow the leads that ran from his body.

"You're in the hospital son, someone found you in the middle of a road. Lucky that they brought you in when they did, you were a hairsbreadth from death."

He nodded again, his eyes scanning the room, "Do you have any food?"

"We'll get you something soon, but first I need you to tell me where your parents are." The doctor entered, and sat on the end of the bed next to Sam's feet. Sam bowed his head, and avoided the doctor's gaze. "We don't have to tell them you are here, if you don't want us to."

He thumbed the edge of the bedding, "They're gone."

"That's alright son," said the doctor, resting his hand on Sam's leg. "I'll have a lady you'll like come and talk to you later today; she will explain what happens next."

It wasn't long after the social worker visited Sam, that he was miraculously placed into a foster home. Two loving parents, a brother and sister, who wanted to spend time with him. For Sam, it was the first time he had known love. To have someone tuck him into bed at night, tell him what a good boy he was. The enrolment into school was swift, but not an easy transition. Having been kept from school for the first twelve years of life, Sam found it hard to keep up with the other children, who had been reading and writing for years. The children in the class were more help than a hindrance, several taking the time to assist him with his studies. For Sam, everything had dramatically changed in just a few short months. If only the story could end here with a happy little boy, a promising future and a forgotten past. But a deal is a deal, and the Devil never walks away from a contract. Six months passed before he made his second appearance.

His homework was scattered across the kitchen table, as he scribbled a few numbers on lined sheets of paper. Sam didn't notice the door open, or the man gently glide into the room. But the hand on his shoulder felt so familiar, the heat from his touch stung.

"Hello, my darling boy, how are my eyes treating you?" He asked, in a lyrical whisper.

The pen dropped from Sam's hand as he began to shake uncontrollably. Peering over his shoulder, there was no one there. Looking forward again, The Man in Black was now comfortably seated at the table, his slender fingers flipping through the pages of his thick leather book.

"H...how...how did you do that?" Asked Sam, his hands trembling.

"I can do a great many things. If I can grant you sight, and extend your life, a mere parlour trick is nothing." His mouth pulled into an awkward, toothless smile. "I am here only to remind you of our deal. You have had six months of pleasure from my gifts, you have but six months more before our bargain is forfeit, and I will return for my eyes and your life."

"I...I can't do this, how can I do this, take someone's eyes?" Sam stuttered.

His smile dropped to a harsh grimace, "Oh but you can my boy, if this life means anything to you, you will. And you will do it over, and over again for me. Remember I promised you only one year for every pair you bring me. No tricks either, I'll know if they were stolen from the lifeless, or a lesser beast. You have six months."

Sam was once again alone at the table, in the place of the man's book lay a smoothly curved, bifurcated knife. The hilt ebony, carved with the body of a ram, its horns formed from the two blades. Sam edged towards the knife, stroking his finger against its intricate body. Picking it up he rotated it in his hands, the blades appeared almost like that of quartz or glass. He quickly stuffed the knife into his school bag, and forced it back under the table. Finishing his homework, he placed his books back into the bag, positioning them to hide his new prize from prying eyes.

For weeks he planned, watching the other children at school, following people on the street, all to no avail. Sam didn't know if he was more scared of betraying the man, or taking the eyes. It was at this point that opportunity appeared, in the form of a new student.

He wouldn't know anyone. Sam thought to himself, watching the new boy meandering through the corridors, back tracking his missteps. If I befriend him, I could win his trust, but then I would have to make him go away. Or if I just attack him, I could take his eyes, but how can I get him alone? He sat and watched the boy at lunch, taking a seat alone from the other children; he drew less attention to himself. Sam hung around later than normal and watched as the new boy was collected by his parents in their ostentatious saloon car, before walking home through the fields to the back of the school. He nodded as he walked, tomorrow would be the day.

Sam packed his bag carefully that night, managing to find some duct tape, and a hammer from the garage. Tears started to form little pearls on his cheeks, as he made his plan of action. His handwriting much more legible than the months before. One: Catch him by surprise. Two: Knock him out. Hammer good, don't hit too hard. Three: Take his eyes. It wasn't much of a plan, but it was enough to make things clearer in his mind. Wiping away his tears, he stuffed his new tools and plan into his bag, along with his knife. That beautiful knife, he could hardly keep from looking at it. Stroking his fingers over the ornate carving, he admired the hair on the ram's body, each scored to perfection.

That morning he ran through the plan, over, and over again he mouthed the words. Find, hit, take. It was his mantra, scrawling it on the back page of his book, as his lessons progressed. So very engrossed in his writing, he barely paid attention to his surroundings. Had he taken the time to look, he'd have noticed the shadow that followed him throughout the day. Creeping closer, haunting his every step. The Man in Black knew his first payment was soon to be made, and watch he would, as Sam approached the new boy from behind, alone, leaning against the back gate waiting for his parents. He watched as the hammer fell with a dull sickening thud, sending a cascade of blood down the boy's pale face.

His body stiffened before he fell forward, bouncing as he hit the ground. There was no sound, he didn't cry out as Sam rolled him onto his back, his body arched over his back pack. Struggling with his own bag, he reached for his tape, making an efficient gag, and tying the boy's hands together. All that remained was the final act. He slipped the knife from his bag, gripping the hilt tightly, his hand damp with sweat. He lowered the blades in line with the boy's eyes, the whites shimmering in the last of the autumn sun. Sam slid a hand under the back of his neck, the blades followed swiftly into the boy's eye sockets, a fountain of blood gushed forth as the blades crawled deeper into his orbits. With a quick jerk his nerves were severed, a motion Sam had practiced many times in his bedroom. The school library had been of invaluable help. Medical dictionaries and biological diagrams had been easy for him to find, to study from, to learn his new trade. He quickly withdrew the knife, carefully hiding it at the bottom of his bag again. The boy was still unconscious, but breathing. Sam slowly dragged him backwards, before propping him up, he let his head loll forward, it made for easier extraction. He wiped his hands down his trousers, before slipping a curved finger into the first torn socket of the boy. He retched; his second hand held tightly over his mouth, he fought back the acidic burn of the vomit in his gullet. With his finger hooked deep into the boy's skull, it took but one swift tug for the eye to bounce gently down onto his lap. The empty socket leaked a slow stream of blood, which splattered soundlessly onto the boy's legs. The second took a little more work before the eyeball was relinquished, and joined its brother.

The Man in Black moved seamlessly from one end of the walkway, to beside Sam in the blink of an eye. He nodded towards the eyes, nestled so carefully among the fabric of the boy's trousers.

"Give them to me, my son." He held out his hand, his long slender fingers beckoning Sam closer. Sam scooped the soft orbs from their new home, and quickly placed them in the man's outstretched hand. "You have done well. Consider your year's debt fulfilled, I will return again when my payment is due."

Sam kept his back to the freezer in the corner of his basement, as if to avoid eye contact. He reached deep into the oversized refrigerator, grabbing a couple of cold beers, before he forcefully kicked the plastic sheeting on the floor back under the lip of the door. Jessica's footsteps echoed across the ceiling, their repetitive pattern mirroring that of her rocking the small baby in her arms. Letting the door guide itself shut Sam ascended the stairs to the sound of a squawking baby and a cooing mother.

Placing his beers on the counter, he snapped the lock shut before fumbling with the combination, the meaningful numbers becoming but a mess of digits.

"…And what is all this noise about buddy," he grinned, reaching into Jessica's arms and grabbing the soft, cherubic bundle.

"Careful he's fussy today." She leant in close for a cuddle with both, before dodging to the side, and scooping up one of the unopened beers, "I believe one of these is mine."

"Well I…" Sam bounced the wriggling bundle against his chest.

"That's what I thought, you just keep on bouncing daddy man," she said with a smirk, cracking the top off the bottle on the edge of the counter. She gave him a kiss on the cheek, followed by a large gulp from her bottle. "We have a delicacy for dinner tonight sweetie," standing on her tiptoes she extended her reach to the top shelf.

Sam stared deep into his son's cool blue eyes, Jessica's eyes. His were harsh and dark, a bottomless blackness. He snapped back into the room, "Delicacy you say, and what must this spectacular meal be?" He said loudly, talking to his gurgling offspring.

"Macaroni cheese," was shouted from a Jessica, who was now fumbling with cartons in the fridge, she leant back popping her head around the door, "from a box!"

"Goodness! We will eat like kings tonight-and queens of course." He quickly mouthed I love you, before returning his full attention to his son.

Sam lay staring at the ceiling, Jessica breathing deeply beside him, curled around her pillow. His life played out like a movie across the blank, white screen. He had always been prepared for the guilt, from his first meeting with the blade, to the woman who lay, in meticulously dissected pieces in the basement freezer. The next would be his fifteenth victim. His first, and only surviving victim, had long since killed himself, after the trauma of the attack. Sam had seen him struggling to adjust as a teenager, and soon after he was no more than an article in the newspaper. Local teen suicide viciously attacked as child.

After his first, Sam couldn't take the chance of the police picking up on a string of eyeless victims. At thirteen, he was only on his second victim. He learned quickly that women were easier to control. Being large for his age, it was no problem for him to overpower them, charm them, control them. He learned to conceal the bodies, and delay the decay, until he knew enough time had passed for them to be found. As he refined his skills, the bodies continued to go unnoticed, storing parts in his basement, until he was ready to dispose of them. He had taken this house for the very reason that the basement was large enough for him to work. He had managed for years to keep the operation clean, The Man in Black was impressed with his work. Jessica had made things more complicated, stumbling into his life at exactly the wrong time. Sam stared harder at the lines in the ceiling, as they floated and weaved, turning to the crimson weeping lines on the faces of so many. He squeezed his eyes tightly shut, but the faces never faded. Turning over he wrapped his arms around her, and nuzzled in close to her neck, her sweet scent calmed him, drifting off into a dreamless sleep.

Jessica was already gone when he awoke, a note hung from the side of the fridge, 'Gone to dad's back for lunch, I love you, Charlie does too.'

The frozen parts rattled noisily against the plastic wrap as Sam pulled them from the freezer. He wouldn't be able to dispose of all them this time. Stuffing several into his duffel bag, he placed the remaining limbs back on top shelf of the freezer. It wasn't until he was close to the front door that the heat hit him. Flowers on the counter began to wilt slowly before his eyes, followed by a soft dripping from the duffel bag, as its contents began to thaw. He already knew why, and yet the fear, even after all these years, held him fast.

"Hello, my boy," his rasping voice seemed to come from all corners of the room, "it's good to see you so well, and your little one."

Sam turned on the spot "No. Not now, I've done what you wanted for fifteen years, I can't do this anymore. I have a family now, things are different."

"Ah, but my boy that was not what you agreed to." With a snap of his fingers the contract hovered in the air, Sam's bloody signature no more than a single scratch. "You're indebted to me, unless you wish to forfeit." The shadow travelled slowly along the floor, creeping closer to him, before The Man in Black rose from within the ground. He stroked a single elongated fingertip down Sam's face, watching as his eyes began to rotate backwards into his skull, until only the whites shone, once again bathing Sam in darkness. He screamed.

"Now, I believe we agree, you will make payment to me. You have one day, or lose your eyes and lose your life." He once again sank into the shadow, which dissipated quickly.

Sam collapsed to his knees, his hands over his eyes. As quickly as it left him, his sight returned. He crawled to the kitchen, pulling down a roll of towels he began to mop up the festering puddle from his wet duffel bag. Gripping the counter Sam pulled himself to his feet; he tossed the towels, and once more made for the door.

The air buffeted against Sam's arm as he threw the parts from his window, watching in his mirror as they bounced into ditches and woodland. The streets were deathly quiet for a Sunday morning, slowing to a crawl he drove street after street looking for someone. A few people walked alone, but they would be hard to convince to get in the car. Parking up, he walked around a few of the back alleys, only to be stopped by a policeman, questioning his motives. Sam was no closer to finding his next sacrifice. The supermarket was not due to open for another hour, there would be little chance of finding a stray shopper in the far corner of a carpark, or loitering in a smoking area. He needed to be home before Jessica returned. Sunday was family day, time for a long lunch and afternoon drinks. His knuckles were white as he gripped the steering wheel, still hoping to cross some unfortunate on his way back. No such luck.

Sam was home, and safely in bed minutes before Jessica arrived, a gurgling bundle in tow. He lay still on his side as she slid the door open, "Do you want to see daddy?" She whispered, placing Charlie on the bed beside him. Which was followed by a scream of excitement, and swift full palm baby slap to Sam's face.

"Well that's a hell of a wake up," he said, grinning as he slid Charlie into a bear like hug, "Someone's excited, huh?" He planted a little kiss on his nose, before scooping him over his shoulder, and heading out to join Jessica in the kitchen.

"I was thinking tea, before beer today." She called over her shoulder, as Sam snuck closer, planting a kiss on her neck.

"Perfect." He whispered in her ear, as Charlie too lent in, and left a rather damp kiss against her cheek.

The stress of the morning was quickly forgotten among playing games with Charlie, watching movies, and the lunch buffet. It was all too easy for Sam to take his eyes off the clock, and forget for a few short hours what awaited him if he failed to keep up his end of the bargain.

With Charlie tucked into bed, they settled down on the sofa for a quiet evening. Flicking through the channels, Sam watched intently for any news of his disposal. It has been at least three years since a body part had been found and reported. He had become more careful with his methods, distributing the bodies in smaller and smaller pieces in larger areas, and road sides where no one would be walking. He would have to make another trip soon. His mind wandered, it was too late to find someone tonight, Jessica would question if he went out. He couldn't risk leaving a body in public, whether he was desperate or not. He still had until midday tomorrow, if he left early enough it would be easy. Jessica would be out most of day, and assuming he was at work, wouldn't question his whereabouts.

"...hey...hello!" He snapped back to the room, Jessica had been waving at him, "beer me please."

"Yes, sorry bit distracted. One beer coming up." Dragging himself from the sofa, he headed down to the basement for more.

"You know, one day you'll have to let me see what you're working on down there," she called from the kitchen, sorting the dishes from dinner. "Agh! Goddamn it!"

Sam launched himself up the stairs, dumping the bottles on the counter, he could see Jessica gripping her hand tightly, holding it above her head.

He grabbed her hand, lowering it "Oh baby, what happened. Let me get the kit."

"Broke a glass, I think all the pieces are in the sink, so be careful. I don't think there is any left in the wound." She released her grip on her hand, a new pool of blood blossomed on her palm, dripping in quick succession into the sink.

"Oh honey, I don't know. You might need stitches." Sam checked the wound quickly before putting applying a bandage. "If it hasn't stopped bleeding like this in the next few minutes, I'm taking you to the hospital."

It didn't take too long for the bleeding to slow; Jessica was resigned to resting on the sofa for the rest of the evening, as Sam cleared the blood and glass from the sink. He watched the blood swirl down the drain, and faded to nothing.

Checking the boot of his car, he ran through a checklist of items in his head. Rope, tape, plastic sheeting, and knife. Sam was prepared to act outside of his basement if necessary, only a few hours remained. He set off towards the city, the sun wasn't up yet, which meant the curb crawlers would still be out in force. He could get this over and done with before the sun was up.

The red-light district was policed well, the women more than prepared to jump in a car, and get out of the area if it reduced the risk of being caught. An instinct Sam was relying on.

It wasn't long before he spotted them, he didn't like to approach the girls in groups. Too much chance of him being recognised, if things went wrong. At the end of the street a girl hovered alone, peering around the corner. Her short skirt and dirty hoodie was a give-away, long sleeves hiding the track marks. She didn't appear to have a handler.

"You looking for somewhere to be?" Sam leant out of the window.

"I might be, for the right price," she shuffled nervously, stepping closer to the window. "Five for a suck, twenty for everything."

Sam showed her his wallet; he made sure to carry an abundance of cash on these outings, the girls were sure to follow the money. Especially if there was more than the asking price. He popped open the passenger door, patting the seat as she climbed in.

"Take me outta here big spender," she said, with a smile.

Heading out of the city, the roads became less travelled. Sam pushed on further into the darkness, his companion seeming less pleased with the arrangement the longer they travelled. It always went this way, the further he took them, the more likely they were to start fighting. It normally ended with a punch to the face, and dumping them in the trunk before he left the city boundary. This time, a pair of lights followed closely behind.

Jessica woke to the sound of Charlie's cries, baby on breast she went about cleaning up from the night before. Moving the empties to the kitchen, and dumping the dirty plates in the sink, before popping a sated Charlie into his highchair. It wasn't until she began a quick sweep of the floor, that she noticed the lock hanging from the basement door. In his rush to attend to her screams the night before, Sam had neglected to lock the door. Pacing back and forth, she fought with the urge to see what special something he was up to down there. He always had an ongoing project for work; nondisclosure meant that no one was to see what he was working on. Or so he told her. Soon the urge became too much.

"I'll be right back baby," she cooed to Charlie, as he rattled his toys around his tray. He beamed up at her as she blew him kisses.

The basement seemed unusually clean, every surface was pristinely painted. Plastic sheeting covered the concrete floor, stretching the entire length of the room. Resting at the edge of the sheet was a large metal table, a fridge, and a large freezer. Jessica could see where the use of the fridge and freezer had worn holes in the sheeting, puckering its edges.

She ran her fingers against the cool surface of the table, as she made her way to the fridge. The door swung open easily, the shelves filled with a variety of beers. Smiling, she grabbed a couple to pop upstairs for later, she doubted that Sam would notice the transfer of bottles. Heading back towards the stairs, the freezer caught her eye. It was much larger than the one in the kitchen. It was odd Sam had never mentioned it; it would have made more sense to store food down here, and save on the space upstairs. Tucking the bottles beneath her arm, she moved to the freezer.

On the top shelf of the freezer were two small packages of meat, maybe pork or chicken. Jessica pulled one out and rotated it in her hand. It didn't take long for her to recognise the distinct shape of a human foot. The package fell from her hand, colliding with the beer, as it too hit the floor. Shattering in a cascade of foam, the beers drenched the plastic sheeting. The frozen foot slowly rocked back and forth amid the glass and beer. Jessica backed away from the mess quickly, the stump of an ankle bored into her across the room. She didn't dare go in for closer inspection of the other package, for fear of what she may find. Leaning across the table she vomited, her arms shaking as she attempted to steady herself, her now ashen grey features reflected in the harsh mirror of the table top. Beside the bottom of the staircase was a cabinet she hadn't noticed before. The door slightly ajar revealed a handgun sitting on one of the shelves. Tucking the gun into her waistband, she ascended to the kitchen.

"I don't know if I want to go this far," said the girl, thumbing the band of her skirt as Sam sped up.

"Shut up." He didn't look up from the road as he spoke. The lights of the car behind still bore down on him. They had to be following; no one would come this far out of the city before six on a Monday morning.

"C'mon baby, don't be mean. Why don't we just pull over here?" She nervously fumbled with her seatbelt, unclipping the clasp and stroking her hand up his leg.

"I told you to shut up!" he shouted, lashing out, and landing a punch on her jaw. It didn't knock her out, but was hard enough to put her in a daze. Sliding her hand along the door she reached for the handle, pulling hard, but it wouldn't budge.

"Let me out! Let me out, and I won't tell anyone," she said, still pulling at the handle, tears and snot now coating her face.

The lights of the car behind changed from a soft yellow glow, to a flashing blue. Sam knew he had to make his move quickly. Pulling the lock mechanism, he released the door.

"Fine, get out!" he screamed.

She pulled at the lock again, flinging the door open. With a push, she hurtled from the car, landing in a heap on the road in front of the police car. Like he had hoped, they stopped just short of the hooker in the road. Sam sped up, leaving the police, and the girl behind. He had to get away from there quickly. Heading to the nearest estate, he parked the car in a side street and waited. Rocking back and forth in his seat, his knuckles pale from gripping the wheel, he waited. An hour passed, and there was no sign of a police car in the area. Maybe they were just trying to stop hookers, and they were never after him. He couldn't risk heading back to the city now, he would have try the town. If he killed a girl in his car, he wouldn't have enough time to make good on his deal.

He set off towards home. With Jessica at her mother's, he would be free to reassess the situation, and prepare for a second attempt. Keeping his car off the road, and maintaining a low profile was his best option.

Sam flung the front door open; kicking off his shoes he headed for the basement for something to calm his nerves. The lock hung from the door. Tearing it open, he flew down the stairs. The puddle of beer and package lay on the floor as Jessica left them. He turned, she was stood in the doorway, gun pointed at him, her face red from crying.

"Sam, what is this. I…I don't understand." Her hands shook, as she took a step down the stairs.

"It's not what it looks like baby. It's part of my project, it's not real," he said, hands raised in front of him.

"No! Don't you lie to me," Jessica moved further down the stairs, "you stay back. All these secrets, you tell me you're working down here, and I find … find this." She pointed the gun at the package.

"Honey, it's not real," he said again, reaching to pick up the foot.

"Don't touch it; I'm going to call the police." Her hands trembled as she spoke, raising the gun to point at him again.

"No, sweetie put the gun down. You don't need to call the police." Sam started towards her, arms out stretched. Backing away from him she tripped on the steps. It was a chance he wasn't going to miss. He launched himself at her, attempting to wrestle the gun away.

The vibration travelled through his body as the gun discharged, the kickback hit him hard in the chest, as a hollow breath sounded from Jessica. He wrenched the gun from her hands, launching it across the floor. Blood poured from her chest. Tearing off his shirt, he pressed down on the wound.

"Baby no, no, I'm sorry. It wasn't meant to be this way." Her body twitched as her face gradually became paler. Slowly her pupils dilated, as her body went limp beneath him. Her life drained away before his eyes. Blood had run down the stairs in cascades, creating a sticky pool at the base. He released his soaked shirt, and pushed back from the body.

He ran his hands under the kitchen tap, letting the blood drain away, ignoring the screams from Charlie in the bedroom. Blinkered on washing the blood from his hands, he continued to ignore his son's cries. The clock began to chime in the lounge, as the kitchen floor started to warp from the heat.

"I have come to collect," said The Man in Black, as he made his way towards Sam, his arms out stretched.

Sam backed away, "No, no, I need more time. I tried, I couldn't. She's dead…"

"I have come to collect," the man repeated, as he moved further into the house.

"Wait… I…" Sam look around him, before tearing open the top draw, fumbling in his desperation. The heat was unbearable, as The Man in Black remained unwavering in his gait.

The screams from his son grew louder as Sam made his way to the bedroom, spoon in hand, swiftly followed by the Devil.

☐

☐

The Lord's Prayer - Kevin J. Kennedy

Our Father, which art in heaven,
Hallowed be thy Name;
Thy kingdom come;
Thy will be done
In earth, as it is in heaven:
Give us this day our daily bread;
And forgive us our trespasses,
As we forgive them that trespass against us;
And lead us not into temptation,
But deliver us from evil:

Every day we had to recite that hymn. Every fucking day. It used to feel good, kind of reassuring to know that someone was watching out for me. Being left in a basket at a fire-station before I had even turned one year old can cause some personal issues. Admittedly I didn't realise I had issues when I was younger but I certainly wasn't a happy child.

The home I lived in was okay. The people who looked after us were mainly cool apart from old Mr Waters. He would shout at you no matter what you did. He could tell you to do one thing and the next day shout at you for doing that very thing but after a while you even got used to him. The worst thing about staying there was I always felt alone. I slept in a room with eleven other boys and still felt lonely. Each morning we would say the Lord's Prayer but each night I would lie in my bed and say my own prayer. I would pray that some family would come and take me away from the home and that I would be theirs. I wanted to belong to someone rather than just a place. I was a ward of the state. How shit is that? So each and every night I would say a prayer to the Lord or whoever was listening...

As each day turned into months and the months turned into years I knew my chances of being picked grew smaller and smaller. The families that came always took the younger kids. Whether they were in some way trying to pass them off as their own or whether they were just watching the full experience of the kid grow it didn't matter. To me it only meant my chances grew smaller as I grew bigger. After a while I stopped praying. What was the point? No one listened anyway. I got fed up hearing you just have to believe or it's all about faith. I did believe to start with and it made no difference. After a while of believing it all just seemed stupid. In every other element of life if you keep doing something to get absolutely no result you would be considered a moron but as long as it's related to religion it's totally acceptable. I found books about other gods and religions and they all seemed equally ridiculous but the ones I did like were the ones about the Greek gods. I'm not saying I believed in those either but they were a lot more interesting to read.

    I remember lying in bed one night when I was around ten and realising I had been there since I was a baby so why hadn't I been picked. What was wrong with me? Was I un-loveable? The other kids seemed to like me and the staff never showed much emotion but they did treat me well. Why did no one want me? My nightly prayer had been replaced with a restlessness that I couldn't get rid of. I would toss and turn, unable to push the feeling out of my head that no one would ever love me. The nights with very little sleep did nothing to improve my mood through the day. I started getting into trouble more and the staff would make me spend a lot of time on my own, writing lines or 'thinking about what I had done'. I didn't really care. As my moods worsened I couldn't really be bothered with the other kids anyway. I would get up in the morning with bags under my eyes and have to stand at the end of my bed in my pyjamas and say the Lord's Prayer with the rest of them. Some of them truly believed in God even though they were old enough to know better. Standing there, chanting like drones. 'Our Father, which art in heaven, Hallowed be……' and on and on. Which father? Which Heaven? Why should he be the one to give forgiveness? What exactly was I seeking forgiveness for? You see, that was the thing, Christians always seemed to want you to think that you've done something wrong. For a forgiving bunch they can be real arseholes. I can't say it helped me any, sharing my opinions with the staff but even as a child I found it hard to just blindly accept things.

I can remember when I was about ten or eleven that my mood swings became really bad. By that point I knew I was in the home until I was eighteen. No one wants to adopt an eleven year old and as I had said, no one wanted me when I was young so it was pretty easy to be realistic with myself and just accept that I was unlovable. What I still couldn't accept was anyone's crazy belief in religion. Although we rarely got to watch the television, on the odd occasions that we did it would often be the news. It seemed that people all over the world had one main problem with each other and it was religion. It seemed crazy to me. It was all fake. It was a little like people killing each other and blowing things up over who was the best ThunderCat or Transformer. I couldn't quite grasp how adults could actually be fighting over make believe stuff. How could people still buy into this bullshit? I was young and I knew it was nonsense.

    I had tried discussing my feelings with the staff in the home but they were never willing to talk or give reasonable answers to my questions. They only ever sent me to the dorm room or made me do chores to punish me. It was as if they were scared to think about my questions in case it brought some realisation that a lot of stuff we were supposed to just believe in didn't make sense.

    I think it was just before my twelfth birthday when I smashed the room up for the first time. I couldn't take it anymore. No one would answer any of my questions; no one spoke to me anymore. I was either saying prayers to a god I didn't believe in, going through some kind of punishment I didn't deserve or thinking about how no one loved me. To say I was miserable was an understatement.

On my thirteenth birthday I decided I had had enough. I stole a knitting needle from the knitting room. I still wonder about that one. The home had a knitting room. I mean, who the fuck knits anymore. Anyway I stole a one and hid it under my pillow. I lay awake until all the other kids were asleep. It must have been about one A.M. when I quietly slipped out from under my covers. The room was never very dark thanks to the street lamp that was inconveniently positioned right outside our window. The threadbare curtains did little to block out its light. I crept across the room and opened the door as slowly as I could. There were only ever two members of staff in the home through the night. Most worked a day shift or late shift. But only two stayed over in the staff bedrooms. A lot of the staff had families of their own and didn't work the sleepover shifts. It was mainly always the same few people who worked it and I knew that on that particular night it would be Arnold and Betty. They were both old. I had no idea what age either of them were but they were definitely among the oldest of all the staff. It gave me a little more confidence that I could manage exactly what I had planned.

I sneaked into Betty's room first. I was as quiet as a mouse. As I stood over her bed I looked to the ceiling for some strange reason and whispered "If you are real God, this is your time to show your will." I positioned the needle directly above Betty's throat and thrust it down as hard as I could with both hands. God didn't step in and stop me. The needle went into her throat pretty easily. I was neither large nor strong but I think the fact that I had picked the needle with the sharpest point coupled with the fact that throats weren't designed to resist long, thin, sharp objects helped me in my goal. A thin spurt of blood sprayed across my face as Betty's eyes sprung open. She looked like a startled deer as her hands automatically sprung to her throat. I don't remember feeling all that much as I covered her mouth to make sure she didn't make any noise. I'm not sure she could have, with a needle buried in her throat but better safe than sorry. It didn't take long before the life drained from her. I removed my needle from her throat and wiped it on her covers.

I think it took me around three hours that night to kill everyone in the home and then another hour to get everything I needed before leaving. I lived on the streets for a while. I spent the majority of my time trying to work out what I did believe in, what was important to me. Did I have a purpose? Did any of us? Were we here by design or by sheer fluke? Was it just an infinite amount of random occurrences that allowed mankind to come into being or was there some reason for our species existing?

As I grew I experimented with a lot of things. Drink, drugs, women being the main three but as the years went on I tried to find myself in many different places. I'm not sure if I looked in the wrong places or if we are truly never meant to find ourselves. Maybe we are all lost or maybe we are just as pointless as everything else, everything only having true beauty if it means something to one specific person at a particular moment in time.

By the time I was sixteen I looked about twenty five and no one gave me money when I begged in the street anymore. The pity for the young kid had gone and now these God fearing people had only looks of disdain for me. I wondered if that's what they would need to ask forgiveness for, should God turn out to be real. People love to preach but very few live by the morals they claim to have.

It was just before my seventeenth birthday when I was picked up by the police. Apparently they had been looking for me since the incident in the home. How they found me four years later I still don't know. They took me to the police station where they lied to me for days, telling me tales of things I had done since that night in the home, people I had killed, and the horrific ways that I had murdered them but I knew it was all lies. I had killed the people in the home. I knew that. I had to, it was the only way I could escape that life but I hadn't killed after that night, I knew that. They told me stories of bodies found with the Lord's Prayer carved into their chest or back, stories of homes found with groups of people slaughtered and the Lord's Prayer painted on the walls with blood. Stories about whole warehouses filled with hundreds of bodies, every square inch of the walls covered in pencil scribblings of the Lord's Prayer. I don't believe a word of it. I can't remember being involved in any such activities and as I said earlier, I'm not particularly large in frame. How could one young man accomplish such feats? I know they are trying to frame me for something I didn't do but I have no way of proving my innocence. I'm going to go to prison for a long time for something I didn't do but it's okay, I am happy now, here in my little six by eight as I await the trial, now that I have found the Lord. He speaks to me. He visits me every night in my cell, He answers my questions, and He makes me believe. I no longer question right from wrong and no longer care about what I never had in this life. I know that when I die the Lord will welcome me into his arms and forgive me, he has to. I ask him every day to please forgive my trespasses and every day he tells me he does. I think I just never needed him before now. The staff at the home always did say he worked in mysterious ways

☐

☐

Author Biographies

Christopher Law

Christopher Law is the author of Chaos Tales, Chaos Tales II: Hell TV and the soon to be released Chaos Tales III: Infodump, plus a gaggle of other shorts and a clutch of novels he will get published. You can find him on Facebook as Christopher Law Horror Writer and at evilscribbles.wordpress.com. Other than that he's rather dull and middle-aged, still has a great view of the castle apart from the hill in the way and is thinking about getting some kittens.

Kitty Kane

Kitty Kane aka Becky Brown hails from the south of England where she lives surrounded by squirrels. She is also one half of writing duo Matthew Wolf Kane, and has been published both in collaborations and standalone stories. Kitty is the author of stories that have appeared in Full Moon Slaughter and Down The Rabbit Hole Tales Of insanity from J Ellington Ashton Press, and has several more stories in forthcoming releases from JEA. She also was part of the first V's charity anthology battle challenge from Shadow Work Publications, in which she won her battle, and made some lifelong friends. She has also has her work in a Christmas anthology from BURDIZZO BOOKS which was called twelve days in which Kitty cheerfully roasted babies in front of the open fire.

Kitty is currently editing her first solo anthology, The ABC of murder coming soon from Anthology House. She has lots of exciting projects lined up this year including her own novella, a MWK collaboration novella, many short stories and lots of general madness. Kitty says of her writing style that it errs on the side of bizarro, but she enjoys writing classic horror also. A lifelong fan of all things horror, you will find her generally up to no good. Her eyes are brown, her hair is subject to change...one steadfast thing with her though, and she can never be accused of being sane.

Paul B. Morris

Paul B Morris is a writer who hails from Walsall in the West Midlands, although he was created somewhere up north.

His stories lean towards dark fiction, horror and the strange, drawing focus from the dark reality of life. He apologises for that.

After falling in love with the work of the great Shakespeare, Morris has also drawn inspiration from Lewis Carroll, Stephen King, Graham Masterton and most notably, Michael Marshall Smith, who is still his favourite author.

In the realms of normality, Paul B Morris is happily married to an Angel, has four children who constantly get the better of him and wishes that he had the time to care for a pet bat. He owns two red t-shirts that don't suit him.

If you're interested, you can follow Paul B Morris @
https://paulbmorrismedia.wordpress.com/
https://www.facebook.com/paulbmorrisauthor/
https://twitter.com/pbmorriswriter/

Mark Nye
Mark Nye is a self-professed metal head, zombie lover and xenomorph fanatic. He has bounced through several (hundred) jobs, but his one true love will always been horror. Having taken up writing in October 2016, he has one published short story so far, available in Rejected for Content 5: Sanitarium. He also has several other stories coming out in various anthologies throughout the year. As well as working on his first novel he is also juggling being a father to three children, three cats, one dog and a husband to one wife.

Mark is also waiting for the zombie apocalypse…
Happy hunting.

Dale Robertson
Dale Robertson lives in the South West of Scotland with his partner, 2 children and pet dog.

He keeps active by playing football and running but also likes to chill out watching films (mainly horror) or playing Xbox. He is also a huge fan of Stephen King, James Herbert and Richard Laymon.

Currently, he has a short horror story called Skee-Bo self-published on Amazon and is working towards getting more work out there.

You can visit his website, www.dalerobertson.co.uk

C. L. Raven.

C L Raven are identical twins and mistresses of the macabre from Cardiff. They're horror writers, as 'bringers of nightmares' isn't a recognised job title. They spend their time looking after their animal army and drinking more Red Bull than the recommended government guidelines. They write short stories, novels, and articles for Haunted Magazine and have been published in various anthologies and horror magazines. They've been longlisted in the Exeter Novel Prize twice, the Flash 500 Novel competition twice, and the Bath Novel Award. Soul Asylum was shortlisted in the 2012 National Self-Publishing Awards and Deadly Reflections was highly recommended in the 2014 awards. Several short stories have also been long and shortlisted in various competitions. They recently won third prize in the British Fantasy Society Award. In 2015, they were published in the Mammoth Book of Jack the Ripper, which makes their fascination with him seem less creepy. Along with their friend Neen, they prowl the country hunting for ghosts for their YouTube show, Calamityville Horror and can also be found urbexing in places they shouldn't be. They also unleash their dark sides playing D&D/RPGs and gracefully fall off poles as they learn PoleFit.

Links: Blog – clraven.wordpress.com
Twitter - @clraven @calamityhorror
Facebook - https://www.facebook.com/CL-Raven-Fanclub-117592995008142/
https://www.facebook.com/CatsTalesOfTerror?ref=hl
Instagram – clraven666 CalamityvilleHorror666

Michael Noe

Michael Noe is a writer from Barberton Ohio, he is the author of Legacy, Legacy 2, The Darkness of The Soul, Insecure Delusions, Out with A Whimper, and has short stories in various anthologies. When not writing, he co-hosts The Cellar podcast, and is an editor for J Ellington Ashton Press. According to his girlfriend he's also a music snob and collects vinyl records.

https://www.facebook.com/michaelnoeslegacy/

https://www.amazon.com/Michael-Noe/e/B00NJG34BO/ref=sr_ntt_srch_lnk_1?qid=1493615377&sr=8-1

G. H. Finn

G. H. Finn is the pen name of someone who keeps his real identity secret to escape the eternal wrath of several of the ever vengeful, trans-paradimensional, eldritchly squamous Elder Gods. And avoid parking fines.

Having written non-fiction for many years, Finn began writing short stories in 2015. He especially enjoys mixing genres (sometimes in a blender, after beating them insensible with a cursed rolling pin) including mystery, horror, steampunk, sword-and-sorcery, dark comedy, fantasy, detective, dieselpunk, weird, supernatural, sword-and-planet, speculative, folkloric, Cthulhu mythos, sci-fi, spy-fi, satire and urban fantasy.

G. H. Finn's links :

Website: http://ghfinn.orkneymagic.com/

Twitter: @GanferHaarFinn

Facebook: https://www.facebook.com/g.h.finn/

Andrew Bell

Andrew lives on the Northeast coast of England, in a small town called Hartlepool. He is the author of three novels (Unguarded Instinct, Every heartbeat counts, and Ephemera: The ghost of Aaron Brookes). He has featured in dozens of short story anthologies, and is very proud to be a part of Burdizzo Books.

Dani Brown

Born in Oxford but raised in Massachusetts, Dani Brown is the author of "My Lovely Wife", "Middle Age Rae of Fucking Sunshine", "Toenails", and "Welcome to New Edge Hilll" out from Morbidbooks. She is also the author of "Dark Roast" and "Reptile" out from JEA. She's the person responsible for the baby blood bath that is "Stara" out from Azoth Khem Publishing. She has written various short stories across a range of publications. There's always more coming soon. As of writing this, "Stef and Tucker" haven't been released but they will be soon (if "Dancing With White Walkers" hasn't happened by the time you read this).

When she isn't writing she enjoys knitting, fussing over her cats and contemplating the finer points of raising an army of dingo-mounted chavs. She has an unhealthy obsession with Mayhem's drummer and doesn't trust anyone who claims The Velvet Underground are their favourite band.

She currently lives in Liverpool, England with her son and 3 cats.

You can contact her on facebook at https://www.facebook.com/DaniBrownBooks/. (Links to less used social media, can be found on the facebook page.)

Amazon https://www.amazon.com/Dani-Brown/e/B00MDGLYAY

Official and sometimes, by sometimes, she means rarely updated website http://danibrownqueenoffilth.weebly.com/

Mark Lumby

Mark Lumby published his first novel 'Most of Me' in 2016. In 2017 he will be launching a charity anthology, published by PSPublishing, called 'Dark Places, Evil Faces' in which he will feature alongside Ramsey Campbell, Brian Lumley, Jack Ketchum and Graham Masterton.

His writing is influenced by Stephen King, Graham Masterton and Iain Banks.

He lives in Tadcaster, England, with his wife and 5 children and many animals.

www.marklumbyblog.wordpress.com

Betty Breen

Betty Breen is still a newbie to the world of writing, but it's in her blood and she loves doing it. This is the second anthology she has appeared in and hopes to continue this trend. A full time mummy and part time university student she spends as much time as possible exercising her creative muscles. Find her on twitter @just_betty5 or you can check out her blog runningonanxietyblog@wordpress.com where she tackles issues surrounding mental health and exercise.

Lucy Myatt

Based in Liverpool, Lucy Myatt AKA TorAthena is an up and coming name in both the international convention scene and online world. While balancing her time between vlogging about comics, cosplay and her personal life, Lucy also manages her own retro video game and comic book shop, Level Up! Expanding upon entrepreneurial exploits, last year saw the release of her first novella, Peekaboo, with her second story in the works.

J. G. Clay

J.G. Clay is a British author, currently residing in the heart of England. Unleashing his unique combination of cosmic horror, dark fiction and science fiction with the first volume of 'The Tales of Blood And Sulphur' in 2015, Clay has turned his attention to Hell, with the murder/mystery novel 'Peace and Quiet. Time and Space'.

2017 will see him poised to unleash yet more Gods, Monsters and weird events upon the world, providing an endless supply of 'Nightmare Fuel For The Modern Age'.

Away from the printed page, J.G is a bass playing, Birmingham City supporting family man with a fondness for real ale and the Baggie/Britpop era of British Music.

Links
Website: www.jgclayhorror.com
Facebook: https://www.facebook.com/jgclay1973
Twitter: https://twitter.com/JGClay1

Edward Breen

Edward Breen is a Kent based writer, husband and father to three cats and a human child. He loves horror and fantasy and writes short stories mainly. One of his many manuscripts will, hopefully, become a novel some day, but for now you can catch him at https://dwreadswriting.blogspot.co.uk/ as well as on Facebook at https://www.facebook.com/edwardbreenwriting and twitter at https://twitter.com/Ed_likes_beer.

Pippa Bailey

Pippa Bailey is an author, independent reviewer, and YouTube Personality (Or so she tells herself), from Shropshire England. She has written for several horror, and alternative anthologies over the last two years, with several due for release later in 2017. She especially enjoys supporting other authors in their endeavours, through her independent review company; The Ghoul Guides. Which she runs with her partner in crime Leif. You can see more from Pippa on www.facebook.com/theghoulguides and under Ghoul Guides on YouTube.

Kevin J Kennedy

Kevin J Kennedy is a horror author and publisher from Scotland. He fell in love with the horror world at an early age watching shows like the Munster's and Eerie Indiana before moving on to movies like the Lost Boys, the original The Hills Have Eyes and Nightmare on Elm Street. (The eighties was a good time to grow up.)

In his teens he became an avid reader when he found the work of Richard Laymon. After reading everything Laymon had written Kevin found other authors like Brian Keene, Ray Garton, Edward Lee, Bryan Smith, Jeff Strand, John R.Little, Carlton Mellick and the list goes on. At the age of thirty-four Kevin wrote his first short story and it was accepted by Chuck Anderson of Alucard Press for the Fifty Shades of Slay anthology. He hasn't stopped writing since. Kevin lives in a small town in Scotland with his beautiful wife Pamela, his stepdaughter and two strange little cats.

Em Dehaney

Em Dehaney is a mother of two, a writer of fantasy and a drinker of tea. Born in Gravesend, England, her writing is inspired by the dark and decadent history of her home town. She is made of tea, cake, blood and magic. By night she is The Black Nun, editor and whip-cracker at Burdizzo Books. By day you can always find her at http://www.emdehaney.com/ or lurking about on Facebook posting pictures of witches. https://www.facebook.com/emdehaney/

Her poem 'Here We Come A-Wassailing' is in the Burdizzo Books 12Days Christmas anthology and her short story 'The Mermaid's Purse' can be found in the Fossil Lake anthology Sharkasaurus. Available on Amazon https://www.amazon.co.uk/-/e/B01MRXV1WR

Matthew Cash

Matthew Cash, or Matty-Bob Cash as he is known to most, was born and raised in in Suffolk; which is the setting for his debut novel Pinprick. He is compiler and editor of Death By Chocolate, a chocoholic horror anthology, and the 12Days Anthology, and has numerous releases on Kindle and several collections in paperback.

In 2016 he started his own label Burdizzo Books, with the intention of compiling and releasing charity anthologies a few times a year. He is currently working on numerous projects, his third novel FUR will hopefully be launched at the convention.

He has always written stories since he first learnt to write and most, although not all, tend to slip into the many layered murky depths of the Horror genre.

His influences ranged from when he first started reading to Present day are, to name but a small select few; Roald Dahl, James Herbert, Clive Barker, Stephen King, Stephen Laws, and more recently he enjoys Adam Nevill, F.R Tallis, Michael Bray, Gary Fry, William Meikle and Iain Rob Wright (who featured Matty-Bob in his famous A-Z of Horror title M is For Matty-Bob, plus Matthew wrote his own version of events which was included as a bonus).

He is a father of two, a husband of one and a zoo keeper of numerous fur babies.

You can find him here:
www.facebook.com/pinprickbymatthewcash

https://www.amazon.co.uk/-/e/B010MQTWKK

Other Releases By Matthew Cash

Novels
Virgin And The Hunter
Pinprick

Novellas
Ankle Biters
KrackerJack
Illness
Hell And Sebastian
Waiting For Godfrey
Deadbeard
The Cat Came Back

Short Stories
Why Can't I Be You?
Slugs And Snails And Puppydog Tails
OldTimers
Hunt The C*nt

Anthologies Compiled and Edited By Matthew Cash
Death By Chocolate
12 Days Anthology
The Reverend Burdizzo's Hymn Book [with Em Dehaney]

Anthologies Featuring Matthew Cash
Rejected For Content 3: Vicious Vengeance

JEApers Creepers
Full Moon Slaughter
Down The Rabbit Hole: Tales of Insanity

Collections
Reasons To Be Fearful Part 1
Reasons To Be Fearful Part 2
Reasons To Be Fearful Part 3

Website: www.Facebook.com/pinprickbymatthewcash